A Nice Clean Murder

by
Kate Sweeney

2006

What Reviewers Are Saying About Intaglio Publications Authors

Lynn Ames
Fast-paced, compulsively readable, and full of twists and turns, *The Value of Valor* will keep you up late into the night.
— 'nTouch Magazine

Once you pick up a novel by Lynn Ames, you will want to read them all. *The Price of Fame* is a five-star novel that you will want to read from beginning to end. You won't want to miss a single word. — Midwest Book Review

Robin Alexander
Murky Waters - The plotting and characters keep the reader thoroughly involved and pleasantly entertained.
— JustAboutWrite

Gloria's Inn - Just the first few pages of this book will tell the reader that the narrator has a wacky sense of humor and that what's in store is going to be a funny romp. And indeed it is. The descriptions and events of the book made me laugh out loud at times. — Midwest Book Review

Nann Dunne
The War Between The Hearts - Nann Dunne has created an unforgettable heroine, a woman before her time, standing at the crux of a new age. This fast-paced and gripping story will keep you up late at night. Highly recommended. Don't miss it! — Midwest Book Review

C. G. Devize
Misplaced People by C.G. Devize begins slowly in what I thought would be a laid back romantic mystery, but I was in for quite the adventure with this electrifying romantic thriller.
— JustAboutWrite

Kimberly LaFontaine
Picking Up the Pace is a fascinating look at the life of a reporter. Anyone who wants an intimate glimpse into a journalist's work will enjoy this first novel by Kimberly LaFontaine.
— Midwest Book Review

Alex Alexander
Alex Alexander has woven an intriguing story, filled with the kind of scenes that sometimes cause goose flesh to rise, true to *With Every Breath's* mystery-thriller content.
— Midwest Book Review

Judith K. Parker
Counterfeit World's conflicts and the plotline are wrapped up at the end, but I've never seen a character or such a unique world set-up that cried out more for sequels. Shon Emerick is a character who deserves a whole string of stories, and I hope Judith K. Parker is up to the challenge. — Midwest Book Review

Verda Foster
Verda Foster's *The Gift* is a romantic mystery novel with an intriguing premise. — OutLook Book Reviews

LJ Maas
L.J. Maas has written a captivating and touching romance of unrequited love and survival against difficult odds in None So Blind. — Midwest Book Review

A NICE CLEAN MURDER
© 2006 BY KATE SWEENEY

ISBN 10: 1-93313-78-2
ISBN 13: 978-1-933113-78-4

First Printing: December 2006

This Trade Paperback Original Is Published By
Intaglio Publications
Walker, LA. USA

CREDITS
EXECUTIVE EDITOR: TARA YOUNG
COVER DESIGN BY SHERI (GRAPHICARTIST2020@HOTMAIL.COM)

Visit us on the web: www.intagliopub.com

Other Titles by Kate Sweeney

She Waits

DEDICATION

This book can only be dedicated to my Aunt Dor. She epitomizes Aunt Hannah's character in the Kate Ryan series. Many years ago, she took me on a merry romp through Ireland. We certainly left our mark on the Emerald Isle, and with God's blessing, maybe they'll let us back one day.

No aunt has loved her nieces and nephews more—Thanks, Aunt Dor.

ACKNOWLEDGMENTS

I'd like to thank Tara Young, who edited *A Nice Clean Murder*. I hope the fates will allow more of the same in the future. I think she did a fantastic job, even if she is nocturnal.

Next, I owe a great deal of thanks to my invaluable beta readers: Den, Mercedes, Maureen, and Tracey. It would have been a very long haul without your keen eyes.

Also, to Sheri Payton and Becky Arbogast, who will take Intaglio into the future. I look forward to tagging along. Thanks for taking the chance on Kate Ryan once again.

And finally, to Kathy Smith, who made me feel at home at Intaglio from the onset. If home is truly where the heart is, then Kat's heart will always be with Intaglio. She taught me a great deal this past year. She is not only an amazing publisher, but a true friend. Thanks, Kat. Now, start writing that sequel!

PROLOGUE

The cold Atlantic gale that blew across the coast of Ireland seemed to chill Brian to his very marrow as he turned his collar up against the howling wind. He started once again down the rugged path that led to his cottage. For a moment, he stopped and gazed out at the vast ocean before him, listening to the waves crashing below. He felt as though he was standing on the edge of the world.

Shivering, he thought how he should have taken Mary's offer and let Sean drive him home. Feeling old and tired, he sighed heavily and continued along the path as the cold wind whipped around him.

"Swift ships are sailing in from the sea, and the banshee is wailing alone by the lea," he whispered, remembering the poem from his childhood. Then he shivered again, but it wasn't from the cold.

It was then he heard the soft keening mixed with the wind. He looked over his shoulder and stopped. Looking behind him, he saw nothing. "Bloody banshees are all over this fine night," he said and whistled as he continued on his way, hoping to God they weren't wailing for him. He remembered back when his mother died. He swore he heard them calling for her.

He heard something behind him again. He stopped and listened. Not a sound. For some reason, he walked a little faster now and stopped whistling. Though it was cold, he wiped the perspiration from his forehead and looked over his shoulder once more. The keening now turned to a low haunting wail. Something, someone was behind him, right at his heels—he could feel it.

As his thatched cottage came into view, he breathed a sigh of relief but kept his quickened pace. Through the wind, he could still hear the low wail. He stumbled over the path and righted himself on the short stone wall that surrounded his property. He looked over it and peered down at the rocks. There was no moon this windy night. He could see nothing, yet he heard the Atlantic waves crashing below. Again, he heard the low wail, or was it the wind howling over the cliffs as he strained to see through the dark pitch of night?

He whirled around, then sighed with relief. "It's you. For the love of God, ya scared the life—" he started to say and was grabbed by his collar and tossed over the short wall. He screamed as he tried to hold on to the edge of his world.

"Where is it? Tell me now, or I swear..." the voice hissed.

Brian tried desperately to gain a foothold, clawing at the loose rock wall that separated him from the sea below. He looked up and cried, "Where you'll never find it."

Now the shadow was all around him, and in a voice so close it seemed to be inside his head, he heard, "Yes, I will."

A heavy boot unmercifully kicked him in the face and his old body gave way. His screams echoed and mingled with the low haunting wail and the Atlantic wind, as he crashed on the rocks below.

Chapter 1

It was a long flight from Wyoming and I was glad to catch a little sleep most of the way. As I walked through Chicago's O'Hare Airport, I realized how much I hated crowds. People were everywhere, pushing and shoving. I had spent two glorious, quiet weeks on the Snake River in the Teton Range on assignment. It was depressing to come back to the hustle and bustle.

"Kate Ryan!" I heard the familiar voice call out. I turned and looked—it was Bob Whittier. I dropped my bag and almost jumped into the arms of my ex-partner.

"What a surprise. God, you look good," he said, stepping back and looking at me. "Same green smiling eyes and lopsided grin. Hmm, a little more gray perhaps."

I smiled back into the blue watery eyes and smirking smile. "Smart ass. You look well, Bob. How are Helen and the boys?"

"Fine, fine. You must be on assignment. Are you still freelancing?" he asked and picked up my bag.

"Yep, just got back, and nope, I've settled down with one magazine. I love it. No more freelancing." I glanced down at his leg. "Hey, you lost the cane."

We both were silent for a moment. Bob Whittier had retired from the Chicago Police Department after my father died. It was then I had the great idea to follow my first love, and I could think of no one else but my father's partner with whom to start my private investigation business.

We had a good business and built a solid name for ourselves until that last case. When the dust cleared, Bob almost lost a leg. I lost my heart—nearly lost my head—and carried the scars to remind me. Looking back on it, we were lucky to survive. Instinctively, I felt the back of my neck, my only visible scar. In my reverie, I nearly missed what Bob was saying.

"Yeah, I lost the cane. However, when this nasty Chicago weather kicks up, I tell you I'm as stiff as a board. God, Kate, it's been what, three years since I've seen you? That was a long haul back for you, kiddo."

"But both of us are fine now," I whispered in a convincing tone.

"Got anyone in your life?" he asked in fatherly fashion. He was not convinced, it seemed.

I gave my patent, noncommittal shrug. "I'm not sure. I—"

"Then you're not fine. Look, we had no way of knowing on that last case. At least you figured it out before we were killed. When I think how close she came to—" he stopped short. He put his arm around me as we walked through the terminal. His limp was still noticeable, but I said nothing. "Trust me, Kate, let it go. Find a nice girl and get on with it."

"Don't you start, too," I said.

"You're too damned independent. Your father was right," he said with a wry grin.

"So I've been told. What are you doing at the airport? You haven't moved back?" I stopped and gave him a hopeful look.

He laughed and pulled me along. "Hell, no. Arizona is great. The climate is perfect for a broken down P.I. I was in New York. I'm on my way to my plane."

We walked toward his gate in a comfortable silence. "Well, Kate, I gotta go. God, it was great seeing you." He pulled me into a fierce hug. "Write or call me if you need anything, kiddo."

"You do the same. I love you, Bob."

He smiled and I felt his hand on the back of my neck caressing the scarred area. He lightly touched his forehead against mine. "Close shave there, Irish."

"Too close," I said and kissed him.

"I'll be in touch," he said. "We were a good team, weren't we?"

I nodded through my tears. "The best. Take care of yourself." I watched him as he limped out of sight. My heart ached for him when I remembered how we almost died saving each other. I started walking back and felt like a salmon going upstream. Did I mention how I hate crowds?

As I walked out of the terminal, forgetting I was no longer in the pristine Wyoming air, I took a deep breath and let out a hacking cough. I was ready to hail a cab when I saw Maggie Winfield leaning against her car. I hadn't seen her in almost a month.

"Can I give you a lift, lady?" she asked, smiling.

I smiled in return. When Maggie Winfield's sparkling blue eyes smiled, you had no choice but to smile back. Well, I didn't anyway. "What in the world are you doing here?" I asked as I tossed my luggage in the trunk.

"I called Teri. Your sister told me when you'd be coming back since you didn't bother to tell me. My shift at the hospital starts in an hour, so I thought I'd pick you up." She gave me a scornful look. "Get in. I don't want a ticket."

We drove in relative silence for a minute or two. "Thanks for picking me up. I-I've thought about you," I said, suddenly feeling warm. *Geez, has she got the heat on?*

Maggie watched the road. "Really? I thought about you, too. I was on call in the emergency room. A man came in who stepped on a rake and the handle came up and broke his nose. I said to myself, now this is something Kate would do." She gave me a sidelong glance accompanied with that damnable sarcastic smirk.

I said nothing as I looked out the window. She was right, though, I was terribly accident prone. I tried to ignore her contagious chuckling but soon it grabbed me and we both laughed. We were still laughing as she pulled into my driveway.

Out of the blue, Maggie reached over and took my hand. "I really have missed you," she said softly.

I looked down at her small warm hand covering mine. "Me too," I replied. I knew there were a few mature sentences rolling around in my empty cavern, but I couldn't think of anything appropriate. It was becoming an annoying habit.

"Wanna come in?" *Oh, much better, Ryan.*

"I'd love to, but I have to get back to the hospital. I'll be on call till tomorrow at noon, then I'm done for good," she said.

"Maggie, your internship is done? Is it that time already? I almost forgot," I said, trying to sound amazed.

The adorable feistiness showed for an instant. *She's about to blow!*

"Well, I don't expect anyone to remember," she answered.

"It's been a long six months, but it seemed to pass so quickly, didn't it? We haven't seen much of each other, with you traveling and me at the hospital. Christ, I haven't seen anybody. I have to call Aunt Hannah."

"Yes, it has. Boy, six months, hmm," I said absently. I glanced at her angry face as I retrieved my luggage. "Thanks for picking me up. How about I call you later tomorrow? Maybe we'll go out for dinner or something and celebrate."

"That sounds fine. Dinner would be great—if you have the time. I'm glad you're back." She got in her car and pulled away—too quickly.

I winced as I heard the tires squeal. She'd be totally surprised the next day, if she didn't kill me first.

I got myself all settled in and called my sister.

"Hey, you're back. How are you?" Teri asked.

"Fine, I'm pooped." I looked over at my wonderful mutt, Chance, who was happy I was home as well… She was sound asleep, sprawled out on the couch.

"Did Maggie pick you up?"

"Yes, she thinks I forgot tomorrow is her last day of internship. What a goof." I balanced the phone against my ear. "You haven't spilled the beans about the party, have you?"

"Of course not. Oh, I called Hannah. She told everybody and they'll be there tomorrow about two o'clock." Teri let out a hearty laugh. "Hannah is a riot. By the way, she said to say thanks again for letting her use your house for the party."

"Well, Doc and Nathan are already here at the university, and Charlie's flying to O'Hare. So it made sense," I said, looking out the window. I thought about Hannah and all the trouble we had nearly six months before. Cedar Lake, Illinois, would never be the same. "I still can't believe Charlie is Maggie's brother. What a mess that was," I said. "I'm glad they came through it safe and sound."

I let out a short laugh. "I miss Hannah. It'll be good to see them all again."

"I still can't believe what we went through last fall. I can't believe you got shot." I heard the amazement in her voice. "Can't believe you solved a twenty-year-old murder and got a girl, too." Now I heard the hopeful tone.

"Maggie is not my girl. We're becoming great friends. Besides, I-I'm no good at relationships, you know me." I quickly changed the topic. "You'll never guess who I ran into at the airport. Bob Whittier."

"No! How is he? God, you haven't seen him since..."

"I know. We talked about it. I can't believe it's been five years since that nightmare."

"How are Helen and the kids?"

"Fine. He looks happy. I'm so glad Helen made him quit the P.I. business. His security business seems to be doing well," I said. "He deserves a good life."

"So do you. I know that whole mess with your P.I. business is still haunting you. You've got to get it out in the open someday. You and Maggie have become close friends in the past few months. Maybe you could tell her," Teri suggested. "At least you can get your head out of your log cabin and join the human race again."

"Teri—" I grumbled.

"Oh, hush. Have you ever told Maggie about it?"

"Nope," I said and watched Chance sleeping. I yawned in empathy.

"Why not?"

"I've tried on a couple of occasions, but hell, how do I start a conversation like that?" I stopped and thought for a moment. "How 'bout this, 'Hey, Maggie, did I ever tell you about my P.I. business that went bust over a lying murderer I fell in love with? Oh, by the way, she about blew off my partner's leg and sliced me wide open from my neck to my shoulder.' So how 'bout a movie?"

"Don't get sarcastic with me," Teri said in motherly fashion. "You can't keep hiding behind sarcastic remarks—or your log cabin."

I put my hand to my forehead. I felt the wave of nausea start as it does whenever I think of that time. "God, I'm a mess of a woman."

"You are not. Look, I know it's hard, but Maggie's a good person. You might do well to tell someone who's objective. She might be the one."

I remembered five years before and a different—someone.

"So—you love me, right?" I asked playfully and Liz snuggled

19

closer.

"More than I thought possible," she replied.

"We'll figure this out, Liz." I looked down into her brown eyes and kissed her. A wave of contentment rippled through me as I pulled her close. "I love you," I whispered.

I thought she was the one, too.

Chapter 2

I was sound asleep the next morning when the phone rang. It was Teri.

"What time is it?" I asked, rubbing my eyes.

"You sleepyhead, it's almost nine. You have to come over right away, I can't believe this," she said, and I heard the excitement in her voice. "Hurry. Everything is fine, just hurry."

I never got ready so fast in all my life. After nearly tripping over Chance a few times, I bounded out the door. I was there in fifteen minutes, completely out of breath.

Teri answered the door with a big smile. "Good grief, did you run?"

"You said hurry. What in the heck is going on?"

Mac came out of the kitchen. "Hey, Sherlock, want some coffee?"

"Sure," I said warily as I looked back and forth from grinning sister to smirking brother-in-law. I gave them both a suspicious look and followed them into the kitchen.

As I sat at the table, I noticed a letter lying there. Mac casually put a cup of coffee in front of me and sat down, and I drummed my fingers on the table. Patience is not a strong point of mine.

Teri drank her coffee and looked at Mac. "Okay, you tell her."

"Somebody better tell me something," I said with my best threatening tone, which rarely works.

"Well, you remember me talking about my Uncle Brian from Ireland?" he asked simply and I nodded. "Well—"

Teri interrupted him. "He's dead," she said morbidly.

My eyes flew open and I gaped at them. "No! When, how—?"

"We have no idea," she said slowly and looked at Mac.

"Can I tell her this?" he asked.

Teri winced apologetically. "Sorry, sweetie, go ahead."

Mac cleared his throat. "It's from an attorney in downtown

Chicago. Read it." He handed me the letter.

I read it and when finished, I looked at them in amazement. "You're in his will?" I asked and looked back at the letter. "It says he died in an accident a week ago, but doesn't say what kind. Poor guy, I wish you had known earlier, Mac, you could've gone over there."

"I only met him a few times when I was younger. I was over in Ireland before I married Teri. We hit it off and I liked him. We've been corresponding back and forth ever since, but I never got back to see him again." Mac stared off for a second. "He was a kind old guy—full of the devil and always smiling. I loved to be around him. I have no idea what in the world I'm doing in his will."

"You obviously left an impression on him. You have to go downtown and see this Marty O'Shea on Monday. I wonder what you inherited," I said.

We sat there staring at the letter. With that, the phone rang and Mac left to answer it.

I looked at Teri and whispered, "How old was this guy?"

Teri leaned in and whispered, as well, "Mac said about seventy. However, he wasn't sick. I have no idea how he died."

"Why are we whispering?" I whispered with a grin. Teri glared at me.

Mac came back to the table sporting a deep frown. "That was the attorney. He wanted to make sure the courier delivered the letter. He called me Mr. McAuliffe four times and wanted to know if I needed a car to take me to his office."

"They want to send a car?" I asked, wild-eyed.

"I can't believe we have to wait the weekend," Teri said in a deflated voice. "Let's get over to your house and make sure everything is set for the party."

By noon, *Operation Dr. Winfield* was in motion. Maggie would be completely surprised. Everyone would be in town and at my place by two that afternoon. I was to pick up Maggie and think of a reason to come back to my place. That shouldn't be too hard, should it? I dismissed the nagging feeling that Maggie wouldn't want to come back to my house. *God, explain that to a houseful of guests.*

"Did you have it delivered?" Teri asked.

"She got it this morning about nine," I said, not able to control the damnable fluttering in my stomach.

"Kate, that was so thoughtful of you."

"The poor kid is a doctor now. I thought she'd like it. I hope it reminds her of her mother, but I don't want her to be sad." I glanced at my watch. "Okay, I'm going to go get her. I'll be back by two."

As I drove up to the hospital, I saw Maggie standing outside the emergency room with several people. Being five-foot-nothing, she looked dwarfed. I couldn't help but smile when I saw her. She was certainly attractive. She had her thick auburn hair pulled back, and her smile lit up her face.

She looked up when she heard my voice. "Excuse me, I'm in need of a doctor," I called out in a grave voice.

She smiled wildly and I grinned like a fool. She had the purple hyacinth plant in her arms and a sarcastic grin on her adorable face. "Yes, miss, the Psychiatric Department is on the second floor."

Dr. Winfield was the queen of sarcasm. I laughed. "Hey, where'd ya get the gorgeous plant?" The gentle fragrance wafted my way. It instantly brought back the memory of six months before and how we met.

"Oh, some considerate woman gave it to me. I don't know how she knew it was my favorite." She looked at me with tears in her eyes and put her hand to my cheek. "Thank you," she said and kissed said cheek.

"You're welcome and congratulations, Dr. Winfield," I said. I looked down into her eyes and had a wild idea to kiss her. Instead, I ruffled her hair as I opened the car door for her. "I think I'm gonna like having a doctor in the family."

Maggie raised an eyebrow. "Whose family?"

My face was red hot. "Uh—"

Maggie laughed and mercifully changed the topic. "Where are we going?" she asked as she settled in beside me. I heard the excitement in her voice.

"Well, if you don't mind, I have to go back to my house. I have some photos I have to pick up."

"You've got work today?" Now I heard the dejected tone.

"No, I have to drop them off. It won't take long," I said casually, stealing a glance at the disappointed look on her face.

We pulled into my driveway and I saw no familiar cars—this was good.

I got out and Maggie didn't. "C'mon in," I said and she stubbornly sat there. "Oh, come on," I urged and yanked her small frame out of the car.

I opened the door, and when we walked in, she saw the banner that read, *Congratulations, Dr. Winfield.* She looked at me in amazement, her blue eyes sparkling with tears.

Her Aunt Hannah came out of the kitchen, with Chance bounding right behind her. "Heavens, it's about time you got here."

Maggie put her hands over her face and started to cry. She turned into me and I instinctively put my arms around her.

One by one, all the people Maggie loved walked out of the kitchen and surrounded us. She slowly pulled away and looked up at me with those big blue eyes and I chucked her under the chin. "Surprise," I said.

"Thank you, Kate," she said, and the sincerity in her voice pulled at my heart. Then as quick as that, someone whisked her away.

I walked over to Teri and shook her hand. "Success," we said simultaneously.

As I watched Maggie with her family and friends, she seemed relaxed and happy for the first time in months.

Mac, bless him, was tending bar. "Good job, Sherlock. She looked completely surprised." He slid a drink in front of me and raised his glass in congratulations.

Maggie's brother, Charlie, joined us and he kissed my cheek. "Kate, you and Aunt Hannah did a wonderful job. You both belong in the CIA."

"Maggie was surprised. This is good for her. It's good for all of you. Six months ago, it was touch and go," I said as Mac got him a drink.

"Then you came along and saved a family. Good Lord, Kate Ryan, what a mess you solved," he said, shaking his head.

When his smiled faded, I knew what he was thinking. We

discovered the horrible truth that almost destroyed two families.

I watched him for a moment. He was your typical, tall dark and handsome man, with deep brown eyes. He and Maggie looked very similar. Speaking of Maggie, she was talking and laughing, and every so often, we'd catch each other's eye.

"Well, Kate, we did it." I heard Hannah's voice behind me. What a handsome woman Hannah Winfield was. Her silver hair shimmered and reflected her cool blue eyes, which were always smiling with mischief. She shared Maggie's vertically challenged stature, convincing me that good things do indeed come in small packages. She was, in a word, adorable.

"This was a wonderful thing you did, Hannah," I said as I watched Maggie.

"She deserves it. She's been through a great deal in the past six months," Hannah said. "If it weren't for you, I don't know where she'd be right now. I don't know where any of us would be."

"You've all been through a great deal. Let's all relax and have fun this weekend—no worries." I gave her a quick peck on the cheek. "I miss you."

"I miss you, too, dear," she said as she hugged me. "Are you happy?" she whispered in my ear.

I pulled back, hearing the curious question. "Sure, I am."

"Margaret tells me you two haven't seen much of each other."

"Kinda hard when she's busy with the hospital and I'm traveling all over. Besides, she needed to finish this," I said as I jingled the ice in my glass.

"And now that she's finished?" Hannah prodded.

"I thought she was going to take over for Doc."

Hannah sighed deeply. "Goodness, you're insufferable," she said. The quiet tone to her voice made me feel like a scolded child.

"I think I'm a *little* sufferable," I mumbled in response.

She laughed then and pulled me down for a kiss. "You're very sufferable, and you know what I'm talking about."

Yes, I knew what she was getting at. It didn't take a brain surgeon. "Look, Maggie and I—" I heard a familiar voice and looked over.

It was Allison. I had forgotten about her. She was hugging and kissing Maggie.

Hannah sighed. "I wish Maggie wouldn't spend time with her."

"Hannah," I said disapprovingly. I looked over at them as they talked and laughed. "When does she have the time to see Allison?" I asked curiously as I watched them, not that I cared. I didn't. I listened to their laughter and took another healthy drink.

"Don't swallow the glass," Hannah suggested with a smirk.

"Have to admit she's gorgeous," I said and watched them.

Allison *was* a gorgeous woman: five-foot-nine and all legs. Almond-shaped green eyes, jet-black hair—not one strand of gray. Yep, she looked liked the actress from the '50s, Ava Gardner. I jingled the ice in my glass once again, as I looked for one flaw. I would be happy to find just one.

I glared at her for a moment and I heard Hannah's soft laughter. "It's just not natural, is it?" she asked as if reading my mind. I laughed openly—I loved Hannah Winfield.

"I haven't seen Allison since we were all embroiled in solving Miranda's murder," I said. Allison was Maggie's first love and was still in hot pursuit despite Maggie denying the possibility.

As I watched Maggie and Allison, I ignored the pang of emptiness in the pit of my stomach. I turned my back on them and playfully slapped the bar. "I guess I have to make my own drink. Okay, I'm tending bar, anyone need a refill?" I walked around to play bartender.

"I could use one," Maggie said.

I hadn't noticed her walk over as I looked down into those damn blue eyes. "Sure, gin and tonic, right?"

"Right," she said. "Aunt Hannah told me you offered your house for the party. Thank you, it was sweet of you."

"Well, *Dr.* Winfield, you're entirely welcome. Congratulations," I replied.

We looked at each other for a moment. I can't explain the pulling sensation, but we smiled and I met her halfway around the bar. She reached out for me and threw her arms around my neck and hugged me so tight that she left me no choice but to wrap my arms around her and hold her in a tight embrace. For a long moment, I felt oddly content to stay right there. "Maggie, I—"

"Mags, look who's here," Allison's voice called out.

Maggie looked her way and turned back to me with a

questioning look. "Were you about to say something, Miss Ryan?" she asked with a raised eyebrow.

I put my hand up to her cheek. "You'd better get back to your guests," I said in a quiet voice. "I'm proud of you, Maggie. Now beat it, Doc."

As she walked away, I felt the eyes of scrutiny upon me. I looked over to see Hannah sporting a smug look.

"What?" I asked. *Must I always feel like a ten-year-old with this woman?*

"Kate Ryan, I love you as I love Margaret, so I feel it my duty to tell you—you're an idiot," she said evenly and patted my cheek. "Nice party, dear."

Now I watched the elder Winfield walk away… *Crap.*

Chapter 3

The rest of the day went very well with people coming and going all afternoon, and by seven o'clock, the party dwindled down to me, Maggie, Teri and Mac, and Hannah, who was sipping a daiquiri.

"It's a good thing Maggie is driving you to the hotel, young woman," I scolded playfully.

Hannah laughed and sipped her drink. "I can never say no to one of Mac's daiquiris."

I plopped onto the couch and kicked off my shoes. "Good grief, Maggie, you know a lot of people," I groaned.

Maggie was about to say something, but a knock at the front door interrupted her. I groaned again and got up. "If this is one more friend of yours..."

I opened the door and a tall young man was standing there. He had black hair and deep blue eyes. His face, however, was as white as a ghost.

"Is Michael McAuliffe here, ma'am?" he asked in an Irish whisper. He had his hand under his coat, holding his side. "If you'd be so kind." He swayed and fell forward right into my arms.

"Mac, help me!" I called over my shoulder.

Mac quickly took the young man on the other side. "Who is this?"

"What makes you think I know him? He asked for you."

"You know the most interesting people, Kate," Hannah chimed in over my shoulder.

We got him into the living room and sat him on the couch. Chance immediately bounded up and sat next to her new playmate. I glared at her. "Get down," I ordered, and since I've trained her well, she sat there.

The young man tried to get up, but Mac put his hand on his shoulder. "Easy there, pal. You look terrible. Are you all right?"

29

Maggie gently pushed Teri and me aside. "You look feverish." She sat next to him. "What's your name?"

He either ignored Maggie or didn't hear her, for he looked at Mac. "I need to see Michael McAuliffe. Would that be you, sir?"

"Yes, I'm Mike McAuliffe. Who are you?"

He closed his eyes and took his hand away from his side. I noticed the blood on his shaking hand.

"Ohh," I groaned helplessly. "Here we go." I glanced at Hannah—wide-eyed and sipping her daiquiri.

"My name is Peter Sullivan," he said in a quiet voice.

Teri offered him a glass of water, which he promptly gulped, finishing the entire glass. "Mr. Sullivan, if you don't mind my saying so, you look like hell."

Maggie had opened his jacket. There was blood all over the side of his shirt. "It looks like you've sprung a leak, Mr. Sullivan," Maggie said as she examined his side.

"It would appear so, miss." He looked at Mac and whispered, "I wanted to make sure you got to Ireland in one piece, Mr. McAuliffe, but I'm afraid I bungled it."

"You're going to Ireland?" Hannah asked and took another sip.

"Ireland? I'm not going to Ireland," Mac advised him.

"I think you might be, sir. I knew your uncle. He was a good friend to me when I needed one. I saw him the day before he died. He knew something was about to happen. He told me about his will and asked me to come get you and bring you to him. Unfortunately, he died the next day. He wanted to see you and tell you."

"Tell me what?" Mac asked. I heard the impatience in his voice, which rarely happens.

"I don't know, sir. He didn't tell me."

"Look, we've got to get you to a hospital," Maggie said evenly and stood.

The Irishman quickly grabbed her arm. "No, no hospitals. Just put a Band-Aid on it. I'll be fine," he said as he stood up and swayed. "There, I'm fine now."

Mac stood in front of him. "Look, Mr. Sullivan, I don't know who you are or how you know so much, but you're bleeding. I can't let you leave in this condition," he said firmly.

"No doctors and you mustn't leave the house," Peter Sullivan said. As Mac put his arm under him, he collapsed.

"Bring him to the spare room," I said.

Maggie ran out to the car and came back with her medical bag. She sat next to Mr. Sullivan and opened his shirt. The young man winced and looked at Mac. "I said no doctors," he warned.

"It's okay, she's family," Mac said.

Peter looked at Teri, Hannah, and me. "We're family, too," Hannah announced.

I was getting a headache. I made the quick introductions.

"I have to clean this wound," Maggie said and looked up at me.

"Go ahead, you're the doctor, Maggie, I—" I stopped at the exasperated look on her face.

"I need hot water and clean towels," she said calmly.

"Oh."

Mac and I bumped into each other trying to get to the kitchen. "Mac," I said as the kettle whistled. "What the hell did you inherit?"

"I have no idea," Mac said. I heard the anger in his voice as we headed back to the bedroom.

I noticed the young man's breathing was ragged when we entered the room. I set the bowl down on the nightstand. Maggie took a small towel and placed it on his side. "Mr. Sullivan, you realize you've been stabbed," Maggie said.

The declaration stunned Mac and Teri. Hannah promptly fell back into a nearby chair. I groaned deeply, "Wonderful."

Maggie glared at me as she tended to the bleeding Irishman.

"Well, I thought as much," he whispered.

"When did this happen?" Maggie asked as she washed his side and took another towel.

"Earlier this evening. He was outside this house. I scared him away and followed him. He got me in the alley."

"Who is *he*?" I asked. He avoided me and closed his eyes.

"No questions yet, Kate," Maggie said as she concentrated on her doctoring skills. "It's not too deep, but I have to suture this. He should be at the hospital."

Peter opened his eyes and quickly grabbed her arm. "No. You can do this. Please."

31

"All right," Maggie agreed after a moment of hesitation. "Let me go to the hospital. I can get what I need and be back in twenty minutes. Let him rest. It's stopped bleeding. Keep it clean and covered and don't let him move."

"You're not going alone," I said.

"Kate—" Maggie started.

"We're wasting time, Doctor," I said and grabbed my keys.

As we drove to the hospital, I told Maggie what Mac told me. She stared at me. "What in the world is happening?"

"I don't know. Mac got a letter from a lawyer. His uncle in Ireland died in an accident. Mac is somehow in his will and now this. I have no idea," I said.

"Let me go in alone. I'll be out in two minutes."

I pulled into the ER parking lot, and Maggie walked casually through the doors. It seemed like an eternity before I saw her come out.

She quickly got into the car. "Okay, let's go," she said.

I stared at her in amazement. She was confident and sure of herself. It struck me how savvy this little woman was. At that moment, I was anything but.

Once back home, Maggie sat on the edge of the bed and did the quick doctor thing. "I need a little assistance here. I need a light to shine on his side."

Mac took the shade off the lamp and turned it on. Maggie nodded her approval and looked at me. "Kate, take this." She handed me a stack of gauze pads. "You have to wipe away any blood you see. Mac, give the light to Teri. You have to hold him down if he moves." Maggie directed everyone like a conductor leading an orchestra. I was amazed at her poise and control.

We all stood at our appointed stations and waited for our next orders. I knelt next to Maggie waiting for her command. She cleaned the wound with a brown liquid. I was sure it hurt this poor guy.

"Hold him, Mac," Maggie said. Mac did as he was told. Teri stood behind Maggie with the light. "Teri, a little to the left, please."

She then took out a syringe and filled it with, whatever…

"Novocain?" I asked and fought the wave of nausea. Just

seeing it reminded me of how much I hated hospitals.

"Lidocaine," Maggie answered without looking at me.

I closed my eyes for an instant. "Th-The difference?" I asked and swallowed convulsively. I really didn't care, but my ego was galloping, and I didn't want Maggie to see how much I wanted to hurl at that moment.

"It's just a different topical anethes... Are you all right?" she asked and looked up.

I scoffed at her question. "Of course," I responded quickly. I saw the dubious glance before she administered the shot into the wound.

Hannah put her hand on my arm and gave me a questioning look. "You look a little pale," she whispered and I shook my head in response.

"Kate, wipe there." I took the gauze and looked at the wound. It wasn't long, but it was jagged. I stared at it and felt my heart beating in my ears. I couldn't move. My mind instantly went back to that time, remembering how I lay, like the Irishman, in a pool of my own blood with my neck and back split wide open.

White-hot pain seared through my back as I heard myself scream. Suddenly, I felt nothing as my body slipped to the floor. I heard another gunshot, another scream...

"Kate?" Maggie said loudly.

I jumped and looked at Maggie. Teri handed the lamp to Mac and gently shook my shoulder and I jumped once again.

"Hey, it's all right. Give it to me." Teri took the gauze out of my shaking hand.

Maggie gave me a worried look as I moved out of the way, feeling like a shivering fool.

Teri swabbed the area. I regained my composure and took the lamp from Mac.

He patted me on the shoulder. "It's okay, Kate."

I gave him a sick, shaky smile.

Within twenty minutes, Maggie was done. It took fifteen stitches to close the wound. She put a gauze pad over it and taped it. The poor kid had passed out long before she started.

"Can you get a clean cloth and a bowl of cool water?" Maggie asked me. A useless feeling tore through me as I merely nodded.

I came back and put it on the nightstand. If Maggie noticed my hand trembling, she didn't let on. She dipped the cloth in the water and cleaned his face and neck. She was so gentle with him. Then he stirred and opened his eyes.

"Lay still. You're fine," Maggie said, and he closed his eyes. "You all did great. I think he'll be fine. The only problem is infection. I brought some antibiotics if that happens. Hopefully, we won't need them."

She checked his pulse again. "He hasn't lost too much blood and the wound wasn't that deep. I think it's exposure and exhaustion more than anything." She stood and stretched her back.

"You're remarkable," Mac said.

"Thanks, Mac. He'll sleep for a while. We can check on him later."

We all stood in the kitchen dumbfounded. Maggie stood at the sink and washed her hands. She looked around and I handed her a towel.

"Thanks," she said and looked at me, searching my face—probably looking for some sign of sanity.

"Mac was right, you were remarkable," I said.

She looked up and smiled. "Well, thanks again." She gave me a concerned look as a doctor gives a patient.

We were silent for a moment until Mac spoke. "When that young man wakes up, I have a few questions for him."

"I have one right now," I said tiredly. "How did Mr. Sullivan know Mac was at my house?"

I glanced at Mac, who shrugged. "Well, he said the fellow who stabbed him was outside this house," Mac offered.

"And what was *that* guy doing outside my house? Mr. Sullivan must have been either following that guy, whoever he is, or he knows him and…" I stopped and looked down the hall.

"He won't be answering any questions tonight, Kate. I gave him a sedative," Maggie said simply.

"I certainly could use one," Hannah mumbled and put a shaky hand to her silver hair.

"Do you think he was serious about not leaving the house?" Teri asked.

I looked at the clock, ten thirty. "I have a bad feeling here. Why don't you all spend the night?" I asked and looked at

Maggie. "Maggie, if he wakes up during the night, I'd feel better if you were here. Mac and Teri, you take my room. Hannah, you can have the other spare room. Maggie can take the couch. I don't know what's going on here, but I would feel better if you stayed."

Maggie stood. "I agree. I'm going to check on our patient. I'll be right back."

We were silent as Maggie left the kitchen. Mac turned to me. "You okay, kiddo? You were out of it for a minute or two."

I walked over to the sink and leaned against it. "All I could see was the blood. I thought about Bob, his leg covered in it—" I slammed my hand on the counter. It was all coming back in a hurry, all the ugliness.

Mac came over to me. "It's okay. It's over and—"

I whirled around to him. "It's not over! Five years and I still can't get over it. Dammit!" I stopped and took a deep quivering breath, trying to calm the anxiety attack I feared was coming. "Okay, enough. I have some stranger bleeding in my spare room, and I'm standing here like a jackass—"

"Kate, you're not a jackass," Hannah said and pulled me down for a warm hug. "Perhaps just an ass, but never a jackass."

As I pulled back, I noticed Maggie standing in the doorway sporting a worried look.

"Hey, how's the patient?" I turned away and got a glass of water as my hands shook pathetically.

"He's still asleep. I'm sure he'll sleep the night," she said. I could feel her watching me.

"Which is what we're planning. G'night, ladies," Mac said, and he and Teri left the kitchen.

"I'll get your bed ready," I said to Hannah and walked past them to the other spare bedroom.

With everyone safely in their rooms, I pulled out the sheets, and together, Maggie and I made up the couch. I could tell Maggie wanted to say something. She always hums to herself when something is on her mind. She was doing this now and it was driving me nuts.

"Okay, okay, what?" I asked impatiently.

She looked up. "What, what?"

"Don't what, what me. You always hum when you want to say something but don't know if you should."

"I do not. Do I?"

"Yes, you do. What's on your mind?"

"I was wondering what happened to you back there. You looked a little rattled. I've never seen you like that before." She threw the cover on the couch.

"N-Nothing happened. I guess I was stunned, that's all," I said quickly. "All set for beddy-bye? In ya go."

"Okay, I know a brush-off when I get one," she said too seriously and walked over to the fireplace.

Not knowing what to say, I wisely kept my mouth shut.

"I know we haven't talked about much for the past few months," Maggie said. "You've been traveling and I've been at the hospital. It's hard to get to know each other. I don't know how you feel, but I'd like to."

"Maggie, there's things you don't know that I'm not sure I can talk about right now. I—" I stopped and ran my fingers through my hair. "Look, it's late. Why don't we get some sleep? A lot has happened."

"I can't make you talk. I'll listen whenever you're ready." She reached up and kissed my cheek. "Where are you going to sleep?"

"My sleeping bag will be fine for tonight," I said and retrieved the bag from the closet. As I laid it out in front of the fireplace, I felt Maggie watching me.

"Thanks for the party. It was sweet of you," she said and slipped under the covers.

I struggled into the sleeping bag and stifled a huge groan. I was getting too old for sleeping bags. "You're welcome. I was glad to do it," I said and yawned wildly. "G'night."

"Good night."

I watched the flames for a time, listening to Maggie's deep breathing. Only when I was sure she was asleep did I have the courage to steal a look at her. She was lying on her side, facing the fire. The fire's light danced around her face and I smiled when I saw her brow furrowed as if she were dreaming. The image of lying next to her and holding her close flashed through my mind. I quickly dismissed it.

Maggie was becoming such a good friend. *I don't know how you feel, but I'd like to.* Her words rang in my ears. Could it be possible to tell her, to let her in on the shame that I carried?

Chance, the loyal but cowardly mutt who was suspiciously absent during this entire mess, jumped up and lay on my stomach. Her nose was inches away from mine. "You understand me, don't you?" I whispered and ruffled her ears. "Don't answer that." She licked my face in response.

I was dreaming that Maggie was kneeling next to me. I opened my eyes and there she was, kneeling next to me. "Kate, wake up," she said.

"What's wrong?" I whispered, rubbing my eyes. I heard Chance growling from somewhere inside my sleeping bag. *How did she get in there?*

"I think somebody's in your yard."

I jumped up, nearly threw out my back, and stumbled to the kitchen.

Through the blinds, I saw a figure roaming about. Chance barked and the figure took off. The fleeing figure in a dark coat hopped my fence and was gone. I reached for the door handle and Maggie grabbed my hand.

"Oh, no, you don't," she insisted.

I watched for several minutes and saw nothing more. "I'm sure Chance scared the hell out of him." I made sure the door was locked.

It was then I noticed Maggie was shivering. I put my arm around her shoulders and felt the silky material of her robe. "Nice duds," I whispered. I heard the soft laugh and chuckled along.

"Are you flirting with me, Miss Ryan?" she asked.

"I'm not sure," I answered honestly.

To my surprise, she reached up and caressed my cheek. *Quit touching me.*

"Well, that's a start," she said.

We made another check of all the doors and windows. Peter was still sleeping.

"What in the hell is going on?" Maggie asked as we stood in the hallway.

"I wish I knew," I said. "We'll know for sure by Monday morning. Get some sleep."

I had a bad feeling we'd know a great deal more on Monday. Much more than we wanted.

Chapter 4

I woke up to the smell of coffee. As I crawled out of my sleeping bag, I fought the urge to continue crawling and grabbed onto the desk chair. I got to my knees first, then stretched my back and finally stood, feeling like *Homo erectus* coming out of a long winter's hibernation. God, I was stiff! It's not that I'm old—forty-four isn't that old, but oh, I felt every bit and then some in the morning.

I heard somebody humming as I ambled toward the kitchen. Maggie was at the stove, putting bacon in a pan. She looked down at Chance the Beggar.

"No, this is not for you. And don't go waking up Kate, either, she spoils you."

My loyal canine then offered her paw. I hid my eyes—Chance was a flirt. Maggie chuckled, ruffled her ears, and offered a piece of bacon. "I hope this doesn't wreak havoc with your cholesterol."

I stood against the doorjamb with my arms folded across my chest. *This is a nice sight.* Somehow, it seemed right to see this feisty woman in my home.

As she stood, she noticed me. "Good morning, did I wake you?"

"No, I smelled coffee. I thought you didn't know how to cook." I looked at the sizzling pan.

"I don't. I thought you might finish," she said sheepishly. She thrust the kitchen utensil in my hand. "I'm going to check on our patient. He should be waking up soon." She dashed out of the kitchen.

"Hey! Get back here," I said and turned off the stove.

I followed her down the hall, and as she opened the door, Peter stirred and woke. Not realizing where he was, he tried to sit up. Maggie put her hand on his shoulder.

"Easy, don't move too much. Let me take a look," she said.

39

She pulled the covers down to his waist and checked her work. "Hmm. I did a good job."

"Thank you. I'm sorry, I don't remember your name," he said smiling.

"Maggie."

He frowned. "Mr. McAuliffe mentioned you were family."

Maggie glanced at me. "Well, Mr. Sullivan, I'm sort of a... sister," she announced dryly and smiled sweetly in my direction.

I offered a slight, albeit dramatic, bow. Poor Mr. Sullivan didn't know what to think.

"I have a few questions, Mr. Sullivan," I said.

"Let the poor guy eat first." Maggie looked at Peter. "Are you hungry?"

"I could use a bite," he said, oozing Irish charm.

Young Peter Sullivan ate as if he never saw food before. Maggie took the tray away and I looked at it. "He didn't eat the plate, did he?" I asked.

Peter blushed and looked at Mac who was standing by the door with his arms folded across his chest.

"Good mornin'," Peter said in a hesitant voice.

"Good morning," Mac answered with a nod.

Peter adjusted himself and sat up. Maggie put a pillow behind his head and felt his forehead. She looked at Mac and me. "Okay, you have ten minutes," she said and sat down.

"Mr. Sullivan," Mac started.

"Please, call me Peter."

"Peter, what in the hell is going on?" Mac asked.

No use beating around the bush.

"Well, sir, as I said, I was sent by Brian to make sure you got to Ireland in one piece. He figured there might be bad feelings. That was how he put it."

"Bad feelings regarding what?" I asked.

Peter shook his head. "I have no idea. That was all Brian said. Then the next day, he was dead and I was bound to come and get ya as I promised."

"You came all the way from Ireland to make sure I was on my way there? Why would I be going to Ireland?" Mac asked.

"Again, sir, I have no idea. Brian said he knew you'd come," Peter said and shrugged.

"That's a pretty expensive ticket, Peter," I said, looking him in the eyes.

"Brian paid for the ticket. There was no way I could get money like that."

"How do you know my uncle?" Mac asked.

"I was his employee. You see, besides owning the woolen mill, he owned a few horses. I'm a horse trainer by profession," he said simply. "He owns a few Connemara ponies."

Maggie's eyebrow rose. "Really? They're expensive."

"Yes, they are," Peter agreed with a smile and a wink.

I watched him cautiously. *Cool your jets, boyo.*

Mac scratched his head. "This is all too bizarre." He looked at Peter. "Who would want to break into this house?"

Peter sat up quickly and turned white. "Break in? When did this happen?" He looked at all of us.

"Someone was in my backyard last night. When my dog barked, he hopped the fence. What do you make of that?" I asked.

"I don't know," he replied.

For the first time, I thought he wasn't being honest. I gave him a look and he looked in my eyes, and I knew I was right. Mr. Sullivan knew more than he let on.

"We see the lawyer tomorrow morning at nine," Mac said, trying to sound confident. "We'll definitely know what I have to do with my uncle's will."

"When were you planning on going back to Ireland?" Maggie asked Peter.

"I have a return ticket for tomorrow afternoon, five o'clock," he said.

"I think you'll be fine by then. You'd better stay put for the rest of the day," she said and patted his arm.

"You're an angel of mercy, Maggie," he said and winked at her—again.

Oh, brother. I left the room.

Mac followed me to the kitchen. "What do you think?"

I scratched the back of my head. "I don't know. It's hard to tell. I don't know why he'd come all this way. Now he's in the right spot at the right time and the intruder stabs him? Something's not right, Mac. However, if he's right, your uncle trusted him enough to send him across an ocean to bring you to Ireland. Let's

41

see what the will says. If you inherit the family dog or something, Mr. Sullivan has a lot more explaining to do. However, if you get something more, then Mr. Sullivan has a lot more explaining to do."

"Gee, thanks, that clears it all up, Sherlock."

I patted his back. "I'm always here to help."

Mac and Teri volunteered to watch Peter for the afternoon. Maggie had to take Hannah back to the hotel.

"So what are you going to do?" I asked Maggie.

"I'm going downtown. Aunt Hannah, Dad, and Charlie are all leaving this afternoon." She stared out at the backyard. "It's still hard to believe what happened last fall…" Her voice trailed off.

"C'mon now. Give yourself some time. It's an adjustment, but you have so many people who love you and I—" I stopped abruptly.

She looked at me and laughed affectionately. "You should see your face, Kate Ryan. How is it that you always know what to say?"

I looked down at my plate and ate the remainder of my breakfast. "Not always, Maggie," I said and I could feel her watching me.

"What have you got planned for the day?" she asked.

I shrugged. "Nothing really."

"Why don't you come with me? We could spend some time with Aunt Hannah before they go back. Maybe you and I could spend some time together. That'll be a first. You don't have to fly off somewhere and I don't have to be at the hospital. Unless you have something else you'd rather do."

I looked up into the questioning blue eyes and tried to think of something else. Nothing came to mind.

"Take care of my niece," Hannah said and looked me. She then looked at Maggie. "Take care of Kate."

Maggie and I glanced at each other. "Okay," we both said obediently. She kissed us and drove off. We watched the car drive out of sight. Maggie took a deep breath and looked at me.

"What now?" she asked. "Now that you've promised to take care of me."

"Let's go to the zoo, then lunch," I said, avoiding the smirk. "I think better when I eat, and I'm trying to figure out what the hell is going on here. Let's go."

The day had turned sunny and warm again as we walked through Lincoln Park Zoo. Maggie and I talked about nothing in particular as we strolled around. I was eating peanuts and Maggie was humming. After an agonizing minute or two, I stopped. "You're humming again," I said.

"Was I?" she asked innocently.

I gave her a stern look. "Out with it, Doctor."

"What do you think Mac will inherit?"

"I haven't a clue. However, this is becoming strange—the Sullivan guy, the guy last night."

"It does seem peculiar," she agreed.

"Hey, you did a pretty good job last night with the bleeding Mr. Sullivan, Dr. Winfield."

"Thanks, I wondered how I would handle it on my own. I might make a good doctor someday," she said.

"Someday? You did fine, Maggie," I said and ate my peanuts.

"Well, I'm thinking of switching to psychiatry. You can be my first patient and make me rich and famous," she said lightly and grabbed some peanuts.

"You're already rich," I reminded her and slapped her hand away.

We stopped for lunch at a little Italian restaurant and got a quiet table by the window. I was checking the menu and could feel her watching me. *I think she does this on purpose.*

"What's on your mind, Maggie?" I asked, still examining my menu.

"I was thinking about how we met."

"Did I ever apologize for knocking you off your horse?"

"I don't think so," she said as she examined her menu. "Did I ever apologize for calling you an imbecile?"

"Nope." I looked back at my menu. "You are a feisty thing, Dr. Winfield."

"And you're an independent woman, Miss Ryan," she said and added, "Too independent."

In the middle of a mouthful of pasta, I saw a man watching us. I thought nothing of it, but he went to my car and looked in. I thought that was curious, so I watched. When he came back to the window and watched us, I had enough.

"Okay, this guy is bugging me. I'll be right back."

When he saw me walk out of the restaurant, he took off down the street. I ran after him, dodging people right and left, trying not to lose sight of him. As he turned around the corner, I followed and tripped on some woman's dog.

I flew ass over end into a garbage can and went sprawling on the pavement, knocking the wind out of myself. I lay there for a moment, staring at the blue sky. I got up with a groan and rubbed my arse.

"Young woman, what is the matter with you? You almost killed my dog!"

I wasn't listening. I was still looking in all directions.

Maggie came running up to me. "Are you all right?"

"Dammit, I lost him," I said. The woman was still yelling at me. I looked at her. "Okay, okay. I get it—I almost killed your dog. I'm sorry," I said, waving my hand at her.

She walked away in a huff with her little ball of fur waddling behind her.

"You ripped your shirt," Maggie said. She reached over and lifted my arm. "And of course you're bleeding. Christ, Kate."

I looked down at my elbow. "It's nothing. Let's go back."

When we got back to the restaurant, a waitress was standing at our table. "You left your credit card, miss," she said and handed it to Maggie.

They had cleared our table. "Hey, I wasn't finished."

"Sit down, you dope," Maggie said and cleaned my elbow. "Would you mind telling me what in the hell you were doing?"

"It was the guy from last night, I'm sure of it. He had on the same navy blue coat," I said quickly and continued, "he was at the window, and I would've caught up to him if I hadn't tripped over the damned dog."

The waitress had retrieved a first aid kit, which Maggie was rummaging through, looking for her implements of torture. "You tripped over a dog?"

"Yes, I tripped over a dog," I mimicked defensively and winced again as she continued to clean my elbow. "Geez, leave some skin."

"Sit still," Maggie said and finished. "There. Should I kiss it, make it better?"

For a moment, we looked at each other. "Would it?" I asked.

Maggie smiled slightly. "It just might. C'mon, let's get you home before a herd of water buffalo roam by."

As we walked into my living room, Teri came out of the kitchen and took one look at my ripped shirt. "Good grief, now what?"

Maggie gasped dramatically. "Teri, it was horrible. Your sister was attacked by a killer poodle."

I glared at her as I told Teri what had happened. "It was the same guy who came by last night, I'm sure of it. I wouldn't be surprised if my backyard visitor is one in the same."

During the late afternoon, Mac and Teri decided to go home and call in the morning. Maggie offered to stay another night.

"You sure you don't mind staying? You can have the spare room. I feel better when you're here. I mean, if anything happens to Peter," I finished lamely.

She gave me a half smile. I think it was more of a smirk. "I don't mind at all...for Peter's sake, of course. I'll check on him and turn in. Good night, Kate."

I started to say something, God only knows what, but I stopped.

She turned back to me. "Sorry, did you say something?" she asked with a slight grin. "I thought I heard you grunt."

"N-No, I didn't say anything. Good night."

"Hmm. Good night."

I heard her mumbling something as she walked down the hall to the bedroom. I watched her small figure disappear as the door closed. I stood there for a moment and started down the hall...then stopped...then started again...then stopped again.

I glanced over to see Chance staring at me. "Oh, shut up."

Feeling like an idiot doing a one-woman cha-cha in the hall, I finally went to bed.

KATE SWEENEY

Chapter 5

I was pacing like a caged lion. Mac and Teri were still at the lawyer's. "It's almost noon. How long could this take?"

Maggie was sitting on the couch. "You're going to wear a path in your carpet. Relax, they'll be here soon."

"I wonder what they inherited." I glanced at Peter. "Do you have any idea?"

"Honestly, Kate, I do not. I know Brian talked about Mac a good deal in the last six months or so. I know he wrote to him a few times. He told me Mac was a good, honorable man."

"Yes, he is a good, honorable man, and I won't have anything happen to him or Teri. Not for all the emeralds in your Emerald Isle," I said, knowing I sounded threatening, but I wanted him to understand.

Peter nodded. "Understood. I don't want that, either."

I walked out into the kitchen and got a glass of water. Maggie was on my heels. "Did you have to threaten the poor guy?"

"Was I threatening? Hmm. I meant it, though. I don't care if he knows Mac's uncle or not." I thought about it and continued, "Come to think of it, we don't know anything about this kid. How do we know he's not in with whoever tried to break in? Sorry, I'm just not that sure about Mr. Sullivan."

"You can be very suspicious sometimes. Did you acquire that from your private investigation business?" she asked, looking at the counter.

I knew Maggie wanted to know about it. She overheard enough the night before. "That's a part of my life I want to forget. I—"

All of the sudden, I was sweating, and when my hands started shaking, I put them in my pockets.

Maggie put her hands on my shoulders. "Look, I may have

47

just finished my internship, but I know the beginning of an anxiety attack when I see one. You're worrying me, Kate."

"We've got a stabbed Irishman in the living room. Some guy tried to break into my house. This place is crawling with men. Watch where you step." I looked around the floor.

"Someday you'll need to be serious," Maggie said.

And the wall goes up. "My neurosis will have to wait. I don't like what's happening here. You might be better off at home," I said evenly.

I knew I was pushing her away. I avoided the stunned look on her face as I walked past her, leaving her there. A pang of regret hit my stomach, but I walked away.

When Mac and Teri finally returned, they told us about the inheritance. I was shocked.

"Here, read this. It's from Uncle Brian," Mac said with a sad smile.

I took the letter and read it.

My dear Michael,

I know we don't know each other well, you being a Yank and all, but I know you'll do as I wish. Keep the land; it's now part of your soul. But if you don't feel it, don't keep it, for it'll do you no good. I know you'll do the right thing if you do what's in your heart.

There will be many who will try to take it from you. If you decide to give it up, I trust you will hand it over to the right one.

The mill belongs to the people of Duncorrib. This is my only last wish: Go to Ireland, meet the people, and work the mill. If it isn't what you want, do as I ask. There are more important things in this life than money. That's what you said to me all those years ago, and I never forgot it or you.

I know I'm asking a great deal from you, but I remember how you looked when you spoke about the land. It's in your soul, I'm sure of it.

Take care of my land, your land. For heaven's sake, take care of the ponies, they're bloody expensive!

Don't worry, if the good Lord will allow, you'll see me around.

Godspeed to you, Michael.

Brian McAuliffe

Teri had tears in her eyes as I handed it to Maggie. "So what exactly did you inherit?" I asked.

Mac took a deep breath. "Thirty acres of farmland and all that's on the property. A main house, a small cottage, stable, and four Connemara ponies. Here, you read it." Mac thrust the document into my hand.

As I read it, my eyes bugged out of my head. Maggie gently pushed me into a nearby chair. "Okay, Kate. Take a deep breath and read it aloud," she said and sat next to me.

I cleared my throat and started. "Brian McAuliffe owned fifty-one percent of the Oceanview Woolen Mill. He has bequeathed that to Michael Matthew McAuliffe. Should you accept the terms of this will, you will be the controlling stockholder of this business. There are terms to this codicil: The bequeathed must stay on the property and work the mill for at least one year. After that, if Mr. McAuliffe decides not to own this company, he must sell his controlling interest back to the people of Duncorrib as it represents the entire village and their hard work. If you, Michael Matthew McAuliffe, should still desire to sell the Oceanview Woolen Mill, it must be according to this will.

"In the event of Michael McAuliffe's, death, or for any reason Michael McAuliffe refuses the inheritance, the entire estate would be sold and the monies therein divided between the brothers of Brian Martin McAuliffe. The fifty-one percent of the Oceanview Woolen Mill will be handed over to Bridget Donnelly, who is to divide the shares accordingly to the townspeople. The other forty-nine percent is divided equally between James E. McAuliffe, Brian's younger brother, and Timothy M. Devereaux, husband to the late Colleen McAuliffe, Brian's younger sister."

Maggie stared at them in awe. "You have to be joking. You own a woolen mill and his estate?"

Peter whistled. "I knew he wanted ya there for somethin', Mac, but saints above, I had no idea." He scratched the back of his head. I watched him. He looked surprised enough.

"What are you going to do?" I asked Mac.

"I don't know," he said. "It's mine, so I guess we're going to Ireland. I know absolutely nothing about running a woolen mill." He looked at Teri and they both laughed. "Good grief. What have I gotten us into here?"

"Brian didn't run the mill," Peter offered. "He owned it, but Rory Nolan runs it and has for twenty years. Most of the villagers work the mill. Brian stopped in every day to see them all, but he didn't have an active hand in running it."

"There would be no reason for me to change anything," Mac said. "The intent of Brian's will was to make sure if I decided to sell my share, it had to be given back to the village. However, I have to keep it for a year. I'm sure he wanted me to take the time to get to know the people and the business."

"It says here you own Connemara ponies. They're rare," Maggie said and looked at Peter. "You take care of them?"

"Take care of what?" he asked.

"The Connemara ponies. You take care of them," she repeated slowly.

He frowned for a moment. "Oh, yes. Yes, I do. I apologize, my mind was elsewhere, Maggie darlin'," he said, smiling. "Yes, they're fine animals."

I gave him a skeptical look. *Oh, Mr. Sullivan, something smells here.*

Teri broke in on my thoughts. "We have to decide when we're going. I don't see why we should wait. We can go for a few weeks and take it from there," she said.

"Three weeks," Mac started, "that should be enough time to get a lay of the land and at least get all the legalities out of the way."

"I hate to be the bearer of bad news, but we're forgetting that someone stabbed Mr. Sullivan here and is still on the loose. I'd feel better if we all stayed close and were careful for the time being," I said.

"With all this, I had forgotten about that," Mac said and looked at Peter. "Have you any idea who it was?"

"No, it happened too fast, but he did wear a heavy dark coat. I remember that," he said.

Maggie stood suddenly. "I'd better be going. I have to clear my luggage out of the residence quarters by five."

Mac and Teri exchanged curious looks. "You can't leave yet." They looked at me.

"Can't you stay longer? I'll take you over there later," I

offered. *Why is she leaving?*

"No, really. I haven't been over there since Saturday. You could drive me if you would," she said coolly.

"Well, sure. If that's what you want." I watched her.

"Yes. You were right, Kate. I need to go home," she said. *That's why she's leaving, you ass.*

Teri gave me a scathing look I tried to avoid.

Maggie kissed Teri and Mac. She shook Peter's hand. "Now you have a doctor take a look at those stitches. They should come out in a week. And stay out of alleys."

He leaned over and kissed her cheek. "I will, my angel of mercy."

We drove back to the hospital in silence. I pulled in by the apartments and Maggie opened her door.

"I hope everything goes well with this. Call me if you need me." She patted my hand, and I watched her enter the building.

"Maggie, wait," I called and walked up to the building. She turned around as she opened the door. "Look, I don't want you to leave like this. We need to talk, I know."

Have you ever tried to sound reasonable while your heart's beating out of control?

She turned to go and I grabbed the jacket she was holding. She tugged at it. "Kate, please. I understand." She tugged at the jacket again.

I tugged back. "Maggie, will you quit with the jacket?" We were now playing tug-of-war on the doorstep. I gave it a healthy tug. The sound of ripping material echoed in the hall.

She let go of it then. "Satisfied?" she asked dryly.

I stood there with the ripped jacket in my hands. "I'm sorry. I—" I sighed heavily. "Look, stay," I said as I rubbed my forehead.

"Stay for what?" she asked earnestly. "Why should I stay?"

"For the fun of it, Maggie," I said. "There's something going on and I, well when you're around, it's... I mean, you and I, we're... Don't you feel there's something going on?"

"Between whom?" she asked flatly and leaned against her door sporting that damnable smirk.

"W-Well, with this Sullivan guy and Mac, of course," I said.

Maggie rolled her eyes and walked into the building and I followed. "You can be the most obtuse person. You want me to stay but won't tell me why. I get close and you push me away. Christ, it's like pulling teeth," she said loudly.

I winced and stepped back. Her fiery temper was about to blow. The left eye was twitching. "I don't mean to push you away. I-It's just that I have so much—" I stopped and threw up my hands in a helpless gesture.

All at once, I didn't want her to go, but I had no idea how to make her stay. *God, I am a mess.* It isn't fair of me to unload my baggage on anyone—especially Maggie.

I felt her watching me intently. "I could help you with whatever is haunting you, Kate. Perhaps, someday," she said and leaned over and kissed my cheek. "Now you go and help Mac sort out this inheritance thing."

Then she turned and walked into her apartment and closed the door.

I stood there for a moment staring at the door. Finally, I turned and walked away.

Chapter 6

They were all still sitting at my kitchen table. Teri gave me a scowling look as I sat down.

"She's leaving?" Teri asked. I nodded but said nothing. "And you're going to let her," she said. It was not a question.

"Teri, she's better off at home. I'm not—"

"I don't know which is worse, your sarcasm or your self-pity," Teri said with a caustic bite.

I shot a look at her. Geez, first Maggie's leaving, now Teri's mad at me. *What the hell is going on?*

Peter looked confused and stood. "Well, maybe I'd better—"

"Oh, sit down," Teri and I said in unison. Poor Peter sat.

"I'll figure this out. I'm—" I stopped. I didn't want to start blubbering. I buried my head in my hands.

Teri put her hand on my arm. "I know it's hard, but Maggie is the best thing that's happened to you."

We had forgotten Peter was there. He listened with raised eyebrows. *Now he knows.*

He cleared his throat. "Is that the way of it then?" He smiled and gave an understanding nod.

"Well," Mac started, "let's get back to the situation at hand. Peter, you're going back to Ireland later today. My uncle trusted you, and now I'm going to, as well. I hope I'm doing the right thing."

"Mac, you're an honorable man, I can see that, sir. What do you want me to do?"

"First, we'll take you to the airport, and I want you settled in. We're going to see if we can leave on Friday morning. Give me a number where you can be reached. When we're ready, I'll call you to pick us up at Shannon Airport and give you the flight information. We can go from there to this Bridget Donnelly in Donegal," Mac said.

"Boy, when did you decide all this?" I asked as I listened.

"When you were talking to Maggie. We decided to go as quickly as possible. Why wait? We have a lot to do in three days. Our passports are in order, and we need to go to the bank," Teri said, making a list. "And you're going with us. I already called the kennel. You can drop off Chance on Friday morning. I know your passport is in order, as well. There's no reason you can't go. I think it'll be good for you."

It was settled, I guess.

We took Peter to O'Hare Airport, and I spent the rest of the day getting myself ready for Friday. I called my editor to check in. I had to laugh when I heard Connie Brannigan's gruff voice. I visualized her sitting there, puffing on her cigarette.

"Ireland? Good, we need photos—"

"Connie, I'm on vacation," I reminded her.

"—of Ireland for an article we're doing," she finished. I heard her take a drag off her cigarette.

"When are you going to quit smoking?"

"When you wear a dress, you nature freak. Check in occasionally," she said.

I listened to the dial tone and shook my head. I decided to call Maggie.

Hannah answered. "She's not in, Kate." I could hear the hesitation in her voice.

"Oh," I said. "I told her I would call."

"Margaret was going out for a ride and Allison showed up. They left about an hour ago. Sorry, dear," Hannah said.

"Oh, that's all right. Tell her I called, will you?" I told her what had been going on that weekend and that I would be leaving on Friday for Ireland. "I'd like to talk to her before I leave. If she wants," I said. "Please tell her I called. I love you."

"And I love you, dear. Don't worry," Hannah said, and we rang off.

I called again on Wednesday. Maggie was at some function at the clinic. On Thursday, she was in Galena with her father. Thursday night, I called, and Hannah answered the phone again.

"Hannah, I love to hear your voice but, geez, she's not in again?" I asked, completely exasperated. "Did you tell her I'm leaving tomorrow?"

"Yes, dear, I did," Hannah said.

"Where the hell is she?" I asked angrily. "I apologize. I have no right to be mad."

"This is true," she said simply.

I sat there like a dope as her words sank in. It was true, I had no right.

"She's at a charity dinner in Galena with Charles. Allison got invited. I have no idea how. Heavens, she's a pest," Hannah continued.

"Well, Maggie doesn't seem to mind," I said, trying to hold the anger in my voice. "Please let her know I called. I'd still like to talk to her before I leave."

"I'll tell her. Give Mac and Teri my love and have a wonderful trip, dear."

"I will," I mumbled childishly.

I was sound asleep when the phone rang. I jumped and fumbled for the phone, knocking it and the clock off the nightstand. "Dammit," I cursed, rubbing my eyes. I picked up the phone and glanced at my clock—four thirty. "This better be good."

"What did you knock over?" Maggie asked.

"Geez, you scared the hell out of me." I sat on the edge of the bed and flipped on the small light. "You're just now getting home?"

There was silence for a moment. "No, I couldn't sleep. Sorry, I know I woke you."

"I'm glad you called," I said. "Did Hannah tell you I was leaving?"

Again, silence. "Yes, this was kind of sudden. You must be excited."

"It'll be interesting," I said to break the awkward silence. There'd never been an awkward silence between us. "This is a first. Neither of us saying anything."

"A first time for everything. Look, go back to bed. I wanted to talk to you before you left. I'm sorry I didn't get back to you sooner. I-I was busy. Have a good time—give Mac and Teri my love, will you?"

"Of course I will."

"Please take care of yourself. Don't go doing anything foolish. I know you. You'll wind up with a broken something or other. I mean it," she said.

"You're a nag," I said softly.

"Yes, I know. Go back to sleep. Call us when you get settled."

"I will, I promise."

Again, there was silence. I stared at the ceiling, not knowing what to say.

"Goodbye, Kate," she said. "Take care."

"See ya, Maggie. I'll call you," I added as she hung up.

I looked up to see Chance lying on the bed, looking at me.

"Don't start," I grumbled and turned off the light.

Friday morning rolled around. I put my luggage by the front door. My insane dog looked at the luggage, then at me and went behind the chair by the fireplace and lay there watching me. She knew the drill. I get ready to leave and she hides. I take her to the kennel and feel guilty—I'm sure she feels vindicated.

I drove back from my guilt trip to a completely empty house, and for the first time in my life, I felt alone. I stood in the living room looking around, and I thought of Maggie. I now felt nauseated. The phone rang and I tripped over my luggage getting to it. With my foot caught in the strap, I dragged it with me to the phone.

"Hello?" I said, while shaking my leg.

"Geezus, what are you doing?" It was Teri.

"This luggage is alive," I growled as I tried to free myself. "What's up?"

"Nothing, the cab's on the way, we'll be there in fifteen minutes. Maggie hasn't called?"

"She called this morning at four thirty. I thought maybe she'd call again. I don't know why."

"At least you got to talk to her. That's good."

"Definitely, I didn't want to go without talking to her or Hannah," I said.

"Hell, the cab's early, it's here. We'll be there in a few minutes."

I could hear the excitement in her voice. Then I wondered

what in the world was waiting for us in Ireland—my excitement turned into anxiety.

The flight was long and tiring. I tried to sleep but couldn't. Mac and Teri held hands most of the way. I put my head back and smiled.

"What are you smiling at?" Mac asked.

I looked over at him and noticed Teri was sound asleep, her head resting on his shoulder. "I was thinking how much in love you guys are. You make it look so easy."

"Easy?" He looked down at Teri and whispered to me, "You may not know it, but your sister is sometimes the most difficult person to deal with."

"And you're a saint."

"Well." He chuckled openly. "Remember when I first asked Teri to marry me? I was petrified."

"No. Really, why?" I turned in my seat to face him. We have never had this kind of conversation before.

"Well, I'm eight, almost nine, years older and thought I was too old for her. I was pretty set in my ways and the thought of waking up and finding someone next to me was scary."

"I know exactly how you felt. I feel that way about me with Maggie. She's a great gal. I really think I'm too old for her. Though I do enjoy the time we spend together as friends."

Mac gave me a skeptical look. "Just friends?"

"I think that's best. It's been so long for me. This business before, I don't know if I can do it again. I don't want anything to happen to our friendship. It means a great deal to me," I said honestly. *I was being honest, right?*

"Why are you so hard on yourself? I never understood that about you."

The flight attendant came up and asked us if we wanted anything. "Yes, two Bloody Marys please," he said and looked at me. "Oh, who cares, we're on vacation. So answer my question."

"It scares me that I could have been so easily manipulated before. I should've seen it coming. I let my guard down, and I nearly paid for it with my life—and Bob's," I finished.

"You have to make a conscious effort to get past that, and not only for Maggie's sake. If she's not the one for you, she's not.

You need to get over this for your own sake. You can't live like this anymore. What happened back at your house is bound to happen again."

"Teri said I can't hide behind my sarcastic remarks or hide in my log cabin. She was right, as usual." I put my head back.

"Don't ya hate when that happens?" he asked. "And you are quite the sarcastic wench. However, your sister has little room to talk. You both get it from your father. I miss him, but you certainly got his instincts. That's one reason I'm glad you came along. I think I may need your expertise. Something is definitely rotten in Donegal," Mac said seriously.

I nodded in agreement as our new best friend the flight attendant came our way.

When I stepped off the plane at Shannon Airport, I felt at home. It was as breathtaking as before. We walked through the small airport and saw Peter Sullivan waving to us. "You all look like happy exhausted travelers. How was the flight?"

"Fine, Peter. You looked rested and well." Mac shook his hand.

"I am. Thank you. Let's be on our way."

We followed him out of the terminal and into the windy, damp late afternoon Irish air.

I took a deep breath and sighed. "Now this is clean air," I announced and noticed the rental car. "How in the hell are we all going to fit in that?"

It was the typical rental—small, complete with shoe horn. How Mac and Peter got all the luggage into that small trunk, I will never know.

Peter drove wildly, as the Irish do. The driving is completely opposite from the States. The last time I was here, it took me a few days to get the hang of it. We drove north toward Donegal, passing through Galway. To the left was the Atlantic Ocean, to the right, beautiful rolling hills of green. It was cloudy, so we really couldn't get a good view of the sunset, but we had plenty of time.

"Who knows we're coming?" Mac asked.

"No one. I've said nothing. Only Deirdre knows," he said as if proud of himself for keeping the secret.

"Who's Deirdre?" Teri asked from the backseat.

"Oh, she's my girlfriend. We're to be married someday when I can afford it," Peter said.

"Good for you," Mac said and patted him on the back.

Teri and I both realized that Mac had already taken the dubious Mr. Sullivan under his fatherly wing.

"I took the liberty of making the reservations for all of ya," Peter said as we pulled up to a small inn, right off the main Donegal road.

After settling into our rooms, we headed down to the small dining room where Peter met us. "I'd best be goin'. I'll pick you up at nine. How does that sound?" He stifled a yawn.

"Peter, sit and eat with us," I offered.

He shifted uncomfortably. "No, no. You enjoy yourselves."

I gave him a curious look. "Do you have a room here for the night?"

He avoided my eyes. "No, I'm stayin' down the road." *I know a lie when I hear one.*

Mac watched him. "Peter, what's going on?"

"Sit," Teri said with a motherly tone and pulled out a chair. "C'mon, what are you hiding?" It appeared Mac and Teri knew it, as well.

"I-I don't have a room," he said, looking at the plate on the table. "I was staying with Deidre since Brian died. However, she's in Dublin. I don't—"

Mac got up without a word and went to the desk. Peter sat there, staring at his hands when Mac came back. "Now you have a room, and now we eat. I'm starving."

Peter smiled sheepishly and agreed. There was something about him, though. I couldn't figure it out. I watched him as he joked and talked with Mac and Teri. Something didn't fit.

"So, Peter, you look young to be a horse trainer, how old are you?" I asked.

"Twenty-seven. I-I've been around horses all my life." He shrugged and continued eating. He hadn't looked at me, though.

"Good grief, you're a baby," Teri said amazed.

He's no baby. I looked at him. He glanced at me, and for a split second, our eyes locked, and I knew I was right. Something's up with Mr. Sullivan.

I slept like a rock, in fact we all did—jet lag. I met Teri and Mac in the dining room at eight o'clock for breakfast. Peter joined us, looking rested.

"Hey, how are your stitches?" Teri asked, eating her toast.

"Oh, I had 'em taken out. I'm—how do you Yanks say it?—fit as a fiddle. Whatever that means," he said and drank his tea. "Maggie, she's a wonder."

"Speaking of Maggie, did you try her again last night?" Teri asked.

"Yes, she was out again." I fought the wave of irritation.

"I called Bridget Donnelly, and she's going to meet us at ten o'clock at her office," Mac said.

It was a beautiful windy, sunny morning as we stood by the car. I put on my sunglasses. "Can I drive?"

"Have you ever driven in Ireland before, Kate?"

I nodded. "Yep, so hand over the keys."

Teri and Mac sat in the back. "Please be careful," Teri said.

I turned around and looked over my sunglasses. "Always," I said and revved the engine and took off. It took me about ten minutes to get the feeling back.

Peter quickly put on his seat belt and gave me a wary look. "I'm impressed," he said as we drove around a curve.

"I'm scared," I heard Mac say from the back.

Chapter 7

Bridget Donnelly's office was at the northern end of Donegal. She was an extremely attractive woman. She was almost as tall as I was, with black curly long hair and violet blue eyes.

"Mr. McAuliffe?" she asked with a thick Irish brogue.

Mac introduced all of us. When she shook my hand, our eyes met, and she shook it for an instant longer and let it go.

"Did you have a nice flight?" she asked. We all concurred it was long but worth it. "That's grand. First I have a few papers here to sign. Mr. O'Shea called earlier in the week and said everything went well in the States. It's my job to make sure everything goes well here. So these are formalities, Mr. McAuliffe."

As they talked business, I glanced around Miss Donnelly's office. It was decorated in soft tones, probably meant to keep irritated clients at ease. I noticed not one, but two diplomas on the wall and raised an eyebrow when I saw something odd, or maybe I'm odd.

"Have you heard anything from Brian's family?" Mac asked Miss Donnelly. I turned my attention back to the conversation.

"Yes, I have. They are quite upset, to say the least. I'm sure they intend to contest the will, although they haven't gone to a lawyer as of yet. The brothers live in Galway. I'm sure they'll come to call once the word is out you're here. Would ya like me to show ya the property and take ya over to the mill?"

We followed her out of town and through some beautiful winding tree-lined roads and headed west toward the Atlantic coast. The temperature dropped a few degrees as the clouds blew in and the pesky rain started. We drove through the woods in silent anticipation. As we reached the coast, we headed south on a typical narrow road.

When the ocean came into view, it was breathtaking. The

landscape changed from a few wooded roads to craggy low sloping hills. Only one or two cottages dotted the rugged landscape. I was amazed at how wild and isolated it looked as we drove along the coastal road. Bridget pulled over and I followed.

As we walked toward the cliff's edge, I noticed a small grove of trees. In the clearing stood a small white cottage in need of rethatching and whitewash. Behind it was a small stone hut of some kind.

The view was magnificent. The wind howled as we stood in front of a stone fence about twenty feet from the edge of a cliff. Good thing the fence prohibited us from going any further. It was a sheer hundred-foot drop to the bottom. The small stone fence stretched as far as the eye could see. In some places, it was almost at the edge of the cliff.

I walked over to the stone wall, which came up to my knee. These walls are found all over Ireland, and they were built with apparently no rhyme or reason. This wall, however, seemed to have a purpose—it saved you from falling off the cliff. I leaned over it and peered down. The waves crashed against the rocks below where small birds were soaring. It was breathtaking and I couldn't wait to get some photos.

"Be careful, Miss Ryan," Bridget said from behind me. "The wind gets fierce at the cliff's edge. I've heard tell people bein' whisked right off."

"Really?" I asked as I turned around. Our eyes met again. "I'll remember that. Is this where Brian fell?"

Bridget looked up and down the craggy stone wall. "Yes, along here, but I don't know exactly where."

I thought it odd, Bridget being Brian's lawyer, that she didn't know where he died. However, I said nothing.

"When do we get there?" Teri asked. I could hear the anticipation in her voice.

"Mrs. McAuliffe, ya *are* there. This is the beginning of the property. This is a private road we turned onto—your road," she said and pointed to the little cottage. "That's your cottage. Brian had a well dug so you have running water and a septic tank. They come out regularly to empty. It's heated by petrol in the winter. Of course, you have a fireplace. It's got two bedrooms. Would you like to see it?"

"Oh, brother, you have your own road?" I whispered to Teri and Mac as we walked up the path.

The wind blew off the cliffs and we all stopped abruptly as we heard it—a low wailing sound. Mixed with the wind, I couldn't tell what it was.

"Hmmm, the banshee wails. *Bwahaahaa*," I joked. Mac and Teri laughed.

Bridget shot a look at me. "Don't joke about those things, Miss Ryan." She was serious. "When the banshee wails, tis for—" she stopped abruptly.

I raised my eyebrows. "I apologize."

She blushed slightly. "We're a little superstitious on this side of the Atlantic, I'm sorry."

"Don't be. We are, too." Mac smiled as we walked up the path and Bridget handed him the key.

The cottage was adorable. Just how you would picture a thatched cottage to look. It had low-beamed ceilings, and the fireplace was to the left, taking up nearly the entire far wall. Two small chairs were in front of it. As I looked right, there was a hallway leading to the two bedrooms. Straight ahead on the far wall was a short grandfather clock situated between the two windows. As we walked in, the pungent aroma of peat, which was used for the fireplace, was unmistakable.

"No kitchen?" I asked.

"It's behind that door." Bridget pointed to the door next to the fireplace.

I opened it to find a very small kitchen. A two-burner stove and a small icebox. A small table and two chairs. Well, what the hell, only one person lived here.

Teri looked around, smiling. I could see the wheels turning already. She was picturing all sorts of changes.

Mac was checking out the rooms and bath. "Boy, this is small. How long did Brian live here? I remember a huge house."

"You're thinking of the main house," Bridget offered. "Brian lived in this cottage for only a few months. For some reason, he left the main house and came to live here. I don't know why."

I saw her steal a glance at Peter.

"I can see why. I'd rather stay here than a lonely big house all by myself," I said. "I'm sure it's cozy with a view of the ocean and a warm fire going."

"You're a romantic, Miss Ryan," Bridget said.

"It's this country, Miss Donnelly," I replied and smiled.

We left and drove farther south down the private coastal road. Then we saw the main house at the end, at the top of a hill. It was a sprawling gray brick estate. Behind it were rolling hills of green. It struck me that it looked like Maggie's house only much more massive. It looked like a museum. The road curved in front of the house, continued in a circular path, and led back, sort of a cul-de-sac effect.

"You have to be kidding me." I was amazed.

It was immense. That's the only word that came to mind. As we pulled up to the house, I saw the stables. There was a fenced area of almost an acre or two, where Peter undoubtedly exercised the ponies.

The foyer of the house was as big as my log cabin. It was finished in a dark cherry wood. To the right was a living room with a massive stone fireplace that looked like an entire tree could fit in it. Books were on every shelf that lined three walls. A couple of couches and several chairs rounded off that room.

To the left was a dining room, with a table to seat ten and yet another enormous fireplace.

We walked through the foyer, all of us looking up and down with our mouths wide open. Bridget took us through the dining room, then through a door that led to the kitchen. Nothing looked like it had been touched in quite some time. Dust covered everything. There were huge windows looking out at the hills behind the house.

When we stood in the main hallway of the second floor, we looked down the other two halls.

I said laughing, "Okay, I give. How many bedrooms?"

"I say six or eight," Teri offered.

Bridget nodded. "Good guess, six it is."

"Six bedrooms?" I exclaimed. "You're going to need a map. Do you two even know six people?"

My family ignored me. However, Miss Donnelly laughed. *Ah, I found an audience.* "You have quite a sense of humor, Miss Ryan." She smiled at me and I smiled back. There was a lot of smiling going on.

Going downstairs, Mac noticed another door in the hallway. "Where does this lead?" Mac asked as he yanked on the locked door.

"I think it's a cellar, but I wasn't given a key to that door. It might even be a closet. I'll see if there's a key back at the office," Bridget offered.

We continued down the hall and found ourselves at the foyer once again. Bridget looked around. "That's about it. I can show you the stables now, if you like."

The stables were north of the house. As we walked toward them, we could see the ponies. They were impressive, but I didn't see the monetary value. Then I'm not a horse authority. Maggie was right, they are a more sturdy breed than American horses and shorter. They looked more like the wild mustangs I've taken photos of in the past.

"So, Peter. What is the big attraction about these horses?" I asked.

"They're indigenous to Connemara, which is south of here. And they're a rare breed," he said.

Boy, that was lame. I expected a little more. So did Mac, by the frown on his face. He looked disappointed in the explanation. I let it pass with an "Oh, really?"

Peter almost looked relieved and he again exchanged a glance with Bridget. "This is it. All thirty acres," he said.

"If you like, I can take you back into town. We can all go to lunch, then go see the mill," Bridget suggested.

So far, we hadn't talked about Mac's uncle. *Enough of that.* "Do either of you know how and where Mac's uncle died?" I asked.

They both stiffened. I thought it was a good question. Mac agreed. "Yes, you must know something. I would like to know," he said.

Peter was the first to speak. "Mac, maybe we can go into this later. I don't want to upset the ladies," he motioned to Teri and me.

Upset the ladies? He should see upset. I gave him a skeptical look.

"I don't think it'll bother them. Tell me what you know," Mac said firmly.

"As far as we know, he was walking home from Sean's when he stumbled in the dark and fell over the stone wall and off the cliff. It was horrible when they found him, Mac. I'm sorry." He did look sorry.

"Seems odd that he would live here his entire life, know every rock in every path, and stumble off a cliff," I said thoughtfully as we walked out to the car.

Neither Bridget nor Peter said a word.

We stopped at a quaint restaurant in Donegal. Actually, it was more of a pub. Mac and Peter got the drinks and we all sat at a small table not saying much until Teri broke the silence. "Can we stay at the main house while we're here?"

I was waiting for the glance to Peter Bridget did before she answered. "It hasn't been lived in for years. You may do better at the inn."

I noticed Teri's disappointed look. "We can stay at the inn for a couple of days, but I would like to stay at the house for a time. Who's been taking care of the house up till now?"

"There were a few young girls in town who dusted and cleaned up till Brian died. I'm sure I can get them to get it ready for you in a couple of days. Is that what you had in mind?" Bridget asked.

"Exactly, thank you."

We talked for a while longer. I walked up to the bar and got another Guinness, and Bridget Donnelly came up behind me. "Miss Ryan, are you free for dinner?" she asked, getting right to the point.

"Sure," I answered without thinking—as usual.

"Grand, there's a little restaurant in town. Why don't you meet me at my office, say at seven? We can walk from there."

"That sounds fine. I'll see you then."

Upon Bridget's suggestion, we took a drive to the woolen mill. We followed her out of town. I looked at Mac in the rearview mirror. "I can't believe you own fifty-one percent of a woolen mill."

"I can't, either. This is like some odd dream."

The winding road seemed to take us higher as we drove back toward the ocean. Outside the village, we turned north and the mill came into view. The one-story brick building had a sign outside reading, *Oceanview Woolen Mill.*

"Well, this is it," Bridget said, as we all stood in front of the small building.

As we walked in, there was a woman sitting behind a desk doing paperwork. She looked up, smiled, and came from behind the desk. "Good day to ya," she smiled. She was about fifty or so, dark graying hair, and blue eyes.

Bridget introduced Mac as Brian's heir. Her eyes widened and she shook Mac's hand and ours, as well.

"Is Mr. Nolan about?" Bridget asked.

"Yes, he's in the back. I'll get him straight away." She hurried to the back.

We waited for a minute or two, and a tall lanky man came from the back. He had curly short brown hair and green eyes. His ruddy complexion made him look as if he had just come in from the cold. When he smiled, his entire face lit up. He looked straight at Mac. "Mr. McAuliffe, it's a pleasure, sir." He stuck out his hand and gave Mac a hearty handshake.

Mr. Nolan took Mac and Teri on a tour of the mill, and I stayed back with Peter and Bridget. We walked outside and stood by the cars.

"I think Rory likes your brother-in-law," Bridget said, smiling at me.

"He's an easy man to like," I said.

"He's a grand man. You're all good people," Peter said. "So was Brian."

"Peter, how in the world did he stumble over that wall?" I asked.

"I don't know."

"Who was the man in America? Do you have any idea?"

"I don't know that, either. I'm sorry," he said and walked away.

Bridget looked at me. "Is this something I should know about?"

"Right now, Miss Donnelly, I don't think so."

"If it's something concerning Mac, being his lawyer, I might be able to help."

"I agree. If it comes to that, I'll let you know," I said, ending the topic.

"You're a mystery, Miss Ryan."

"I don't mean to be, and please call me Kate," I said.

"If you'll call me Bridget."

With that, Mac and Teri came out with Rory Nolan. "Well, Mac, that's the mill—small but efficient. All the workers are from the village, been workin' the mill all their lives," he said proudly.

"I see no reason to change that, Rory." Mac shook his hand. "I'm glad we got the opportunity to talk. My wife and I will be staying at the house in a day or two. We'll have you and Mrs. Nolan over for dinner."

Rory beamed. "That would be grand." He shook Teri's hand and went back into the building.

"Seems like a nice guy," I said.

"If you'll excuse me, I have to be getting back. I have a client at four," Bridget said and turned to me. "Kate, I'll see ya at seven."

She gave me a quick wink and I smiled, then caught the glare from my sister.

Chapter 8

As I showered and dressed, there was a knock at my door. It was Teri of the scowling face.

"What is the matter with you?" I asked. "You've been giving me dirty looks all day. God, you look like Mom."

"What are you doing?" she asked.

"I'm only going out for dinner. I'm on vacation. Geez," I said and buttoned my shirt. I glanced up and laughed. "Will you quit with the looks? Christ, it's just dinner."

"It better be," Teri said with a maternal tone.

I gaped at her. "I'm an adult. I know what I'm doing. Good grief, you complain that I lock myself up in my cabin. Now... Great, now I feel guilty, and I'm not doing anything wrong. You *are* like Mom."

"Have you called Maggie again?"

"Yes, and she's out again, probably with Allison. Maggie is an adult, too," I said frankly, ending the discussion.

I stood outside Bridget's office for a minute or two before I looked up to see her jogging across the street.

"I was delayed at the police station. I had to post bail for a client. I'm sorry," she apologized.

"That's all right, I understand. So where's this restaurant?"

We walked down the cobblestone pavement. It was chilly, my neck and back were starting to ache. I could never live here year-round.

"So Peter tells me you're a photographer. That sounds exciting. You must have seen a great many places," she said.

"I've been around the States mostly. I've been to Ireland before, but this is the first time I have an assignment abroad," I said. "This is a beautiful country. I hope I can stay awhile with Mac and Teri. I think I could get some beautiful photos of this countryside. It's so wild and has an untamed feel about it. There must be a great many tales spun around the fire at night."

"There is a great history in this part of the country. Our religious men were forced to hide themselves away. Sailing ships, pirate ships, Viking and Spanish invasions. This coast was quite busy a few centuries ago. So many countries have invaded Ireland. You know America is the only country we've invited," she said as we continued down the walk.

"And we appreciate the invitation." I smiled as she laughed. I was finding it easy to talk to her. "I know Mac and Teri are glad to be here, but sorry about the reason."

"Yes, it was a shame. Brian was a good man. A quiet, simple fellow—a humanitarian and a patriot."

"He sounds like he should've been knighted."

"I guess I was partial to Brian. He was a good man."

"Loyalty is an admirable quality."

"Thank you, Kate," she said politely.

We got to the restaurant where, it seemed, everyone knew Bridget. "Same table, Brig?" the waitress asked.

"You must come here often," I said as I sat down.

"I do like this place," she said, putting the napkin in her lap. "The prawns are marvelous."

We talked of nothing in particular as I looked at her over the candlelight. I noticed how attractive she was. Her raven hair curled about her face and her blue eyes sparkled. Our eyes met for an instant and she grinned and quickly looked at the menu.

We ordered and Bridget cleared her throat. "I think you and I are cut from the same cloth, so to speak." She looked right at me and smiled knowingly.

I raised my eyebrows. Well, any doubts I had were quickly dispelled. "So to speak."

"Grand, wanted to make sure before we go any further," she said and drank her wine.

I coughed nervously and ate my prawns. "These are good. We usually don't get shrimp this big back home." *What did I say?*

She laughed heartily. "We've lost many a fishing boat to them, that's for sure."

I laughed out loud at that one. She had the Irish gift of talking easily with anyone.

"What shall we discuss?" she asked.

"Brian McAuliffe," I said frankly.

She frowned and sat back. "I thought you might want to talk about something a little more pleasant." She looked disappointed, but I felt this topic would do fine. "What more can I tell you?" She had her lawyer's voice now, as she smoothed the napkin in her lap.

"Why wouldn't he leave his estate to his immediate family?" I asked, drinking my wine.

"I don't know. He didn't get on with his brother, he's the greedy one. Then there's Tim Devereaux, he was married to Colleen, Brian's younger sister. She's been gone these past four years—left her share of the mill to Tim. They've been harping at Brian for years to sell. They're all younger, you see. Brian was sixty-nine and the oldest. Let's see. James is sixty-six and Colleen would be fifty-nine. Mother and father died twelve years ago. Brian never married, no children. I don't know why he never married, and I don't know why he didn't stay at the main house. And before you ask, I'll look tomorrow for the key to that door," she finished in a huff.

I had my wineglass up to my lips and stopped. "I-I, well, thank you," I ended foolishly.

"I'm sorry. I have a frightful temper."

"Don't apologize. It's my lot in life to be surrounded by ill-tempered women." I laughed and raised my glass to her.

"Ya poor lass. It's a fate worse than death," she said, smiling as she watched me over her wineglass. "So if ya don't mind my askin', why are ya here alone? I can't imagine a woman as attractive as you unattached."

"There's nothing wrong with being unattached. How is that you are not otherwise engaged for the evening?" I countered affably.

"Actually, I had a decision to make for this evening. I'm content with my choice," she said, grinning over her wineglass.

"Young woman, you need to set higher goals for yourself," I said and continued eating.

She raised her eyebrows and drank her wine. "That was a sour thing to say."

I looked up at her and realized that it was. "I'm not a very good dinner partner. You're right. I apologize."

We talked absently over coffee. "So tell me about the

banshee," I said.

I waited for a good story. Bridget did not disappoint. "They are very real entities. Every family has one. The banshee wails foretelling a death. If ya hear her wailing, someone in the family is near death, ya can be sure of it."

I watched her. She was serious. My grandmother used to tell us of the banshee, but I always thought it was an Irish ghost story. Bridget looked at me so seriously, she scared me. "Good grief, woman. You believe in them?" I asked as my skin crawled.

She nodded and finished her coffee. "I do indeed. It's no joke." She looked at her watch. "Jaysus, it's almost midnight. I've got court at nine. I'm sorry. I've got to get goin'. Do ya mind?"

"Of course not," I said.

We walked through town back to her car in silence. "Thanks so much for dinner. It was grand." She held out her hand.

"I had a good time, too."

"The fog is settlin' in. Can I give you a lift to the inn?" she asked and I declined. She leaned over and kissed my cheek. "You're a grand one, Kate. I'll be seein' ya, you can be sure." She got into her car and slowly drove down the narrow road.

The wind picked up and it started to drizzle. *Great, I shoulda let her drive me back.*

The light fog had indeed settled in. There was no one on the street. The fog-shrouded street light was the only illumination. I turned up my collar, as if that would help, and headed up the cobblestone walk. I heard something behind me and turned around, but there was no one. I continued and heard it again. I was sure someone was following me. I stepped up my pace and still had a feeling someone was behind me. Then I stopped and heard nothing. I continued but didn't hear anything. *Geez, this country— spooks everywhere.* At least I wasn't hearing my banshee wailin' for me.

I came to a corner and was about to cross the empty street, when someone grabbed me from behind. I yelped as a hand clamped over my mouth.

"Shh, now, lass," a voice said in my ear. He had his arm around my neck and held tight. "Go home, Yank." Then whoever it was unceremoniously tossed me down and I rolled ass over everything else I owned. I could hear him running as I finally got to my knees and looked back. I only got a glimpse of a dark coat turning the corner.

In the light fog and darkness, all I heard was the eerie sound of clattering footsteps on the cobblestone. I limped back to the inn, thanking God it was only a half block away. I flew through the doors and into the lobby.

The desk clerk jumped. "Heavens, miss, are ya all right?"

I limped to the desk and leaned on it. "Fine. Fine. I tripped over a patch of fog," I said, wheezing. I limped upstairs to Mac and Teri's room and knocked.

Mac answered the door and was shocked. "What happened? Get in here."

"What in the hell happened to you?" Teri asked anxiously as I plopped myself into the chair.

I took a breath and explained the entire ordeal. I must admit I was a little rocked by it. I flexed my knee and winced. "I must have banged it on the cobblestone when he threw me."

Mac was extremely angry, to say the least. He left the room and Teri watched as he left.

"Where's he going?" I asked.

Teri shook her head. "Are you all right?"

"Not damaged, just scared."

"I called the police," Mac said as he came back. "I know you didn't get a look at him, but I don't want this to continue. If the word is spread that the police are involved, they'll stop." He looked at me. "Don't argue with me on this."

I stared at him. "I wasn't going to argue with you. I agree."

"Mac, take it easy, sweetie."

Mac softened. "Sorry, Sherlock. I'm getting a little rattled."

The police arrived quickly. Constable Reardon entered the room. He was rosy cheeked and looked like he was fifteen. We all stared at him, saying nothing.

"Well, good evenin'." He took off his cap and looked at me. "Now what happened to you?"

I looked at him closely, searching for signs of puberty—like facial hair. I explained what happened while trying not to laugh. I don't know why I wanted to laugh. I avoided Mac and Teri's faces as I finished.

Baby Face Reardon looked serious, taking notes and nodding.

He cleared his throat professionally. "There's not much to go on, is there now?" he said simply and scratched his head. "I don't want ya to be thinkin' bad of us now. We really love you Yanks."

"Constable, we wanted to make you aware of the situation. That's the point I want known. We're staying," Mac said. It almost sounded like a threat. Teri put a cautious hand on his arm.

The young policeman turned red and said with more authority than I thought he had in him, "Mr. McAuliffe, I assure you this will be brought to the chief's attention, and I will personally make sure the word is out. I liked Brian McAuliffe. You remind me of him in a way. He was protective and loyal as yourself. I'll do me best, sir. If you need anything at all, you call me." He shook Mac's hand.

On his way out, I stopped him. "Constable, was there an investigation into Brian's death?"

The young officer gave me an odd look. "It was an accident, Miss Ryan. There was no investigation and no sign of foul play."

"Would it be possible to meet me at the cottage tomorrow morning and show us the scene of the accident? I'm very curious and my family would like to be sure."

He scratched his head and nodded. "I understand. I'll met ya there around ten o'clock. How's that?"

I shook his offered hand. "Thank you."

"What was that all about?" Mac asked after the constable left.

"I don't know. Just a feeling," I said with a shrug. "I'm going to take a hot bath and go to bed."

I gave Teri a wink. "Mac, you savage. Go to bed. Tomorrow we've got some figuring to do, now that the whole town will know we're staying."

I got up early the next morning and met Mac and Teri in the dining room for breakfast.

"How was dinner?" Mac asked as I poured a cup of coffee. "We didn't get a chance to ask you with all the excitement."

"It was fine. She's a nice woman and we had a nice talk," I said and drank my coffee. I looked up to see Bridget coming our way.

She looked worried and came over to me. "I heard what happened. Are ya all right?" She put a hand on my shoulder and searched my face.

"Boy, word gets around fast," I said. "I'm fine, thank you. Would you like to join us?"

"For a minute, if you don't mind," she said as she sat.

I poured her a cup of coffee and Teri was once again giving me the eye. *Just like Mom.*

"Did ya not see him at all?"

"Nope. Only a fleeting glimpse of a dark coat," I said.

Bridget frowned but said nothing. "Oh, I nearly forgot." She handed Mac a large skeleton key and a much smaller one on the same ring.

"The large one is for the cellar door I'm thinking, but I don't know what the smaller one is. It's an odd-lookin' key," she said and looked apologetic.

Mac studied the keys and handed them to me. It was an odd-looking key. "This will keep you busy for a while, Sherlock," Mac said, smiling.

"Mrs. McAuliffe, the girls are tidying up the main house as we speak. They should be done by this afternoon if that's to your liking."

"Thank you, Bridget. Maybe we can stay there tonight?"

"If you like," Bridget said. I heard a tone of uneasiness in her voice.

We decided to look at the property once again. The day had turned cool and cloudy as we pulled up to the thatched cottage. The girls had certainly been there. The place was spotless and there was wood in the fireplace ready to go. They had the fridge stocked and the bedrooms were cleaned. Teri was impressed, I could tell. So was I because basically, I'm a slob.

"Boy, I'd love to stay here. Why don't you guys stay here? This is great."

Teri shook her head. "I want to see how the big house looks after it's all cleaned up and ready to go."

As we left the cottage, I glanced at my watch. The constable should be arriving soon. As if on cue, I saw his car coming up the private road.

"Good morning, all," he called out.

"Good morning," I said. "You're right on time, thanks."

"I know you'd like to get on with your lives and I want to

help. So let me show ya exactly where the accident took place."

He took us about twenty yards down the road and stopped at the section of stone wall as it curved slightly. "Right about here. This is where we figure he stumbled and fell."

"You don't know for sure?" I asked and glanced at Mac who frowned deeply.

"He was alone when the accident happened. When I came here in the morning, I found his pipe right here," he said and pointed to the spot.

I squatted with him and looked closely at the wall. "Who called you?"

"Mary Farrell. She and Sean were worried about him. He had a bit too much to drink, they said, and with it being so late, I came out that morning and had a look. I found his pipe, which I thought was curious. I had a look around. It was then I saw his body lying on the rocks below. I'm sorry," he said.

I examined the area while he talked. "Constable," I said and stood. "If he stumbled and fell over this rock wall…" I stopped and leaned against the heavy rocks. As I pushed them, a few gave way. "Wouldn't there have been some rocks misplaced? I mean this wall isn't cemented. It's just built layer on layer, am I right?"

The constable frowned and nodded. "I see your point, Miss Ryan. But who would want to kill Brian? It was late, Brian had too much to drink, and he fell. Also, the wind was fierce that night, believe me."

"If he stumbled, hit that wall, and fell over it, those rocks had to move. A man who was stumbling drunk falls into a pile of rocks and just falls over?" I asked absently and leaned over the edge. As I leaned against the rocks once again, a few of them moved. Bridget and Mac reached out and grabbed my arm.

"Christ, Kate," Mac exclaimed.

I gave the constable a questioning look. "See what I'm getting at?"

He swallowed and nodded. "Well, Miss Ryan, with no evidence of foul play and nothing unusual at the scene of the accident, if what you're saying is right, the killer replaced the rocks and tidied up the area. That *would* make it a nice clean murder."

I shot a look as he hid his grin. "Okay, I get it. It's just a thought."

Constable Reardon held out his hand. "I'm not making light of Brian's death, miss. I truly believe it was an accident. I'll tell the chief of your theory, nonetheless. How would that be?" he asked kindly. "Now if you'll excuse me, I've got to be goin'."

We watched him drive out of sight. "What are you thinking, Sherlock?" Mac asked.

"I don't know. Something just doesn't seem right to me. I must be over-tired," I said with a shrug. "Let's get to the main house before I come up with another theory."

We walked back to the car and drove up to the main house. There were four girls cleaning, one in each room. We left them to their work, walked around the property, and noticed something we hadn't seen before. Behind the house, about a hundred feet or so, was a gray stone mausoleum set on the edge of the woods.

"How did we miss this monstrosity?" I whistled and shook my head.

"What in the hell?" Mac said as we slowly walked up to it.

The heavy door was locked. Mac looked up and across the top of the door in big letters carved into the stone was the name *McAuliffe*. There was a crucifix on the roof and gray pillars on each side of the door.

"Good grief, is that what I think it is?" Teri asked and looked at Mac in horror. "Behind the house?"

I grinned. "Yep, the family—buried right outside your kitchen."

We looked at each other and burst into laughter. "How many do you suppose are buried in there?" Teri asked, amazed.

"I don't know, but it gives me the creeps."

We stood there staring at it in silence.

"What are ya doin', folks?" Peter said from behind us. I noticed Peter was wearing glasses—those black horned-rimmed kind. It changed his appearance completely.

"Checking out the family plot," I said and Teri nudged me in the ribs.

"Is my uncle buried there?" Mac asked.

"Heavens, no. He wanted to be buried in the ground, not in a tomb. He's laid to rest in the cemetery outside of town. We drove by it when we came in the other day."

"Who's in there?" I asked and looked back at the mausoleum.

Peter scratched his head in contemplation. "I think there's four McAuliffes laid there. Going back two hundred years, I'd say, from the looks of it." He looked at us suspiciously. "Ya don't want to see 'em now, do ya?"

"Good grief, no," Teri and Mac both said, grimacing.

I was curious, but didn't want to be the odd man out, or a ghoul, so I declined.

Peter breathed a sigh of relief. "Grand, you had me worried there. I thought you might turn out to be morbid Yanks." He laughed nervously and Teri and Mac joined in.

"How can you tell its two hundreds years old?" I asked curiously.

He looked at the mausoleum, took off his glasses, and cleaned them on his shirt. "See that column structure, I'd say that's definitely circa eighteen twenty. Now if you look at the top—" he suddenly stopped, as if saying too much, and put on his glasses. "I read somewhere about these things."

"Let's get out of here, shall we?" Mac said and we walked to the stables.

Once back at the house, we found the girls had finished the cleaning. They had their buckets and mops in hand all lined up ready to leave. They stood there looking at Mac. I sat on the stairs and watched.

Mac turned to Peter and whispered, "How much have they been getting?"

Peter turned red. "Well, not much, see the money's been tied up. But usually, they get five pounds each."

Mac looked amazed. "That's all? That's not enough for all this work."

"It's plenty," Peter whispered insistently.

Teri was shocked, as well. "I agree. That's not nearly enough."

I sat there shaking my head. *The Rockefellers at work.*

Mac turned and walked over to them like the lord of the manor. "Well, ladies," he started and looked at me as I cleared my throat. He turned red and coughed. Ignoring my grin, he continued. "Thank you for all your help. You did a fine job." He handed each of them a ten-pound note. I raised my eyebrows and

Mac gave me a superior grin.

They all stared at him in amazement. They shrieked and picked up their buckets and ran out, stopping to thank the generous landlord and lady. Mac stood there bursting with pride with his hands in his pockets.

Peter gave him a curious look. "Just how much did ya give them, Mac?"

"Ten pounds," he smiled broadly and so did Teri.

Peter put his hand to his forehead and groaned. "Each?"

Mac nodded confidently and Peter sighed. "It'll be all over town by this evening."

"What will?"

"That there's a daft yank throwing ten-pound notes to people who probably have never seen more than a fiver." Peter let out a short laugh. "You'll be crawlin' with maids by mornin'."

The Rockefellers looked at each other. "Oh."

Chapter 9

After all that expense cleaning the house, we had to stay the night. What else could we do? The fireplace in the living room was roaring and there was plenty of food in the fridge. Mac and Teri asked Peter to stay, as well. I watched him. He seemed fidgety or maybe it was me.

Teri was thrilled and went into the kitchen to make dinner. I was sitting in the most comfortable chair imaginable. "I didn't know you wore glasses."

"I misplaced them. I only need them for reading," Peter said quickly.

"You know we've never talked about what happened in Chicago. You never explained the incident," I said evenly as I watched him.

Teri came into the living room. "Okay, we eat in an hour."

She sat next to me. She caught me rubbing the back of my neck. It ached horribly. "It's this weather, isn't it?"

"Yes, and there's nothing I can do about it. It's a constant reminder of my stupidity. I don't ever want to be in that position again."

"It was years ago. You've been locked up too long. Please don't be so hard on yourself," she said and turned her attention to Mac and Peter. "What are we discussing?"

"I was asking Peter about Chicago and the run-in he had with a knife," I said. "So what about it, Peter?"

Peter stood by the fire and took a long drink of his whiskey. "There are those who don't want you to own this property. I don't know exactly who they are, but the man in Chicago sorta works for them," he said and took a deep breath.

Mac sat next to Teri. "I don't know what this is all about," Mac started. "All I care about is my family, so if you have any influence or know of anyone who does, you'd better spread the word. I don't scare easy and no one harms my family."

Peter looked hurt as he gazed at the fire. Teri said, "Peter, Mac's not implying that you're involved in anything. Are you, Mac?" She gave him the look of a wife about to clobber her husband.

I have no one who'll clobber me, so I continued for Mac. "No one is implying that, Ter. We're curious. There's too much going on that we have no answers for, and that bothers me." I kept an eye on Mr. Sullivan.

"Peter," Mac said calmly, "I'm not accusing you of anything, either, but you seem to know more about whatever this is. I've trusted you, and so far, you've come through. I'm extremely grateful. You've made this transition go without a hitch. However, I am serious about my family. When I took this inheritance, I made a promise to do what I thought was right. I keep my promises."

Peter looked at Mac with what I considered close to hero worship. "You're an honorable man, Mac. I'd like to think I am, too. You say you trust me, well trust me a little longer. I've lived here all my life and I can help you."

"Help with what?" I asked firmly.

With that, there was a knock on the door. Mac got up to answer it. A thin elderly gentleman and woman stood at the door.

"Yes, can I help you?" Mac said affably.

"Well now, I don't know. I would like to see Michael McAuliffe," the gentleman said.

"I'm Mike McAuliffe. Won't you come in, please?" Mac stepped back and Teri came to the door.

"This is my wife, Teri, and her sister, Kate."

"I'm Sean Farrell and this is my wife, Mary. Brian was a dear friend of ours."

"Please, come in out of the rain," Teri offered.

Mac took their coats and brought them into the living room. They instantly reminded me of the vicar and his wife from the John Wayne movie *The Quiet Man* filmed here in Ireland.

"Please, sit down. Can I get you a drink?"

"Whiskey would be grand," he said, smiling.

"A small glass for me," his wife said.

Sean looked at Peter and frowned. "Hello, youngster. What

are you still doing here?"

"I'm trying to help them, Sean." I noticed the tension between them. Mary coughed and gave Sean the wife look.

"It's nice to meet you," Teri said cordially. "Do you live close by?"

Mary nodded. "Just down the road, about two miles. It was a nice night for a walk."

Teri looked outside. "In the rain?" she asked.

Mary laughed. "You Americans. This isn't rain. There's a storm coming in a day or two, then you'll see rain, my dear."

We talked for another half-hour or so before anyone brought up Brian's death. Of course, I did the honors. "I understand you called the police about Brian," I said.

Husband and wife exchanged a quick glance. "Yes, we were worried that he had too much to drink. When we paid a visit the next morning, he was nowhere to be found, and that wasn't like Brian."

"So you believe Brian stumbled and fell?" I asked.

"I don't know what else it could be, Miss Ryan," Mary replied.

The topic was dropped and the conversation turned to the weather and the woolen mill. Twenty minutes later, they said their goodbyes and left.

Mac turned to me. "It seems like an accident, Kate."

I heard the impatience in his voice. "I know. I'm sorry," I said.

Teri put her arm around Mac. "I have an idea. How about we have dinner for some of Brian's friends?"

"That would be fine, honey, but how many people are we talking about?" It appeared to me that Mac sounded relieved to be talking about something other than Brian's accident. I couldn't blame him.

"Peter knows all of them, I'm sure," I said and looked at him. "Don't you?"

He looked me in the eye, and once again, our eyes locked for an instant. I couldn't figure him out, and it was beginning to annoy me. Sean Farrell and his wife didn't seem too happy that Peter was still around. I'm assuming they meant after Brian's death. I wondered why it bothered them. It seemed natural that he was taking care of the stables.

"Of course, I can give you a small list of, I'd say, four or so. How would that be?" he asked and looked away from me.

Teri whistled. "Four or so. With us, that makes seven. I've never cooked a formal dinner for seven." She looked at me as I tore my eyes away from Peter.

"Hey, I love to cook, but I haven't a clue about this," I said, holding up my hands. "But according to Peter, we'll have a lot of help in the kitchen."

"That you will, Kate. Now if you'll excuse me, I have a few things to attend to."

"Peter, one question," I said. He stopped and cocked his head to one side and waited. "Sean Farrell seemed surprised that you'd still be here."

"Yes, he did," he said simply and shrugged. "Well, good night." He smiled and left the room.

"Okay, what was that about?" Mac asked.

"I don't know. There's something that doesn't sit right with me about Peter."

I was glad Mac and Teri let me stay in the cottage. I started a fire and got the place warm and cozy. I tried to think about what was going on here. Someone didn't want Mac to be here, that was a given. If I wasn't sure of it back home, after being tossed around in the fog, I certainly was sure of it now. But why? And what did Peter have to do with it? He wasn't what he seemed, but I couldn't put my finger on it.

It was late, but I couldn't sleep. I sat there gazing at the peat fire. Maggie's face flashed through my mind. I should have asked her to join us on this odd trip. I knew why I didn't. Maggie is a good woman and I know she cares for me. I also know that I'll have to spill my guts if we should get closer. My heart started the familiar pounding in my ears. My skin crawled and I shivered violently. I quickly rubbed my eyes, hoping the vision would not appear again. Wiping the sweat from my brow, I took a deep calming breath.

I walked over to the window that overlooked the back property and looked out into the dark night. The moon was drifting in and out of the clouds, briefly illuminating the hills and the woods. I looked toward the main house and could barely see their lights.

It was then I heard something at the front door. I quickly turned around to see the old doorknob twisting back and forth. As I ran to the door, I gracefully tripped on the ottoman and landed with a heavy thud. "Dammit," I exclaimed through clenched teeth and rubbed my foot.

I heard something again; it sounded like someone running. As I looked out, I caught a shadow flying by the front window. I quickly got to my feet and ran out into the windy night.

The wind was whipping around as I saw the fleeing figure stumbling his way to the top of the hill. I quickly followed, not giving any thought as to what I would do if I caught up to him.

As luck would have it—well, my luck anyway—I slipped on the craggy rocks and stumbled against them, completely losing my balance.

Sliding down the rest of the way on my backside, I came to a halt at the foot of another small hill.

Well, that was interesting. I stood and rubbed my sore ass. So much for being a finely honed private investigator.

Whomever I had seen was long gone and I did not intend to wander around in the dark any longer. I meekly walked back to the little thatched cottage and the safety of my bed.

It was a cloudy and damp morning, making my neck and shoulders ache like the devil as I walked to the house. There was a light fog and the wind was blowing off the cliffs as I made my way up the road. Even in the daylight, it was eerie.

Mac and Teri were in the kitchen with Mac at the stove. "Good morning, Lord and Lady McAuliffe."

Mac grinned and bowed slightly. "Good day, you lowly peon."

"Landlord," I grumbled playfully and took the offered cup.

I noticed Teri's worried look. "How'd you sleep?" she asked.

I raised a curious eyebrow and glanced at Mac who shrugged as he read the paper. "Fine, why?"

Mac said from behind the paper, "Mother hen was worried about her chick."

I laughed as Teri hit the paper he was reading.

"I think you must be psychic," I said with a weak smile. Mac immediately lowered the paper and sat forward.

Teri's blue eyes got as big as saucers. "What happened?"

"Somebody was outside the front door. He took off and I followed him—"

"You what!" Teri exclaimed and Mac winced and gently pulled her down in the chair next to him.

"It was nothing, Teri. I lost him along the ridge of the hill out back," I said and drank my coffee.

"And?" Teri asked.

I let out a sheepish laugh. "I fell on my ass."

"Something different!" Mac exclaimed, and before I could answer, he put the paper down. "Let's put on our walkin' shoes and check out the woods. Maybe it was just kids playing around with the crazy Americans."

It was still foggy and damp as we walked behind the house toward the mausoleum, and we slowly made our way in the direction of the ridge.

"This is kind of eerie," Teri said and shivered while she pulled her sweater around her.

I agreed. "Is it me or do you guys feel like we're being watched?" I asked and looked around.

The light fog dulled our senses and I felt my heart beating in my ears. We heard something in the woods. A twig snapped, which sounded like a gunshot, and we all whirled around. It was Peter.

"Christ, will you wear a bell or something?" I exclaimed, putting a hand to my heart.

"Good morning. Takin' a nice walk in the beautiful Irish weather this fine morning?" His smile faded when he saw our faces. "What happened?"

"Nothing," I said with a shrug. "Just had a visitor at the cottage last night. Or maybe it was my imagination."

I noticed the look of concern on Peter's face. "Any ideas, Mr. Sullivan?" I asked and once again looked right in his eyes.

"No, I haven't a clue," he said and scratched the back of his neck.

"You stay at the house tonight, Kate," Mac said as we walked back to the house.

I was about to argue with him when Bridget came around the

back of the house. "There ya are. I knocked but got no answer. How is everyone this morning?"

I explained my visitor and watched Bridget as she shot a questioning look at Peter, who shrugged. "Any ideas?" I asked her.

"None," she said.

"What brings you out here this morning, Bridget?" Teri asked.

"Oh, I wanted to see Kate," she answered and smiled at me.

Mac and Peter headed back. So did Teri, but not until that certain scowl flashed across her face.

"I have a client at eleven, but if you like, I have the afternoon free. Perhaps I can show you the countryside," Bridget suggested with a slight shrug.

"I'd like that. How about one o'clock?" We agreed to meet at her office.

With Bridget gone, I wandered back into the kitchen. "What are your plans for the rest of the day?" Peter asked Mac and Teri.

"Mac and I are planning a dinner on Friday evening. I hope that Rory Nolan and his wife, Anne, Bridget and you, and Sean and Mary Farrell will attend. Wow, that's ten. I've never planned a dinner party for so many," she said.

Peter coughed. "If you don't mind a suggestion. You're the woman of the house, you should be having someone doin' the cookin'. They'll expect that. Why not let me get you a cook and a server for the evening? How's that?" He smiled broadly.

Teri was amazed. "I won't need all that, will I?"

Peter nodded. "Believe me, Brian told me how he used to have people over all the time. The people in the village really loved him. They'd be glad to do it for ya, I'm sure." He smiled wickedly. "Besides, you pay far better than Brian himself."

"Landlord," I grunted playfully.

Chapter 10

I was at Bridget's office at one o'clock. She was locking the door when I arrived. "Well, good afternoon," she said, smiling. "I thought we'd go for a drive, how's that sound?"

"Sounds fine. Shall I drive?"

"No, you'll be wantin' to take in the scenery. I'll do the drivin', you relax."

We drove south along the coastal road; the view was breathtaking. The sun had come out and it was unusually warm. I noticed a basket in the backseat as Bridget picked a spot near the cliff and parked the car.

"Where in the world are we?" I asked.

"Clew Bay. Isn't it grand?" she asked, gazing out at the ocean.

We found a spot on the grass, and she put the blanket down. "I hope you like cold chicken."

"I didn't know this was going to be a picnic," I said as I sat down.

She gave me a sly grin. "I figured if I told ya, you might not come."

I looked out at the bay. "Clew Bay, huh?" I asked. "Any history there?"

"God, yes. Many a ship has been scuttled against those rocks. Legend has it that a ship from the Armada was sunk somewhere out there," she said, gazing almost lovingly at the ocean.

"You really love it here, don't you?" I asked and sipped my wine.

"Yes, I really do."

We sat and talked about nothing in particular. "I don't know what to make of last night, with whomever it was outside my door," I said, stealing a glance at her. "But it does seem strange. With all these things happening, it's somewhat scary."

"I don't blame ya. Maybe you shouldn't be staying at the cottage alone," she said.

"Well, that's the consensus of opinion." I laughed and ate my chicken.

She gave me a curious grin. "You're an independent woman, Kate." It was not a question.

I stretched out on my side and leaned on my elbow. "I guess so. I never really thought about it, but in the past few months or so, I've been told that incessantly."

"Well, there's nothin' wrong with being independent. Just as there's nothin' wrong with bein' unattached. If that's what ya want, of course," she said as she munched on a chicken leg.

I scowled as Maggie's face flashed in my mind. I changed the topic. "Tell me about Brian. I'm curious as to how he died. Seems strange that a man lives all his life in one spot and one night trips and plunges to his death." I shrugged and looked out at the ocean. "Doesn't mesh."

"I don't know, but ya don't live here. The night plays tricks on ya."

I raised an eyebrow. "Banshees again?"

Bridget laughed and looked out at the ocean. "Who knows? Sean and Mary said he had far too much to drink. It's sad. Brian was a good man. I only saw him when he came to town and had business with me. He came to me with his will. I'll admit I was a little surprised, but I figured Mac must have some great qualities in him," she looked at me and continued. "About two years ago or so, some people from Dublin came to see Brian. He never said a word about it. We never knew who they were, but they came several times. Different people," she said with a shrug.

"How do you know they were from Dublin?" I asked and she blushed.

"I asked Constable Reardon to check the license tags. It was not a rental and they were from Dublin."

"Very clever, but why ask? What did it matter who called on Brian?" I asked curiously. She hesitated for a moment. I thought a moment too long.

"We're a small village here. Unexpected visitors are a curiosity, and ya know we Irish are a curious lot and love a bit of gossip," she said with a wink. "Now finish your chicken, or you'll have me thinkin' ya don't like my cooking."

I chuckled nervously, not sure why I should be nervous around this woman. She was smart, attractive, and amusing. Maggie's face flashed through my mind, clouding all my reason.

I looked at Bridget, who was watching me. My detached emotional loop had me by the ankle, dragging me back once again. I did the only thing I could think of—I ate my chicken. "What do you think they wanted?"

"I don't know, but they looked very high class. Ya know, impeccably dressed. There was the same woman and man, they came three times," she said. "I have no idea what in the world I'm talkin' about. You have a way about you, Kate Ryan. You're easy to be with."

I let out a rude snort, which I did not intend to do. "Wait till you get to know me, you won't think I'm so easy," I said, trying to keep the conversation light and on track. That was not going to be easy with Miss Donnelly, who leaned in and gave me a sly grin. I instinctively leaned away.

"I didn't say you were easy, but I would like to get to know ya, to find out for myself," she said as she handed me an apple.

I looked at it cautiously. "Don't worry. I'm not Eve, but I am temptin' ya," she said with an evil grin and laughed, I'm sure, at the dumbfounded look on my face.

I immediately thought of Bette Davis in the movie *All About Eve*. Her distinctive voice rang in my ears—*"Eve, Eve, little Miss Eve-il."* I took the offering and a healthy bite.

We sat there the rest of the day talking about our childhoods and Irish history, then not saying very much at all. I was leaning against a tree, eating another apple, looking out at the ocean. I leaned over, poured her another glass, and refilled mine.

She was giving me a strange look. "What are ya thinking about?" she asked.

"Nothing really. It's a beautiful country—a country of poets."

Bridget nodded as she looked around. "Yes, it is. My favorite? Oscar Wilde," she said and gazed out at the ocean. I said nothing, not wanting to break her pensive mood. "Each man kills the thing he loves…" she said wistfully.

We were silent for a moment. "Well," I said with a nervous chuckle. "*I* was thinking of a little Thomas Moore. I wasn't expecting you to recite from *The Ballad of the Reading Gaol.*"

She looked right in my eyes then and a cold feeling swept through me. Then she laughed. "You should see your face. We Irish can be romantically morbid, it's true. This was a grand afternoon, but the clouds are comin'. We'd best get back."

"So did you have a nice afternoon?" Teri asked absently as we were finishing dinner.

I had my fork to my mouth and stopped. "Yes. I had a very nice time. Bridget's a nice young woman."

I told them what Bridget said about the visitors from Dublin. "She was curious and found out where they were from, but that's all." I sat back and thought about that.

"Who are these people? What has this land got? Okay, let's look at this. Some people from Dublin visit Brian. For two years after that, his family bothers him, probably till his death, to sell. Brian falls off a cliff. You inherit his estate. Someone tried to break into my house. Peter shows up stabbed. I get mugged and told to go home. We've got to find out what is so important about this land. Is it the mill they're after? Peter knows something..." I looked around. "Hey, where is he anyway?"

"He told me he had a few things to do, but hell, that was this morning."

I glanced at my watch. "Let me give Maggie a call," I said.

The phone rang and rang. The answering machine came on and I took a deep breath and waited for her message to stop. "Hi, it's Kate. I thought I'd give you a call, but you're out. Hope everything is fine. We're not at the inn. We're staying at the house now. Anyway, this damned machine will cut me off. I'll call you on Friday. G'bye, Maggie," I said and banged the phone down.

Teri was standing in the hallway. "Did you get in touch with Maggie?" she asked.

"No!" I snapped, not knowing why I was getting so irritated. *This whole inheritance thing is getting to me.* That was it. "I called over an ocean and got a stinking answering machine. I told her I would call. Where could she be? Anyway, I left her a message. Hell, I'm going to bed."

I lay in bed staring at the rain beating on the window. What in the world was happening? I needed to clear my mind and think about this. Someone tosses me down the cobblestone walk, probably the same guy who stabbed Peter. What next, I thought as another burst of thunder shook the window.

I turned on my stomach and put the pillow over my head as the thunder rolled.

I had a fitful sleep, dreaming about disembodied people chasing me. Bob was in it, Mac and Teri, Maggie; hell, everybody was in it. They were calling for me, screaming, and I couldn't get to them. The harder I tried to get to them, the slower I went. I could feel someone coming up behind me.

I woke up in a sweat and sat on the edge of the bed breathing heavily and wringing my hands. Trying to calm my racing heart, I sat on the window seat, waiting for this wave of panic to subside. I ran a shaky hand through my hair. *Christ, I hate that dream.* I put my hand to the back of my neck; it ached horribly as I stretched it from side to side. As I lay back against the pillows, I drifted back to a restless sleep.

None of us slept much. I know the storm kept me up most of the night. Mac and Teri were in the kitchen, looking exhausted. I grumbled a good morning and they groaned back. I plopped down in the chair and Teri poured me a cup of coffee.

"What a storm," I said, yawning. "Did you hear that thunder?" Both gave me an exasperated look. "Stupid question."

We were finishing breakfast when we heard someone at the front door.

"I'll get it," Mac and I said at the same time.

I waved my hand tiredly. "Be my guest, lord of the manor. I wonder if Brian had as many visitors as you've had in the past two days." I heard a man's voice and was immediately curious. My fatigue forgotten, I followed the voice to the foyer. There stood two older men with Mac.

"Mike McAuliffe?" one of them asked. The other just stood there.

"Yes, can I help you?" Mac asked. I poked my head around to get a good look.

"I'm James McAuliffe and this is Tim Devereaux. We're your uncles," he said sourly. *What a grump.*

"Family, Mac darlin'," I whispered in his ear. Teri pinched my arm.

"Well, come in, please," Mac offered and pushed me out of the way.

Both men sat on the couch looking at us.

"Can I get you some coffee or tea?" Teri asked a little shakily.

"Thank ya, no," James said with a frown.

"Yes, I would like some tea, thank you, ma'am," Tim said in a kindly voice.

Teri went into the kitchen, and Mac stood by the fire. "So, gentlemen, I take it you know about the will. I'd like to talk to you about it."

"I'll tell ya right now, we don't like it one bit. I'll be honest with ya, we wanted Brian to sell the mill," James said.

Tim said nothing but looked at his hands. I kept my mouth shut for the moment.

"I can only imagine how you feel. However, Brian had controlling stock, and it was his wish to keep the mill open." He stopped as Teri came into the room with the tea and gave me a curious glance.

James looked at Teri. "Will you excuse us? We're discussing business."

Oh, that was such the wrong thing to say. I winced and looked at Teri, whose face was now the color of her red hair.

"I *beg* your pardon?" she asked with her hands on her hips.

Mac said quickly, "No, I will not excuse you. You will not come into this house and insult my wife. Now I think it's time for you both to leave." He ended the conversation.

"I meant no disrespect. However, this is not over." He nodded and walked out. "Let's go, Tim."

Tim stood there looking apologetic. "I'm sorry for James's behavior." He extended his hand to Teri and she took it hesitantly. He smiled sadly and left.

"In all my life, I have never been so insulted. The nerve of that man. Who does he think he is?" Teri fumed.

Listening to Teri's tirade, none of us noticed Peter standing in the foyer until he cleared his throat. "Did I see James and Timothy drive away?"

"Yes, and James is quite the rude thing," I said, avoiding my sister's glare.

"I guess I can't blame him," Mac said.

"Mac, don't trust him," Peter said.

Mac nodded. "I know. I do not intend to sell this mill, Peter. Not to anyone."

There was another knock at the door. "Good grief, it's like Grand Central Station," Teri exclaimed.

"Are you guys on some sort of schedule?" I asked. "We could pay for the maids if you charged admission."

Mac laughed as Teri opened the door. A tall thin man stood there with a briefcase in his hand. "Is Mr. McAuliffe about?" he asked.

Teri let him in and took his coat. Mac came up and shook his hand. "I'm Mike McAuliffe."

"Well, sir, it's a pleasure to meet you," he said, shaking Mac's hand. His accent was definitely British.

Mac brought him into the library by the fire. Teri offered tea and he gladly accepted. "It's a bit chilly. The weather certainly changes quickly up here," he said in a friendly demeanor. *C'mon, get to the point.*

"Well, Mr. McAuliffe, I'm Jarred Collins. I've spoken to your late uncle several times in the past. I won't take much of your time. I represent The Omega Group." He offered Mac his card. "We've been interested in Oceanview Woolen Mill for quite some time. The last time I was in this country, I spoke with your uncle and he was very interested in selling the mill to our company. Unfortunately, before we could settle anything, he had the accident. I am sorry. I liked Brian, he was a good man," he said.

Mac looked at the card. "Well, Mr. Collins, it's my understanding that Brian didn't want to sell. I have a letter from him that states that. So I'm afraid you came all this way for nothing."

"That is curious. Brian seemed very interested five months ago. When was your letter written, if I may ask?" Mr. Collins said politely.

"I'd have to look. I don't have access to it now," Mac replied.

Mr. Collins nodded in understanding. He opened his briefcase. "This was the proposal I gave Brian. Perhaps you can read it over, take it to a lawyer, and think about it. I know it's very soon after your uncle's untimely death. However, I think you might be pleasantly surprised at the offer." He stood and shook Mac's hand

and Teri's, as well. "Mr. McAuliffe, it was a pleasure to meet you and you, Mrs. McAuliffe. I'll be staying in Donegal for a few days. Please let me know."

I watched as Teri and Mac walked Mr. Collins to the door. It was then I noticed Peter, who had been conspicuously quiet the entire time.

Chapter 11

The Omega Group? What in the world is that?" I asked as I held the business card. "They're based out of London." Then I had an idea.

"I wonder if Charlie's still in London. Maybe he can find something out about this company," I said thoughtfully. "I was going to call Maggie anyway."

Of course, Maggie wasn't in, which was now beginning to annoy me. Hannah, on the other hand, was delighted to hear from me. I told her all that had happened. She was shocked.

"Good heavens, Kate, what is happening? You were mugged?"

"Hannah, I was not mugged, and don't tell Maggie about that. She said something like this would happen. All I need is an 'I told you so' from your niece. What I need to know is if Charlie's in London." I explained the situation.

"My, your timing is perfect. He flew to London after Margaret's party. I have his number."

I called the number Hannah gave me. Charlie's voice came over the phone and I had to laugh.

"Well, I'll be! Kate, what in the world are you doing calling me?"

I explained the entire mess to Charlie and told him what I needed.

"The Omega Group. Hmm. For you, Kate, anything. What have you gotten yourself into this time? I can't believe Mac inherited that, good Lord. So how are you treating my sister?"

"Please, Charlie, one predicament at a time," I said. Teri motioned for me to hand her the phone. "I think Teri wants to talk to you. Call me when you find out something." I handed the phone to Teri.

Mac was in the kitchen reading brochures of Ireland's points of interest.

"Typical Mac, checking out the history."

"Hey, you should read these. This place is crawling with history. Read the one about Grace O'Malley. She was a pirate, an honest to goodness pirate," he said.

I read the brochure. "Hmm. Apparently, she was pretty successful in her day, which was about four hundred years ago," I said and continued reading. "Boy, she plundered quite a bit. Feisty little wench. Wonder if Maggie's related," I said absently.

Teri came into the kitchen. "Charlie says to give you this," Teri said and planted a big kiss on Mac.

"Remind me to thank him," Mac said.

"I hope he can find something on this company. Where's the proposal Mr. Collins gave you?" I asked. Mac handed it to me. "I still can't get over how much he offered. I think you'd better show this to Bridget. Four million euros seems steep for a small, village-run woolen mill," I said, handing it to Teri.

"There has to be some mistake." She handed it back to me.

"Whoa, that's a lot of wool," Mac said, staring at the paper. Teri nodded in amazement.

"They all made me hungry. I'll make breakfast," I said and rubbed my hands together.

As we ate, I picked up the brochures that were still on the table. "Mac, everywhere you go, you get these brochures. Grace O'Malley, tough cookie for those days," I said. I handed the brochure to Teri.

"Hmm, plundering the Spanish Armada, pirating treasures."

I thought of Maggie, I don't know why. I could see her on the bow of a ship, yelling orders at everyone. *That's why.*

"You know what we haven't done yet?" Teri asked.

I got very nervous, and as I glanced at Mac, I could tell he felt the same. A look of terror flashed across his face. "What, honey?" he asked.

"We haven't gone into Duncorrib and met some of the locals. You're their bread and butter. You should meet them."

Mac perked up, grateful she didn't mention a shopping spree, I'm sure.

"You're right. Let's get squared away here and go into town and hobnob with the local gentry," Mac said. "First I'll call

Bridget. Maybe she can meet us in the village. I want to show her this proposal."

We drove into town about midday. The day had turned cloudy, but the sun made an appearance every now and then. At least it wasn't the constant dampness. People knew who we were before Mac could introduce us. They all shook his hand and slapped him on the back. They told him how they loved Brian and how he took care of the town. Mac was gracious and assured them that he didn't want to change a thing. In short, they loved him.

Teri put her hand in the bend of Mac's arm. "They love you, honey. This will work fine. I feel much better."

"Me too. It'll take time to get adjusted. I want to talk to Rory Nolan again. I want to make sure everything is status quo."

I stopped and looked down toward the end of the village. There was a man in a dark coat with short black curly hair. I was thinking about the guy in Donegal who attacked me in the alley. I remembered his coat. It was black or navy wool. The guy back home looked the same.

The man was standing there, smoking a cigarette, and talking with two other men. One was a redhead. The other was bald with a gold earring in his right ear.

The man in the dark coat threw down his cigarette, turned up his collar, and walked across the street. The other two young men split up and went their own way. "Those two certainly don't look like they fit in this quaint little village," I said as I watched them.

Mac slapped me on the back. "You need a pint," he informed me. *He could be right.*

We were to meet Bridget at a small pub at the end of the village at one o'clock. We sat there having our drinks when she arrived.

"How are the happy McAuliffes and Ryan this fine day?" she smiled and sat down. She looked at me. "You look well, Kate." Her hand lingered on my shoulder.

Mac told her about Mr. Collins and the proposal. She scowled as she listened. "He's back, is he?"

"What's the deal with him?" I asked.

"He came round about two years ago. I think he might have been one of the ones from Dublin, but I can't be sure. He's been a pest ever since. He wants the mill, why I don't know. It doesn't produce enough for a big company."

"I don't know, Bridget, they seem to want it bad enough." Mac sighed and handed her the proposal. "He suggested I show it to a lawyer."

Bridget frowned and took a drink of her beer while she read. She showed little emotion, like any lawyer. She finished and took a very long drink of Guinness. "Well now, this is quite a sum of money," she said, frowning.

"That's putting it mildly. Why would a company offer so much for so little? It doesn't make sense," I said. "There's more to this."

I wished Charlie would call. I felt sure he'd find something. All this was connected. I was sure that the Irishman back home who had stabbed Peter was the same man who tossed me around the alley. Now a company is willing to pay four million for property that's not worth one. I ran my fingers through my hair in a frustrated gesture. Now where in the world was Peter?

"Sherlock, are you with us?" I heard Mac ask.

"Sorry, I was thinking," I said absently.

Bridget gave me a curious look. "My, you were far away. Sherlock? As in Sherlock Holmes?" she asked. "Are ya a detective then, Kate?"

"No, I'm curious, that's all," I said, trying to end the discussion before it got started.

Bridget looked to Teri, who explained about our father being a policeman. Bridget looked at me. "I'm impressed. Maybe you can figure out why The Omega Group is willing to part with four million," she said.

"Maybe," I said as I watched her, and for a moment, our eyes locked.

"What are ya thinking, Sherlock?" she asked. "Professor Moriarty?" Bridget was about to continue when Peter walked in looking tired and dirty.

He came over to the table. "Good afternoon. How's everyone?" he asked, smiling.

I noticed he had boots on that were muddied and his pants were wet.

"Where have you been?" Mac asked.

"Oh, I've been at the stable's cleanin' up," he said and sat down. He glanced at Bridget for a moment.

I looked up as the door opened and in walked the two young men from the morning. They glanced at our table and sat at the bar.

"Know them?" I asked Peter as he watched them.

Peter shrugged. "No."

Mac, Teri, and Bridget continued talking about the proposal. I noticed a short older man walk in. He smiled and waved at Peter. "Well, Sully, what in the world were ya doin' down by the shore? You daft boy, you could've been swept away."

Peter immediately sprang up, went to the old man, and put his arm around his shoulder and guided him to the bar.

Once again, *The Quiet Man* came to mind. This little man looked like Barry Fitzgerald from the movie. Short, funny, with an unquenchable thirst, he had the devil in him for sure.

I watched Peter for a moment. *The shore? What was he talking about?* Peter had said he was at the stable. I looked at Peter's boots. They were muddy, but also his pant legs were damp below the knee. I was sure he was up to something and I was determined to find out what.

The two young men were standing next to Peter and one of them bumped into him. Peter turned and apologized. The bald youngster gave Peter a shove. Peter looked angry but apologized again. Then the redhead also stood by Peter. "Whattaya mean, shovin' me friend," he said to Peter.

"I apologize. I didn't see him," Peter said affably and turned away.

"Don't be turnin' your back to me," the redhead said.

Mac got up and walked over to them. "Hi, fellas. What's the problem?"

The bald Irishman said, "Stay out of this." He then pushed Mac.

"Uh-oh," I said and pushed my chair back.

Teri fumed and started to get up. I looked at her. "Sit down, for chrissakes."

"Look, I don't know what my friend did here, but I assure you he meant no harm. Let me buy you a drink and be done with this," Mac said and put out his hand. The redhead slapped it away.

"Oh, this is going to be very unpleasant," I said and

instinctively sat on the edge of my chair. I had no clue what I could do, these were big boys.

Mac glared at him and put his hand on Peter's shoulder. "Let's go." He turned and the redhead grabbed him by the shoulder and took a swing at Mac, who ducked in the nick of time. Mac grabbed the young man by the back of the neck and threw him across the bar.

Peter was standing there amazed as the bald kid tried to hit Mac. He grabbed the young man, and that was all she wrote.

Bedlam...Never have I seen such flailing arms and flying fists.

Teri screamed for Mac to stop and started for the middle of the foray. I grabbed for her as she flew by me.

Mac had the redhead and as he reared back, he hit Teri in the face with his elbow. She let out a yelp and Mac turned toward her. As I got to her, I noticed the redhead coming for Mac again.

"Mac, behind you!" I yelled and took a chair and quickly threw it at the man's feet.

He tripped over the chair. Mac whirled around, hauled off, and punched the redhead dead in the face. His eyes crossed and he stood there a second, teetered back and forth, and fell to the floor.

Peter had the bald one in a headlock, the poor kid looked like he was about to pass out.

"Peter, let him go. He's turning blue," I informed him.

Peter unceremoniously let him go and the young man fell to his knees, grabbing his throat and coughing.

Mac was breathing like a bull as he wiped the blood from his cheek. He picked up the young man. "Now pick up your friend and get the hell out of here."

We watched as both staggered out the door. I looked at Teri in amazement. "Oh, God, Teri," I said and covered my mouth, trying not to laugh. "Your cheek is turning purple, Lady McAuliffe."

Peter sat down at the table. His lip was cut and bleeding, but he was smiling. "I haven't been in a brawl like that since I was at university," he said proudly.

"It's been that long for me, too," Mac said as Teri put a wet towel against his face. "Sorry, honey," Mac said quietly and touched Teri's bruised cheek. "A little makeup will hide it."

"A little?" I asked and avoided the glare from my sister.

Bridget was sitting there clearly amazed. "Well, I have to admit, I'm impressed with all of ya."

"Thanks, Kate, that was quick thinking," Mac offered.

I found Bridget smiling at me. "That *was* quick thinking. You could've been hurt, though. You're reckless, Kate Ryan." She smiled wickedly.

The bartender came up and slapped Mac on the back. "You did fine. Those two are a couple of ruffians. I'm glad to see someone take care of them. The drinks are on the house," he said and turned away.

The little man called after the bartender. "And it's high time, too." He roared with laughter. "Wait till the village hears about this one." He laughed and walked away.

Within ten minutes, the bar was filled with villagers.

I felt Bridget at my side. "I've got to be going. Walk me to my car?" she asked and I followed her out, avoiding Teri's motherly look.

I was humming as we walked to Bridget's car. "You've had an interesting day, Miss Ryan," she said as she opened her car door.

"Yes, and I wasn't even hurt. I've got to tell Maggie about that one," I announced.

Bridget grinned, and out of the blue, she leaned over and kissed me. I heard a soft moan as she pulled back. I think it came from me.

"Tell her about *that* one." She winked and drove off.

I stood there for a moment, then walked back into the tavern to see Mac, who looked like the mayor, shaking hand after hand, as did Peter. The Guinness was flowing freely—we all made sure it passed the taste test.

I watched Peter and thought of what he had just said about his college days. Then I looked over at the old man who had said something about Peter being down by the shore. Something wasn't right here. I walked up to the bar and the little guy looked at me and smiled; his Guinness definitely passed the test. "Well, there, lass, you should be proud of Mac and young Sully."

"I am. I'm sorry, I don't know your name," I said, smiling.

"Murphy, Patrick Murphy at your service," he said with a bow and gave me an inquiring look.

"Kate Ryan," I said.

He smiled broadly. "And a fine Irish name it is, Kate," he said and drank his beer. "I was impressed when ya threw the chair at the redhead."

"Patrick, what in the world was Peter doing down by the shore? I've told him it was dangerous, too," I said as I took a drink.

"I know. He's daft that young Sully. He's always down there looking for something. He'll break his fool neck if he's not careful. The Atlantic wind plays tricks on those cliffs and on the rocks below. He goes down there at the most peculiar times." He leaned in and so did I, as he whispered, "I told him to bring his young woman here. That way he'd have something to occupy his time instead of going down there in the wee hours of the morning and late at night. The young fool."

"I see your point. Wonder what he's looking for." I drank my beer. I noticed his glass was empty. "Can I get you another?"

"Thank you. One more, then I should be gettin' on home."

I motioned for Seamus to get another round for everybody. I made friends quickly. Soon I had three or four local men standing around talking about Peter and his cliffs.

I listened as they argued back and forth, about when and why he goes down to the rocks below. As they argued, I looked over at Peter, who was laughing with Mac and Teri and feeling no pain, drinking another black beer. I turned back to the conversation.

"If you ask me, the young boy is a bit touched," one man said and put a finger to his temple.

"He's down there no matter what the weather," another agreed.

"What's down there that could be so fascinating?" I asked, and they all looked at me as if I had run out of Guinness. "What?"

"Don't tell me ya don't know about the legend?" Patrick asked.

"What legend?" I asked, completely intrigued. "Tell me."

One old man coughed, holding his empty glass.

"Okay, okay," I said and called Seamus over for yet another round.

Patrick cleared his throat and looked around as if to make sure no one else was listening. The others huddled closer; I leaned in, as well.

"The pot o' gold is down there," he said and looked at me.

I leaned back and gave him a sarcastic look. "Well, if you're not going to be serious, Patrick."

He grinned wildly. "I am serious. The legend has it that there's a cavern deep down inside the cliff. However, no one can find it. The wind whips around the rocks somethin' fierce and the waves and tides have taken many a man with them. I am serious about that," he said and drank his beer.

"You think that's what Peter is looking for? A pot of gold?" I asked, extremely disappointed. I thought it would be a real legend. This was a great Irish tale to be told at the pub or around the fire on a cold night.

The Irish blarney was flowing better than the Guinness, if that were possible. After a few hours, we were ready to leave. Mac and Peter had their arms around each other's shoulders singing some obscure Irish rebel song.

We dragged the hero of Duncorrib grudgingly home to his castle. We no more than opened the door and the phone rang. It was Charlie. I told him about the day and he roared with laughter. "I missed it!"

"So, Charlie, what did you find out?"

"Plenty, but I can't go into it on the phone. I'm done here and was going to fly home. Could you stand a houseguest for a couple of days?" he asked.

"Of course. When?"

"Tomorrow I can get a flight and be at Shannon by midday. Oh, do you think I might bring a guest for the weekend?"

"Charlie, you devil, of course. We've got plenty of room, that's for sure. Teri's having a dinner party on Friday," I said cheerfully. "Wait, let me ask Teri."

I turned and jumped, startled. Teri was standing right behind me. "Geez, don't do that!" I said. "Charlie wants to come for the weekend and bring a houseguest," I said and wriggled my eyebrows.

She gave me an exasperated look. "Give me the phone."

I frowned and handed it over. I listened as Teri talked to Charlie. "Not a problem, Charlie. Should we pick you up? No. Okay." She gave him directions. "See you about one or so."

We went into the kitchen to find Mac sitting there. Teri put on the coffee and sat next to him.

"Well, Sherlock, what did you find out? I saw you talking to the locals," Mac said.

Teri put coffee in front of Mac. "Drink this, my hero."

Mac blushed and drank it. "I'm sorry about hitting you, sweetie. It was purely accidental," he finished with a weak smile.

The black and blue of her cheek was not as bad as Mac's jaw, which was turning a wonderful shade of purple. I got some ice, put it in two different towels, and handed one to each of them. They sat there drinking coffee with the ice on their faces. I put my hands on my hips in a motherly fashion.

"Don't ever tell me I get into strange situations again, children."

They both scowled at me. "It would take us a lifetime to catch up with you," Mac said.

"This is true." I hate it when they're right. "Peter said today that he was at the stables. I found out he was down on the shore skulking around. He's been doing it for a few months now."

"What's he looking for?" Teri asked.

"A pot of gold. That's the legend anyway," I said rather disappointed.

"What legend?" Mac asked.

"Apparently, there's gold buried in them thar cliffs," I said, laughing.

Mac shook his head. "Oh, brother, another Irish tale."

"Probably, but remember after the fight, Peter said he hadn't gotten into a brawl like that since college?" I asked.

"So?" Mac asked.

"I thought he was a poor kid and has been around horses all his life? How does a poor kid in this country go to college and wind up a horse trainer, making little or no money at all? There's something not right with him, Mac."

Mac shifted uncomfortably. "I don't know. That's a good point, but he fought like a son today."

"Maybe I'm way off. I hope so," I said, rubbing the back of my neck. It ached horribly. "My barometer is working. I bet it rains tomorrow."

"Hey, what did Charlie find out?" Mac asked.

"Oh, I nearly forgot. He couldn't talk over the phone but asked if he could come for the weekend and bring a houseguest," I said and raised my eyebrows.

Mac laughed. "This should be interesting."

"Yes, it will be," Teri said absently while drinking her coffee.

I noticed she looked like the proverbial cat that ate that poor canary. She looked far too much like our mother at that moment— it scared me.

Chapter 12

I woke on Friday morning stiff as a board. It had to be raining. I looked out my window—cloudy and damp but no rain. I thought about Peter and the rocks as I made coffee. Legends. Those old guys thought it was amusing, I'm sure, to get the goofy Yank, and I fell for it. I sat there at the table and shook my head.

It was peculiar, though, that he'd been down there so much. Maybe I'd take a trip and see what was so fascinating. I went upstairs, put on some heavy clothes and my boots, and grabbed my camera bag. I left a note for Mac and Teri and left.

The cliffs were so close I probably could have walked. The mill came into sight and I took the small road as far as I could. The ocean was magnificent. Indeed, a small rugged path led down to the shore. It was about a forty- or fifty-foot drop. It was steep but not impossible...sort of. I stood for a moment. If Maggie were here, she'd say no—I grinned childishly and started down the rocky path.

I made my way down little by little, slipping a couple of times. I looked back and was amazed at how little I had accomplished in ten minutes. This was steep, and for a moment, I thought of going back. However, I continued slowly. It took me the better part of an hour, and I was only halfway down and breathless. If I went any faster, I would surely slip and fall at least thirty feet. The wind was fierce, whipping and swirling around. I stopped and leaned against the cliffs. *I need to get into better shape.*

Finally, I reached the bottom. There certainly wasn't much shore to walk along. The huge rocks and boulders made for precarious maneuvering. I slipped on several occasions, scraping my shin badly. I looked down to see my jeans torn at the knee. *Why does this always happen to me?* I winced and looked at the blood running down my leg. I took the bandanna out of my pocket, tied it around my shin, and continued. There was a small clearing, and all at once, a huge wave crashed on the shore and I was soaked with the icy Atlantic. At that moment, I was glad I left my camera equipment in the car. *This was a mistake.* I felt and looked like a drowned rat.

I saw a small cave opening. I stared at it and walked closer. The opening was about seven feet, as high as it was wide. I looked closer and thought—bats.

"Yuck," I said openly and shivered.

I tried to get closer, but the waves were crashing and there was no way I could make it the thirty feet. Huge rocks and boulders surrounded it. Looking up, there was a sheer wall. No one could possibly come down here any other way but the path. Unless they rappelled like a mountain climber. I shivered and decided to make my way back. It took me the better part of an hour to get off those rocks, all the while being soaked by the icy waves. When I got to my car, I was freezing. Mac and Teri are going to be so pissed. Fine, now I felt like a ten-year-old.

Maybe I'll plead insanity. People tend to be nice to the insane.

I pulled up in front of the house and saw a strange car. It must be Charlie, I thought, smiling. It will be good to see him. I was freezing and soaking wet. I looked down at my shin and cursed myself for my clumsiness. I shivered and couldn't wait for a warm shower. Maybe they're out and won't even know.

I tiptoed into the foyer and headed for the stairs with my boots squishing. If I could only get to my room…

"Where the hell have you been?"

I stopped dead in my tracks. *Mom?* "So close." I sighed helplessly and turned to Teri. "Hey, you'll never believe what happened," I started innocently when Mac and Charlie walked out of the library.

"What happened?" she asked and noticed my makeshift bandage.

I chose to ignore her. I am an adult after all. "I'll fill you in later. Right now I'm freezing," I said and looked at Charlie. "Hi there. How was the flight and where's your houseguest?" I asked and winked. He motioned to the top of the stairs.

I was stunned. There stood Maggie sporting a wicked smile. "Surprise," she said flatly.

No longer stunned, I stood there dumbfounded and shivering. My heart raced—she looked good. She was wearing an Irish sweater, a green turtleneck, and brown wool slacks.

"What are you doing here?" I asked as I walked up the stairs.

"Teri invited me," she answered dryly and looked at my shin. "What did you do?"

I stopped and looked down at myself. "Oh, I slipped."

She rolled her eyes and stepped aside. "Go take off those wet clothes."

As I passed by, she lightly touched my shoulder. "Are you all right?"

The damned soft voice sent a chill through my already chilled body. *I wish she'd stop touching me.* "Yeah, I'm fine," I said. "I'll be right out."

"Do you need me?"

For an instant, our eyes locked. "I think so, but not for this," I said and motioned to my scraped shin. We both let out a nervous laugh as I walked by.

After getting warm and dry, I headed downstairs. They were all in the library and looked my way when I came in from the hallway.

"So where did you go? You had us worried," Teri asked.

"I thought I should see for myself if there was anything to this pot of gold business, so I went down there. I got a little bath from the Atlantic, so I turned back. However, I did see a cave entrance," I finished, and Mac gave me an astonished look.

"You're kidding."

Teri put her hands on her hips. "You went down there alone?"

"Yes, Teri. I went down there alone. Now for a second, stop being Mom and listen. Why would Peter be playing around down there? There's something to this, I can feel it," I said. I turned my attention to Charlie. "So, Charlie, what did you find out?"

We all took places around the fire. Maggie sat on the hearth and leaned over. "Charlie told me what's been going on. You've been busy," she said, and I could hear the worried undertone in her voice. I looked into her blue eyes and smiled.

"I like being busy," I said as I reached over and held her hand, giving it an affectionate shake. "There's something going on here, Maggie."

Charlie cleared his throat and took a note pad from his breast pocket. "Well, Kate, this is strange. The Omega Group, based out of London, is a company that does pretty much the same as we do. They buy smaller companies and sell them for a profit, blah, blah," he started.

"However, this is a big company. Much bigger than ours, it's worldwide. They don't usually go after small potatoes like Oceanview Woolen Mill." He looked at Mac. "No offense, Mac, but your mill's real worth is to the village. You'll make a nice living, but I don't see the attraction to a mega business like Omega."

Mac nodded in understanding. "I don't, either." He picked up the proposal and handed it to Charlie. "See for yourself. I don't know what they're thinking."

Charlie frowned as he read it, turning the pages back and forth. "Wow, that's a chunk of money." He handed the proposal to Maggie.

Maggie read it and agreed.

"Did you take this to a lawyer?" Charlie asked.

Mac nodded. "Bridget Donnelly was Brian's lawyer. She's taking care of us now. She read it and can't figure out why they want the mill, either."

"Bridget did say that this Mr. Collins has been up here on several occasions in the past year or two, bugging Brian to sell. I personally think his family knew and that's why they wanted him to sell." I paced in front of the fire.

"What would a multi-bazillion-dollar company want with a tiny woolen mill? Brian's family wanted him to sell. They don't have the sentiment that Brian had. They want the money pure and simple." I thought for a moment and continued to pace. "The more I think about it, the more I don't believe Brian's death was an accident. I have a big hunch that somebody tossed him over the cliff because he wouldn't sell. Whoever killed him didn't know he made Mac his beneficiary. That's why we got the visit back home and why I was attacked in the street. Someone wants us out of here."

"Wait a minute, what happened to you?" Maggie asked.

I explained simply as she and Charlie listened in disbelief. "So you see why I'd like this solved soon," I said earnestly. "This company is the key. Charlie, how much more can you find out?"

"I've got three people working on it. That's how big this company is. I gave them twenty-four hours to come up with something. They're burning the midnight oil. I should be hearing from them by tomorrow."

"I'm going to get dinner ready," Teri announced. Maggie offered to help and Teri shook her head. "Oh, no. You're a guest for the next few days. Besides, it'll keep my mind busy. Kate, take Maggie out to see the horses. We showed them around a little this afternoon while you were swimming, but I didn't get to the stables."

Maggie and I strolled across the field to the stables. It was still bright. The sun hadn't fully set over the ocean.

"My God, it is beautiful. I've never seen so much green," Maggie said as she looked around the landscape.

"I know. It's because the weather is so foul," I said and rubbed my neck.

She looked at me. "You're not upset that I'm here?"

I stopped and looked down at her worried face. "Of course not."

"Charlie said it was my duty as a wealthy woman to hop on a plane at a moment's notice."

I grinned at the sarcastic tone. "Well, he's right. You have an obligation to throw your money around," I replied. I looked into her eyes. "I should have never told you to go home. I wanted you here. I-I should have thought of inviting you, I'm sorry."

I could tell she was caught off-guard by my statement. To tell the truth, so was I. The dimpled grin started and my heart skipped. Suddenly, I felt the need to explain.

"Well, I mean you needed a little getaway, too, after six months straight in an emergency room." I took a deep breath. "S-So it's good that you can relax and—"

Her warm fingertips were suddenly against my lips. "Don't say another word, Kate. What you said was perfect. Thank you."

I was sweating. My mouth was dry. My heart was pounding and my hands were shaking. *What a mess.*

She grinned slightly and walked toward the stable. I obediently followed, when my legs stopped shaking, and pulled the heavy door open. Maggie was still grinning as she walked by.

"Oh, quit your grinning," I grumbled and pushed her into the stable.

She was amazed, as I knew she would be. The Connemara ponies were in their stalls. She immediately went to them, took a handful of oats, and fed them. I watched in quiet amazement.

"Boy, you're good with animals. Maybe we can take those two out for a ride tomorrow." I motioned to the chestnut mares in the last stall.

"That would be wonderful. I forgot you do know how to ride. We haven't done that since last fall."

"That's true. Then we'll definitely take them out," I said as we started back.

"You've been rubbing your neck since I've seen you. What's wrong?" she asked as we walked.

I realized what I was doing and quickly put my hand down. "I hurt it a few years back. This weather bothers it," I said frankly and shrugged.

Though I was grateful she didn't pursue it—it didn't matter. Now I was thinking about it and I felt my body tremble. *Don't start now,* I begged the gods above. The ringing in my ears started. I know Maggie noticed. She notices everything, which for some reason, unnerves me.

The gods ignored me as I felt my palms getting sweaty and my hands shaking. I quickly put them into my pockets and we walked to the stone wall.

Maggie looked out at the ocean. "Magnificent. I've seen the ocean from both shores back home. This, however, is—" she stopped and looked at me.

I barely heard her. My mind was back to five years before. I blinked and shook my head, but I couldn't get the bloody images out of my mind.

"Kate, are you all right?" she asked me.

I looked at her and nodded. "Fine." My voice cracked and I sat on the stone wall. I wiped my forehead again and she sat next to me.

"C'mon, let's go in," she said.

I buried my head in my hands, the anxious feeling rippling through me. I felt like breaking into a dead run. "Goddamit! I can't do this. Maybe you shouldn't have come. You're better off—" I almost lost it. I took a deep breath. I was on the verge of a real crying jag. I felt the tears coming as the sweat dripped down my back.

"Kate, take a deep breath," Maggie said firmly as she rubbed my back. I obeyed immediately. "Again."

I took another and it subsided a bit. I put a shaky hand to my forehead. "Sorry," I whispered, feeling pathetic.

She reached over and took my shaking hand. I felt her soft hand caressing mine. I was amazed at how reassuring it felt and how I was instantly calmed.

"Better?" she asked.

I nodded quickly and took a deep breath. "Thanks," I whispered. I don't know why, but a feeling of shame swept through me. "I-I'm sorry," I said.

"That's the second time in three minutes you've apologized. For what, Kate?"

"I don't know. I just, I don't know," I said and felt awkward. My hands were still shaking and I didn't know what to do with them.

Maggie reached over and held them. I stopped shaking when I felt the warmth of her hands.

"What is it?" I heard the soft plea in her voice. God, I wanted to tell her, but I couldn't look her in the eye. "Whatever it is, I'll understand."

I looked down at my hands as she held them tightly in her own. "I can help you," Maggie whispered. I barely heard her; my mind once again had traveled back.

"I'll help you, Liz. We can get through this. It was an accident," I said and gently shook her. She blinked and looked up into my eyes.

"Yes, it was, wasn't it?" I heard the hopeful tone in her voice and pulled her close.

"Yes, it was." I pulled back and cupped her face. "We'll have to go to the police, Liz. Don't worry, I'll be there for you, always," I said. I saw the doubtful look flash across her face. "I will be there for you."

Maggie's soft hand on my cheek brought me back to reality. "C'mon, let's get back," she said.

By the time we got to the door, my panic attack had subsided. I stopped and turned to her. "Thanks, Maggie. With all this going on, I'm out of sorts," I offered the lame excuse as I opened the door.

"You know I'll listen if you want to talk," she offered and winked. "But let's do it inside. I'm freezing."

After dinner, we sat in the library and had a delightful conversation of murder and Bridget's banshee.

Charlie raised an eyebrow and asked, "So which room has the ghost?"

Teri laughed. "None," she replied. "So far."

"Well, which room did you give me?" Maggie looked at me suspiciously.

Teri laughed. "You've got the room next to Kate's. Charlie is next to ours. So at least we'll be together if anything happens," she said.

As I walked into my room, the connecting door was opened and Maggie and I stood there looking at each other. "I didn't know this was a connecting door." I reached over and started to close it. "I'm glad you're here," I said and winced, knowing I had said that several times now. I looked down into those blue eyes, which I've searched so many times before.

Maggie stood there for a moment. "Thank you. So am I. Good night, I'll see you in the morning."

I stood there looking at the closed door. Visions of the previous autumn flashed through my mind as I remembered meeting this feisty woman and just how much I enjoyed Dr. Winfield's friendship... *But damn those blue eyes sparkled.*

Chapter 13

The thunder and lightning was horrific and I lay there looking out at the show. Sleep did not come easy, so I sat on the window seat and watched the storm. I froze for a moment and held my breath when I heard the door creaking; it was Maggie standing there in her robe.

"What's wrong, are you all right?" I asked quickly, my heart beating like a drum. *Why must this happen every time I see this woman?*

"I hate thunder," she said in a shaky voice. She was shivering, and as the thunder boomed, she quickly walked over to me. I met her halfway.

"C'mon, sit, we'll watch the storm," I whispered. I grabbed the extra quilt off the bed.

She sat on the other side of the window seat facing me. The lightning flashed, and for a moment, I saw her face. She looked sad. I handed her the quilt and she wrapped it around herself. She brought her knees up to her chest. I inched closer and tucked the quilt around her feet.

"Thanks," she said.

"You're welcome. I didn't know you hated thunder," I said softly.

Maggie snuggled into the blanket. "When I was a little girl and it stormed, my mother would always let me climb into her big bed and hold me. I felt so safe and protected. When she died, I no longer had that feeling. Oh, Aunt Hannah was always there and she did her best. But—"

"It wasn't your mom," I finished for her. My heart ached when I saw the tears welling in her eyes. "I *am* sorry, Maggie."

She sniffed and wiped her eyes. "I feel like a big baby. I'm a doctor, for chrissakes," she grumbled and let out a nervous laugh.

"It was hard for you growing up after Miranda died, wasn't

it?" I asked and reached over and tucked the blanket under her feet again. It was perfectly fine; I just needed contact with her, I suppose.

"Oh, I was fine. I was just…" she stopped and looked out the window and watched the rain.

"Lonely," I whispered and she nodded without looking at me. I didn't want her to be lonely anymore. However, I didn't consider myself the best candidate to comfort her.

"You know, there's quite a bit we don't know about each other, Kate. Why is that?" she asked and stretched her legs and put her feet on my lap. I smiled slightly and adjusted my legs.

"Hey, your feet are freezing, even through these wool socks," I said and rubbed her feet, avoiding her question. She knew it and repeated.

"Why is it that we've known each other all these months and we're still strangers?" For some reason, that cut right through me. *Were we strangers?*

"We're not strangers, we know each other. I've been traveling and you've been at the hospital—"

"And now? I'm done with my internship. Soon, I'll be taking over for Doc at the clinic. Then what will be our excuse?" she asked and I didn't have an answer. *God this woman was direct.*

She sighed and looked out the window as the lightning flashed. "Maybe you and I are not... You've got something on your mind. I know it has to do with your P.I. business years ago. Something happened to you. I'm your friend, and I'd like to help. You can't go the rest of your life carrying this in your heart." She said this quietly, but the truth rang loud and clear.

I ran my fingers through my hair as I listened to the heartfelt concern in her soft voice.

Why not? Suddenly, I felt the inexplicable urge to tell her everything. Perhaps the soft worried voice eased my heart. Perhaps it was the fact that we were sitting in the dark—I felt safe there. And perhaps after so many years, it was time.

"I do want to tell you about this. I suppose now is as good a time as any." I looked over at her and I could tell she was shocked.

"I've got to get this out," I said almost to myself. Maggie was a good friend, that much was definitely true, and I knew I could trust her.

Pacing in front of the window seat, I started. "Eddington, Elizabeth K."

I took a deep quivering breath. Maggie will never know how monumental that was—just to say her name out loud. "You know I had a private investigation business. My partner was Bob Whittier. He was my father's partner on the police force. We started the business after my father passed away. We struggled for a couple of years. When business was slow, Bob hired himself out in security. I had my freelancing. Then our reputation got around and business was good. We made a good name for ourselves, not a lot of money, but good honest work, and for nearly ten years, it flourished. Then Liz walked in and our worlds were torn apart.

"We were hired to find her husband. I felt uneasy from the get go, but she offered a vulgar amount of money. Bob had four boys and a wife. So we took it," I said, feeling as though I was defending my actions. I looked over at Maggie. She was watching me in the darkness.

"You don't mind if we keep the light off, do you?" I asked. Somehow, I didn't want to see the pity on her face.

She shook her head. "This is fine," she said in a tender voice.

"To make a long ugly story short, the whole mess was weird, and I should've used my head. Liz offered more money. Bob, he needed it, and we took it and..." I sighed and looked out the window.

"I fell in love with her. She gave Bob money and she gave me herself, plain and simple, no excuses. However, I made the sad discovery that her husband wasn't missing, she had killed him. She said it was an accident. I believed her. I was wrong. What she really wanted from us was to find some money her husband had embezzled. We found it hidden in the cellar. Instead of using my head, I used every other part of my anatomy," I said as my anger rose. I took a deep calming breath. "When I put all the pieces together, I confronted her, telling her I would help any way I could. I believed her when she said she'd give herself up. I was completely foolish," I spat out, disgusted with myself all over again, "and I left her alone for an hour."

I was pacing in front of the window like a caged lion. My hands were shaking and I was perspiring as if I'd run a race.

"Why can't we just leave? There's enough money here for

your partner and his family. We take the rest and go someplace. Please, Kate, we can be happy..."

I thought of Bob and his family. Surely, they could use the money. For a moment, I thought of doing just that. Who would care? It was an accident. John Eddington was an asshole and Liz was finally out from under him. My heart said take the money, take Liz, and go. My heart...

"Liz, we will be happy, but you have to tell the police. We don't need money, sweetheart," I said.

Liz looked into my eyes and nodded. "Come back for me, Kate. I need to get a few things in order. I have to call my lawyer. You believe me, don't you?" she begged as she held onto my shirt.

"I love you, Liz, and I believe you. Now I'm going to call Bob and tell him everything. I should have told him sooner. You call your lawyer. I'll be back in an hour and we'll get this resolved. I know a lieutenant in Chicago, he can help," I said and kissed her deeply. "Don't worry."

I rubbed my eyes and glanced at Maggie. She sat there watching me, not saying a word. I could only imagine what she thought of me now. Probably what I've been thinking for five years—a pathetic loser.

"That's what I am, Doctor," I said as I paced in her hospital office. I turned around to see Dr. Tillman sporting a wary look and continued. *"Look at me. I fell in love with a murderer and nearly helped her get away. Because of me, Bob is lame. I'm... fuck!"* I growled and slammed my hand on her desk.

"What happened, Kate?" Maggie's voice broke into my wandering thoughts.

I took a deep shaky breath and continued. "That was enough time for her to get to Bob before I did. She told him I was hurt and in the cellar of her house. Her plan was to get both of us there and kill us, I imagine. It almost worked."

I stopped pacing, sat on the bed, and buried my head in my hands. I couldn't help myself. I took a deep breath and let out a sob. I could see Maggie start to get up and I said quickly, "Don't, please." She stopped and said nothing.

I finished as if in a trance, staring out the window. "I was in the cellar. Bob came down with his gun drawn. When he saw me, he looked relieved and he lowered his weapon. I don't know where she came from, but she had a shotgun. The noise was deafening. I whirled around, and when I tackled her, the other shot fired aimlessly. I looked over at Bob, who now was lying in a pool of blood. His leg was covered in it. As I got up to go to him, I felt like I was hit in the back with a hot poker and collapsed."

Suddenly, I was exhausted. All the ugliness, laid out in front of me, once again. "Later Bob told me that she had a sword or small saber. Her husband collected guns and antique weapons, whatever. I suppose she was trying to cut my head off. She missed," I joked, as Maggie caught her breath. I finished quickly.

"In the end, Bob was lame, his knee shattered. I was in the hospital for two months. We both decided to quit. Wise decision, don't you think?" I laughed ironically and gazed out the window. "Bob lives in Arizona with his family and I…well, you know what I'm doing."

Maggie spoke. "What happened to her?"

"Bob shot and killed her," I said slowly. "In twenty years on the force with my father, he'd never killed anyone. Then he works with me, and because I lost all perspective—" I let out a pathetic laugh. "Sounds like something out of a dime novel, doesn't it?"

"So you blame yourself for all of it," Maggie said.

I felt as though I was in Dr. Tillman's office once again. Then lightning flashed and the rain continued. I peered at her through the darkness. "Yes. I blame myself because it was my fault. I knew better. I allowed my emotions and passion to control the situation. Never again." I knew those words came out with a nasty bite.

Maggie graciously rose above my childishness. "What happened to you medically?"

"She missed my spinal cord by inches, but she did do some damage to my neck, which is why I ache in this godforsaken weather," I said and continued. "Nothing permanent, mostly emotional. Hence the anxiety attacks, which, as you know, I haven't been handling very well. I was seeing a hospital psychiatrist for a while," I said with a shrug.

"Why did you stop?"

"I wanted to choke her," I said and chuckled at her odd look. "I suppose she got too close and I got scared. I thought I could handle this on my own. Look, I don't want any pity from you," I snapped at her again. *Good, maybe she'll quit this and leave.* I felt the tears catch in my throat at the thought of it.

"Why did you tell me?" she asked, ignoring my anger.

"I wanted to tell you. You deserve an explanation for my actions for the past months..." My voice trailed off. I looked at her. "That's not entirely true. I knew someday this would come out. We're getting closer and I, well, I appreciate you listening and I value your friendship. Believe me, I can't imagine talking like this to anyone else. I value that," I said, meaning every word.

"I'm glad. We've become good friends and I value it as much as you do," she said as she stood. "That's what friends do. They help each other." She put her hand on my shoulder.

"God, Maggie, please don't pity me, I couldn't stand that."

"I don't pity you. Although I think you're taking way too much of this on your shoulders. You've locked yourself up in this self-imposed prison, taking all responsibility, all blame. You seem to forget that you had a partner. Don't you think he feels his culpability in this?"

Visions of the hospital psychiatrist saying those exact words flashed in my mind. I glared at Maggie in the darkness, knowing I couldn't choke her. "Maggie, he has a family, four boys and a wife. Now he's lame and struggling to get a business going. I think his culpability is..." I stopped and sighed. "I don't want to argue."

"I don't, either, but understand this: You were not alone. Yes, you fell in love and you weren't thinking straight. However, while you might have taken her love and lost all perspective, Bob took the money and did the same. You can get as mad as you want with me, but if you would stop blaming yourself for one minute, you might see I'm right." When I didn't answer her, she continued. "Or you can be stubborn and think it's all you. Either way, I'm glad you told me. Maybe now, getting over it won't seem so hopeless and your anxiety attacks will be less frequent. I hope so. You know I'm always willing to talk to you."

She caressed my shoulder and I looked up into her blue eyes. "Now get into bed. Enough for one night," she said like the doctor she was, and without a word, I got into bed.

The lightning flashed and the thunder rolled. I saw her flinch and her small body tremble. I did something then I never thought I'd do again. Not in this lifetime, anyway. I scooted back in bed and pulled back the covers. "Climb in. I think both of us could use the connection right now."

Maggie looked at me, seemingly searching my face. I don't know what she expected to find. I certainly had no clue. Without a word, she slipped off her robe and I chuckled at the flannel pajamas. "Nice, pjs," I said.

"Oh, shut up. I get cold easily," she said and I heard the slight tremor in her voice.

It's funny. I never thought Maggie would be nervous about this. I, of course, was petrified. Maggie slipped in and lay on her side with her back to me. I pulled the quilt over her and as I moved away, she reached back. "Could you stay close until I fall asleep?"

I felt a pang of sadness ripple through me at the quiet plea in her voice. "Sure," I said and prayed to God I didn't faint as I felt her shaking body against mine. It's been quite a while.

As if it were the most natural thing in the world, which scared the hell out of me, I spooned behind her and wrapped my arm around her small waist. I felt her cold hand holding mine.

"Thanks," she whispered.

"S'okay," I answered and closed my eyes, breathing in the fragrance of her hair. "What shampoo do you use? It smells like apricots." *Oh, no, did I just ask her what shampoo she uses? Apricots? God, Ryan, why don't you tell her she smells like a frickin' fruit salad? So pathetic.*

She chuckled and held my arm. "I don't remember. I bought it last week. It has a built-in conditioner."

There was a moment of silence as we lay in the darkness. Then we started laughing. "I'm sure it was *not* on sale," I said through my laughter.

"Heavens, no," she replied and snuggled closer. "I spent a vulgar amount of money on it. What do you use?"

"Whatever Walgreens has," I answered seriously and she roared with laughter.

I reached up and put my hand over her mouth to quiet her. "Shhh, you'll wake the banshee."

She stopped laughing and I felt her warm lips against the palm of my hand. I quickly took my hand away. "I-I'm sorry. I—"

"It's okay. Thanks for talking about this. I feel honored that you'd let me in," she whispered.

She's honored? Oh, Maggie, if you only knew. "Thank you for listening." I wanted to say so much more, but lying next to her was good enough for now. Actually, it was near overwhelming for me.

"Anytime, Miss Ryan," she whispered through her yawn. "Thanks for taking care of me," she mumbled, on the edge of sleep. Her small body twitched as the thunder rolled in the distance.

I swallowed back a few tears and thought how nice this would be, if it were ever possible. The visions of Liz still held me captive as I felt my eyelids get heavy. I let out a deep sigh and fell sound asleep, holding Maggie.

Chapter 14

I woke early, as usual, but not stiff and achy. I stretched and realized I had company. I was lying on my back with Maggie plastered to my side. Her arm was thrown across my waist and her leg across mine. I swallowed with difficulty and my body ached in a way I never thought possible again.

I glanced down and saw nothing but a mass of auburn waves and green flannel. *Somewhere in there is a feisty doctor.*

Maybe she'll be embarrassed when she wakes up. Thinking that was a distinct possibility, I eased out from underneath her. She didn't even budge. I stood there and looked down at the comatose figure. Giving in to my inner child, I lifted her arm and dropped it. It hit the mattress with a quiet thud. Nothing, not one move, only a gentle snore. I shook my head, covered the slumbering woman, and gathered my clothes.

I showered and dressed and made my way down to the kitchen, limping. I couldn't figure out why I was limping until I remembered slipping on the rocks. I looked out the window. For something completely different, the morning was foggy and damp. At least it wasn't raining.

I made coffee and sat there lost in so many thoughts I gave myself a headache. My main thought for the moment was the night before. What was I thinking? *Good God, Ryan, of course she had to sleep with you, you pathetic dope.* I didn't even want to think about the shampoo debacle. I shook my head in disgust. Okay, the bus for Stupidville is leaving in ten minutes. Pack a bag. *God, what an ass.*

"Good morning."

I jumped and spilled my coffee at the sound of Maggie's soft voice.

"Hey, g'morning," I said quickly and reached for a napkin. My face was red hot.

"Ah, coffee," she sighed and poured a cup and sat opposite me.

"How did you sleep?" I asked casually.

"Like a baby. I didn't even hear you get out of bed. How about you?" I heard the smile in her voice.

"I slept okay," I said with a shrug. "Thanks for listening last night. It meant a great deal to me."

"You're welcome. I was glad to be there," she said.

I could feel her watching me. "Kate, about last night—"

"Hey, no problem. It didn't mean anything. So—" *My stupidity has no boundaries.*

"It didn't?" she asked angrily as her left eye twitched.

With that, Mac and Teri came down, as did Charlie, and soon I was making breakfast for all of us. We didn't discuss much as we ate. I was too busy avoiding Maggie's glaring eyes.

As I watched her, I couldn't help that inner child again. I've grown accustom to seeing the feisty pose. I walked over to her and gently pulled her arm. "Come on. You need some fresh air and I need to run off this breakfast. Let's take the horses out."

The sun burned off the morning fog, and as we made our way to the stable, Peter pulled up and waved.

"Maggie? What in the world are ya doin' here?" he said and walked over to us. "Ya couldn't stay away, is that it?" He winked at me over her shoulder and I scowled at him.

"Something like that," Maggie said. "Kate and I thought we'd take the horses out. Would that be all right?"

"Sure, that'd be grand. I suggest, though, not to take the ponies. Two mares might suit ya better. If anything happened to those Connemara ponies, I would never forgive myself," he said, smiling.

"That's fine with me," I said and Maggie agreed.

Peter stood there with his hands in his pockets. I looked over at the English saddles. I turned to Peter. "I'm not used to these saddles. Can you give me a hand?" I asked helplessly and I noticed Maggie give me an odd look but said nothing.

Peter looked horrified. "Of course I can," he said a little shaky.

He picked up the saddle, and as I suspected, he had no clue what he was doing. He was holding it backward, for one thing.

Then he tried to put it on the poor mare without a blanket. The horse was no fool. It got jittery and snorted. "Whoa there, girl."

I couldn't let it go on. "Okay, Peter, get out of there before you kill yourself or the poor horse," I said hastily.

He came out of the stall. "This horse never liked me."

Maggie had already saddled her horse. She was watching Peter with a great deal of curiosity.

"Give me that," I said impatiently, and he handed over the saddle.

"You ladies seem to have this under control. Have a grand ride now. Be careful." He smiled and quickly left the stable.

"What was that all about?" Maggie asked as I saddled my horse. "You know how to saddle a horse."

"He has no clue about horses. He's hiding something, I can smell it." I cautiously sniffed the air. "Then again, maybe it's these horses."

We rode for a while taking in the Irish landscape. It was beautiful, with rolling craggy hills on one side and the ocean on the other. Finally, we stopped and gave the horses a breather. We sat by a lone huge oak tree and looked out at the ocean.

"It is beautiful, isn't it?" Maggie asked.

"It's wild and free, so untamed," I said.

"Like you," she said with a small smile and nudged my shoulder.

"Me?" I asked. "Is that how you see me?"

She nodded, looking out at the ocean. "You have an independent spirit."

"Always have," I said and stole a glance at her. She was smiling as she gazed at the water. "What are you thinking about?" I picked a small wildflower that was blooming by the tree. The little flower gave off a sweet fragrance as I absently put it to my nose. I looked up to see her watching me.

"I was thinking how grateful I am that you came into my life last fall and what good friends we've become," she said and ran her fingers through her windblown auburn hair.

"I'm grateful, too," I said and offered her the flower.

She took it, and our hands touched. Maggie pressed her soft fingers against mine for a moment. She put the little flower to her nose and smiled as she looked back at the ocean. "That's nice to know."

"Look, Maggie. I…We've…" I started and stopped.

Maggie grinned slightly as she played with the wildflower. She saw my frowning glance, let out an amused laugh, and patted my leg. "Sorry, you're too much fun to play with sometimes." She kept her hand on my thigh. "You can say anything to me, you know that."

"Oh, I know," I grumbled and took a deep breath. My thigh was tingling.

We heard a car pull up and horn blare. Both of us jumped as Bridget pulled up next to us on the road.

"Well, good mornin', Kate. How are ya?" she asked, smiling, as she walked up to us.

"Bridget, g-good morning. What brings you out here?" I asked as my heart rate returned to normal.

I introduced Maggie and avoided Bridget's grin. They exchanged pleasantries and now, for some reason, I also avoided Maggie's glance. I felt the color rise in my cheeks. My detached loop screamed for me.

"I thought you might want to know I found the license tags from the Dublin car. I thought you might be interested. Maybe Reardon can check it out again," she said.

I thought for a moment. "It couldn't hurt. What's your day like?"

"I've a ten o'clock appointment. Why don't we go to the police station at say, noon? Maybe I can buy ya lunch."

"Good, see you at noon," I said and started to get up.

She waved me off. "Ya look far too comfortable. See ya at noon. It was a pleasure meeting ya, Maggie. I'm sure I'll be seein' ya again," she said and was gone.

Maggie watched the car pull away. "She seems like a nice girl."

"She was Brian's lawyer and now she's taking care of all the legal stuff for Mac. Hey, why don't you come with me? We'll go to lunch and I'll show you around Duncorrib."

The moment between us was gone and I had no idea how to get it back.

She shook her head. "Charlie and I are going to take a ride into Donegal later. He's getting a fax from his office in London.

Besides, you've got to go with Brittany," she said simply, twirling the little flower.

"Bridget," I corrected her.

"Sorry." She got up and quickly mounted her horse. "Race you back."

She took off and left me in her dust.

Bridget and I drove to the police station. Constable Reardon informed us we could have our information by late the next day.

We walked down to the same restaurant where we had dinner and sat at the same table. It looked out over the town and the Atlantic Ocean beyond. I stared absently, my mind wandering.

As I set my attention back to our table, I noticed Bridget playing with her fork. "Poor Bridget. You could have picked someone with better manners. I apologize."

"Your manners are just fine," she said. "So tell me where ya got the nickname Sherlock. Other than your father being a detective."

I hesitated for a moment before I told her of my private investigation business. I knew I was being vague and glossing over much, but I really didn't want to get into detail because I felt the sweat dripping down my back. "So the business ran its course and I went back to photography." I looked up to see her watching me intently. I quickly continued before she asked anything further. "I hope your friend can find out something fast."

"I do, too," she replied and looked at her watch. "I've got to run. I'm sorry. I forgot I have to be in Donegal by two o'clock. See ya tonight."

I decided to take a walk to the cliffs after lunch. The day had turned cloudy, cool, and very windy as I walked over close to the edge. I watched the Atlantic and heard the waves below. My mind raced, trying to get a handle on things, when I suddenly realized I had been sitting there for two hours. I heard a car pull up and noticed it was Charlie and Maggie.

Charlie called out, "Don't jump, Kate. We can figure this out."

Maggie walked past me and stood precariously close to the edge. She peered over the cliff, then gave me an incredulous look. "You went down there? Are you insane? Really, I know you have an adventurous spirit and I admire you for it, but for God's sake, woman, you went down there all that way? Alone?"

"Yes, yes. I'm insane, I know. There's a cavern, and Peter goes down there all the time. There's something down there, I know it. Aren't you curious?

"You have to admit, it's weird. I can see why no one has seen it, it's nearly impossible to get to, but I think we can if we're careful. Don't you want to know what's in the cave?" I laughed with excitement.

Maggie looked at me as if I were nuts. "You are without a doubt the most juvenile, irresponsible—"

"Okay, enough with the love talk." I stopped abruptly when I realized what I had said. "Answer my question," I went on quickly and gave her a challenging look.

"Well, I have to admit I'm curious. But," she said insistently, "you are not going down there alone. Maybe tomorrow we can take a closer look," she said thoughtfully.

"Now you're talking," I said enthusiastically. I looked at Charlie. "You'll go, won't you?"

"I can't let you go alone. Can I?" He looked over the edge and looked at me. "That requires an answer, Kate."

"No, you cannot let me go down there alone."

He gave me a sour look. "Not the answer I was hoping for. Maybe we can get Mac to come with us."

Charlie and I walked closer to the edge. Maggie grabbed our arms. "Will you please be careful? Christ, you're like two children. C'mon, let's get back before one of you gets swept over."

We looked down one more time. "You really think something's down there?" Maggie asked.

"Yes, I do," I replied. "And I'm going to find out what."

Mac and Teri were sitting in front of the fire when we returned. "Shouldn't you be in the kitchen?" I asked Teri. For a frightening moment, she really looked like our mother. "Just kidding," I assured her. "Seriously, what time is dinner?"

"Well," Teri started thoughtfully, "the cook will be here at three, servants at five. We eat at seven thirty. Good Lord, what a production." She looked up as Maggie and Charlie walked in behind me. "Hey, how'd it go?" she asked.

Mac noticed the bags Charlie carried. "Oh, took your sister shopping, eh?"

Charlie groaned in agreement and plopped down in a chair. "Good grief, you have a finely honed pecuniary skill, sis."

Maggie laughed. "I picked up a few things in Donegal." She handed a box to Mac and one to Teri. "A little something for the new landlords, as Kate says. Thanks for inviting us."

She bought Teri a beautiful pair of earrings and a handsome Irish tweed tie for Mac. Teri gave her a big hug and Mac affectionately kissed Maggie on the cheek. "Thanks, kiddo," he said with a wink.

Charlie groaned. "It took her an hour to pick out that tie, Mac. You better wear it to bed."

Both Winfield siblings then excused themselves to call Hannah. "Give Hannah our love, will you?" I asked. "And then we can discuss what you found out, Charlie, before the guests arrive."

I sat in the unbelievably comfortable chair and stretched out my legs. "I told Maggie last night...everything." I laughed at the stunned looks of both faces.

"Everything, everything?" Teri asked slowly.

"The whole enchilada," I replied.

"I'm glad you told her," Mac said. "She's a good woman, Kate."

"Yes, she is and a good friend. I should have told her before." I stood up and stretched. "Well, milord and milady, I shall ready myself for dinner," I said and bowed dramatically. "But you're still a landlord," I called out as I headed for the stairs. A pillow caught me nicely in the back of the head.

I was filled with excitement as I showered, wondering what Charlie found out about The Omega Group. This could be a big break. The hot water beat on my neck and back. It ached terribly and I knew I'd be stiff. It dawned on me that my stiffness wasn't followed by thoughts of Liz, as it usually was.

As I dried off, I looked at the scar and had a moment of shivering and a wave of anxiety. I closed my eyes and it passed—I still felt like throwing up. Well, if nothing else came from this trip, I was on my way to putting the whole ugly thing behind me. I had

Maggie to thank for that.

I walked into my room drying my hair and noticed a box on my bed with a note that read—*Open me.*

I felt like a kid at Christmas as I opened it. It was a gorgeous hunter green Irish wool cardigan. There was a small card with it. I noticed it was Maggie's handwriting.

This screamed, "Buy me for Kate!" Thanks for letting me in last night.

I smiled and held up the sweater. "She is *too* sweet," I said. I put on the sweater and looked in the mirror. It fit perfectly. I knocked at the connecting door.

"Wow," Maggie said as she opened the door. "It looks even better on you. Turn around." I did and she brushed my shoulders off and turned me around. "Perfect fit," she smiled.

"Thank you. You didn't have to do this." I shook my head. "It is gorgeous, though. May I come in for a moment?" I asked, smiling, and she stepped back.

"Poor Charlie followed me around all afternoon. I—"

Without thinking, I reached over and cupped her soft cheek. "Thanks, Maggie," I whispered, and kissed her lightly on the other cheek.

Maggie looked up and blinked several times. I grinned at the flustered pose as I walked out.

Chapter 15

Teri busied herself with the servants, handling them as if she'd done it all her life. She was remarkably calm and ready.

As I walked over to the bar, Mac on the other hand, looked jittery. "You look nervous there, milord," I said jokingly, but I could tell he was bothered.

"I *am* a little uneasy. Hell, these people don't know me from Adam and here I am taking over Uncle Brian's estate. How do I look?" he asked and straightened his tie. He looked behind me, wide-eyed and said, "Whoa."

I turned and saw a young woman standing in the doorway. After a comical double take, I realized it was Maggie. She wore a wool skirt with a tweed blazer and an ivory satin blouse. She wore her thick auburn hair down and flowing. *Christ, she has legs.*

She walked over to the bar and smiled. "You both look very nice."

"So do you," I said and smiled slightly as I saw the little wildflower in the lapel of her blazer. She followed my gaze and turned an adorable shade of crimson.

Mac stood next to me, prepared himself a drink, and looked up. "Excuse me, ladies." He walked around the bar and toward the doorway.

In the doorway stood Teri in black slacks, a Kelly green plaid top that complemented her gorgeous red hair, and the earrings that Maggie had given her. She was stunning.

Charlie came bounding into the living room. He wore a tweed sport jacket and black slacks. When he smiled, he looked so much like Maggie. He walked over to us while rubbing his hands together. "Okay, let's get this clambake started. Kate, I'll have a scotch and water."

"Charlie, you look very handsome this evening. You

Winfields certainly have a strong gene pool," I said and fixed his drink. "So before everyone gets here, what did you find out?"

We all gathered around the bar as Charlie started. "It appears that your Mr. Collins works for a company called British Isles Excavation, based in Glasgow, Scotland. They're one of over a hundred smaller subsidiaries of Omega. Unfortunately, that's all we've found out so far, but my staff is still digging. They're going to call me later tonight," he said and took a drink.

Maggie said, "Maybe they use this company when they buy a company and are going to level it."

Mac nodded. "Maybe they want the land for some shopping mall or something."

"Why would you offer four million for land that wasn't worth one?" I asked and rubbed my forehead. "If they only want the land for that, why are we having all the problems? No, that doesn't make sense. There's something to this British Isles whatever. There's something at that mill. Charlie, is your staff checking how often and when Omega uses this company?"

"I'll call and make sure they do. Can you think of anything else?"

"Can your staff also check on people?"

He gave me a curious look. "Sure, we check backgrounds all the time."

"Could you have them check Peter Sullivan, I believe he said he was from Kenmare, but his girlfriend Deirdre Morrissey lives in Dublin. Also, Peter said he went to college, but I have no idea where. Maybe we can get more information out of him tonight." I noticed Mac looking at his glass not saying anything. Teri looked upset, as well.

"I don't want anything to happen to anyone in this room," I said to both of them. "If Peter knows something, I have to find out what it is. The sooner we know the better. Too much has happened for us to play around."

"I know, Kate. I agree. I want this solved. You know what you're doing," Mac said.

I looked for Charlie who was already on the phone with his office. We heard him say, "No one goes home. Get whatever you need, do whatever you have to. I don't care about the money, please get this as quickly as possible, Jess." Then he said a little gently, "I know, honey, I will."

The four of us looked at one another as Charlie walked back in the room.

Maggie was smiling. "Honey?"

Charlie turned bright red. "It's against the law to eavesdrop on a person's phone call. She's the vice president of research. Hell, we're dating," he said and took a drink. His sister laughed and playfully nudged him.

There was so much more information I needed and too many people coming here that night. I'd never be able to talk to all of them. "I need to ask you all a favor," I said. "Start conversations if you can and listen to what they say about the mill, about Brian, but don't scare anyone. We don't know who's who. Seriously, it could be anyone."

"I think that's a good idea. We can all exchange notes at the end of the evening," Maggie offered.

I walked over to the fireplace and Maggie joined me. She picked up the poker and lazily stabbed the firewood but said nothing. We stood for a moment in silence.

"You and your fires," she finally said. "I still think you *are* a pyromaniac."

"I've got a huge fireplace in my log cabin. I go through a chunk of firewood each winter," I said. My mind was back on the previous night with Maggie lying next to me.

"You keep talking about this log cabin," she said and poked the fire.

I took the poker out of her hand. "Good grief, woman, you have no idea how to stoke a fire."

"Before you go to bed, I have something that might help the stiffness in your neck," she said frankly. "I picked up something today for you."

I knew I was smiling. "Thanks. You know, I-I didn't wake up with any stiffness this morning," I said with a shrug.

"You didn't? Hmm, I wonder why," Maggie asked as she stared at the fire.

With that, Charlie joined us. "I think Jess will have her staff hopping and we'll have some answers later. She has a way about her, that woman."

"Obviously, if she's got you calling her honey," Maggie said, smiling.

Charlie reddened again. "I know. It's disgusting," he laughed. "I'm hooked and she's reeling me in."

Maggie kissed his cheek. "And you love every minute of it, Charlie Winfield."

The doorbell rang and one of the girls came rushing from the kitchen to answer it. It was Rory Nolan and his wife. Mac walked up to him and shook his hand soundly. He introduced his wife, Anne, to Mac. She was a little woman with a happy face. She had dark hair, deep blue eyes and—as my mother used to say— alabaster skin.

In my odd musings, I missed Mac's introductions, so I tended bar. "Well, folks, what'll it be?"

Anne looked around the immense library in awe.

"Pretty big, isn't it?" I offered.

"As a little girl, I used to imagine what this house looked like on the inside. It is big."

"Did you know Brian?" I asked casually. I noticed Charlie talking to Rory Nolan.

Anne nodded her response. "Brian had been here since I can remember. He was a grand man, always around and cheerful. Rory said Mac reminded him of Brian in some ways. I'm glad he's not thinking about shutting down the mill. That was a load off Rory's mind for sure," she said, looking at Rory. She looked at me and smiled. "I saw ya around town today, but ya didn't come down my way."

"Your way?"

"Yes, I run a little shop at the other end of the village. It's like an apothecary, ya know, only I sell healing herbs and lotions. Maggie stopped in and bought something. She said she had a friend who," she stopped and thought for a moment and laughed. "Ah, yes, who was a pain in the neck with a stiff neck."

"Yeah, that's very funny," I agreed and glared at Maggie.

With the ring of the doorbell, Sean and Mary Farrell arrived. Mac and Teri were talking to them. Charlie and Maggie were talking to Rory. The Brothers McAuliffe hadn't arrived yet— that'll be interesting.

The doorbell rang again, and one of the girls scurried out from the kitchen to answer it. In walked Bridget wearing a wool dress, and she had her long curly black hair pinned up. She looked like she was ready for the opera. She had a package under her arm.

"A little housewarming present," she said, smiling. Teri thanked her and Mac took her coat. She then saw me. "Good evening."

"Good evening," I said.

We walked over to the bar, where everyone seemed to be gathering. Bridget said hello to Rory and Anne. I introduced Charlie and Maggie again.

"Yes, we met earlier. It's nice to see ya again," Bridget said affably.

"What can I get you?" I asked, standing behind the bar. *Why did I feel safe here?*

"Ya know what I like, Kate. Whiskey neat. No ice, remember?" she said, smiling at me.

As I poured her drink, I glanced at Maggie. She was watching Bridget. *That's why.*

"Bridget is Mac's lawyer," I said. "Well, she's not Mac's lawyer, she was Brian's lawyer and now she's helping Mac with lawyer things. So…" I finished lamely, not knowing why I felt as though I needed to explain.

"I get the general idea," Maggie said candidly and turned her attention to Bridget. "Is your practice in the village?"

Charlie and I watched them as if it were a tennis match.

"No, my office is in Donegal, but lately I've been spending more time in Duncorrib for some reason," she smiled, sipped her whiskey, and glanced at me. *Game.*

"It's a handsome village. I'm sure there's a lot to keep you busy," Maggie said, sipping her drink as her left eye twitched. *Set.*

"Oh, yes. Lately, I've grown very fond of this village."

"I hope your practice in Donegal doesn't feel neglected by your absence, Bridget," Maggie said with a thin smile. *And match…*

Mac mercifully came over to the bar. "Bridget, can I borrow you for a moment?"

I was grateful. With Wimbledon over, it was sure to be an intriguing dinner party.

Chapter 16

Tim Devereaux showed up, alone and apologetic. "It's nice to see everyone again," he said and shook hands with Sean and Peter. "I'm sorry, James couldn't make it," he said a little embarrassed.

I watched Tim curiously. *Hmm. Translation: He didn't want to come.*

Mac shook Tim's hand. "I understand. I appreciate you coming."

"James has no manners at all," he said and handed Mac his hat and coat. "It's a fine soft night out there," he said and rubbed his hands together as Mac took him to the fireplace.

"Soft night?" I asked with a grin. "Tim, it's pouring rain. I don't understand why the Irish insist on calling that a soft night."

Tim and the others laughed. I watched them and glanced Maggie's way. She was ignoring me completely. I knew her well enough to know when she was irritated—her left eye twitched.

Not wanting any part of Dr. Winfield's glare, I followed Teri into the kitchen. I wanted to tell her about Anne. As I walked in, Charlie followed me.

He was smiling and stood there with his hands on his hips. "Are you two-timing my sister?"

Teri looked at both of us. "Who's two-timing who?" She looked at me.

"No one is two-timing anyone. I'm not even one-timing your sister," I said and pinched the bridge of my nose.

Charlie gave me a suspicious look. "Are you sure?"

"Yes, I'm not doing anything with anybody," I said, feeling very rankled. "Anyway, the reason I came into the kitchen..." I explained about Anne.

Teri listened and was very intrigued. "Tomorrow, let's go into the village and check out her shop. I'm very curious. I'll bet your log cabin that she knows something about the people in the woods."

Dinner was ready. Mac and Teri sat at either ends of the table—that was the only arranged seating. I sat at the end next to Mac and Tim sat next to me. Then Sean and Mary Farrell. Peter sat directly across from me. Next to him were Bridget, Rory and his wife and Maggie all the way at the other end next to Teri I glanced at her and smiled and she gave me a slight grin, well more of a smirk.

The young girl had come out and served a delicious-looking soup. I had my spoon poised for a taste when Mac raised a glass of wine. "I would like to say thank you to all of you for coming. You don't know my family or me, but I would like that to change. You were dear friends to my uncle. I only hope I can keep this land as he would have wanted it."

Sean Farrell smiled. "Well, Mac, I'll tell ya. If you're half the man Brian was, you'll do fine."

"I couldn't agree more," Peter said.

Everyone concentrated on dinner and the conversation that goes with it—which was no murder, no mayhem. As the girls came out and cleared the bowls away, I had a chance to watch Sean. My father's words haunted me— "Everything is important, discount nothing." What did we know of Sean and Mary?

I glanced at Tim, who looked sad in a way, as he looked around the dining room. Everyone was having his or her own conversations, so I asked Tim, "Did you grow up here, as well?"

He nodded. "In Duncorrib, yes, though I was never home. When I was young, I joined the Merchant Marines. I was away from this place up to two years at a time, only home long enough to get another ship. Brian was the homebody. He never left this country. I doubt he ever went to a big city like Dublin or Cork in his life," he said. "He deserved this place. He worked hard for it. James…" he stopped and continued eating.

"I'm sorry he couldn't make it," I said while eating.

"He's a dark one, James is. He's bitter, and to be honest with ya, he doesn't think your brother-in-law has a right to it, but that shouldn't come as a surprise to ya," Tim said.

"I understand where he's coming from, but Mac has no intention of ruining the mill. He plans on keeping it as it has been.

You will still make good money from it."

He looked at Mac while speaking to me. "Ya know, I don't know him at all, but there's something about Mac. I think it's the eyes. He does look like Brian. James said as much and it spooked him. Anyway, James is a greedy one. When the man from London came, he was so excited he almost fainted. He thought for sure Brian would sell. When he didn't, there was a tremendous fight and Brian told James never to speak of it again," he said and drank his wine. "They liked to fight, those two." He looked at me. "He and I argued about me comin' here tonight. He didn't want me to come, but I couldn't refuse after he was so rude to Mac's wife the other day."

"He's been through a lot. This has to be hard on him," I said.

"Don't waste your compassion on James, he has more money than he knows what to do with," he snorted and continued eating. He leaned over to me. "I'll be honest with ya, Kate. I don't think Brian stumbled over any wall in the dark."

Everybody at the table stopped talking. Tim looked around and said, "Well, I don't. He knew every inch of this property and those cliffs. He lived here all his life. Don't be tellin' me he stumbled." He looked at Sean and Mary.

"We tried to take him home, Tim. He had too much to drink that night. He was upset with James," Sean said defensively.

Mary put her hand on Sean's arm. "It's true, Tim. We tried to drive him back, but you know how stubborn he could be."

"He knew every inch of this place. I don't care how drunk he was. Someone..." he stopped and drained his wineglass. He looked at Mac. "I apologize, Mac. This is unpleasant dinner conversation."

I thought it was fine dinner conversation, but that's me.

"It's all right. We all understand," Mac said.

Rory Nolan coughed and stood and raised his wineglass. "I'd like to be sayin' a couple of things. I'd like to say thank you to Mac and Teri. They're gracious hosts and a welcome sight to this house," he said and looked at Tim. "No offense, Timmy."

He continued, "I think Brian made a grand choice in Mac. You're a fine man, from what little I know of ya, that is." He winked at Mac and we all laughed. "It's a grand meal. God bless ya both," he said. "And you're the talk of the village now that ya took care of those two young fools."

"Speaking of which, does anyone know who they are?" I asked.

Rory shook his head. "No, but I've seen them with another fellow on occasion. Come to think of it, I saw him today in Donegal," Rory agreed. "He drove a black car. Dark curly-haired fellow in a dark coat?"

"Where in Donegal?" I asked.

"Comin' out of the Donegal Inn, where you were staying."

I thought for a minute. Mr. Collins was staying at the Donegal Inn. "I may take a drive to Donegal tomorrow," I said absently.

It was getting late, and the Farrells were at the front door saying good night to Teri and Mac. "We had a fine time, Mac," Sean said and gave Mac a hearty handshake. "I think your sister-in-law is a bit of a detective, maybe she can figure this out." He patted him on the shoulder and was gone.

The Nolans soon departed and I walked Bridget to the door.

"Well, Kate, it was a grand night," she said and once again kissed me lightly on the lips, then winked and walked out the door.

Tim sat by the fire nodding off. Teri knelt down by him. "Tim, why don't you spend the night? We have plenty of room."

He looked at her and patted her hand. "I would like to stay. I've missed this house. Thank you," he smiled.

He got up slowly and followed Mac and Teri upstairs. I watched them, wondering what Tim knew about Brian and what, if anything, he might be holding back. And where was James?

Peter had left, leaving Maggie, Charlie, and me sitting by the fire.

"Tim's almost sound asleep," Mac announced as he walked into the room. "This was a lot for him, poor guy. However, I think the evening went very well."

"It was a fine time, Mac," Maggie said and stifled a yawn.

Teri came downstairs and sat next to Mac and rested her head on his shoulder. "I agree," Teri said with a yawn. "It went well. Rory Nolan likes you, sweetie. I can tell."

Maggie agreed. "All of them complimented both of you. You did a fine job, Lady McAuliffe."

"Did you find out anything?" I asked.

Among the four of them, they found out a good deal. I was impressed. They all knew about the man and woman who were impeccably dressed and first came almost two years before to see Brian and returned on several occasions, but no one had any idea why. Then Mr. Collins showed up from time to time to offer Brian money for the mill.

Maggie eagerly sat forward in her chair. "I was talking to Rory and Anne about the mill. He said this Mr. Collins came on several different occasions. Rory remembers Brian laughing, saying something like, 'It gets bigger and bigger.' He thought it might be the amount of the offer."

Mac joined in. "I was talking with Bridget, and she told me about the car and the man from Dublin. She has someone checking it and should have something by tomorrow. She hopes."

I sat and listened to each of them. Maggie retold her conversations with enthusiasm. I could tell she was enjoying herself; she wanted to make sure she remembered everything. When they had finished, they all sat back and looked at me.

"What do you think?" Teri asked.

"They all saw the same thing. Now I'd like to find out who these people are. Bridget said she had Reardon check the license tags and they're from Dublin. That's a big city, by Ireland's standards anyway. I wonder if he knows in whose name the car was registered. That might be a help." I stood and paced in front of the fire. Suddenly, there was a flash of lightning. We all looked out the window. *Great, yet another storm.*

"Now as far as Peter goes," I started and a clap of thunder rang out. "I definitely think he knows more than he lets on. I know he told you that Brian sent him to make sure you got over all right, but something doesn't ring true. I have a feeling he isn't all he appears."

Mac looked disappointed and I didn't blame him. Peter was involved in this somehow. "Mac, we don't know what he's doing."

"I've become fond of him, that's all," he said.

Charlie glanced at his watch. "I'm going to give Jess a call," he said and headed for the phone.

He was on the phone for a few minutes. As we heard him ring off, another clap of thunder shook the house, and the lightning flashed.

Charlie came into the room frowning. He glanced at Mac and stood by the fire.

My impatience showed horribly. "What gives, Charlie?"

He took a deep breath and started. "First of all, British Isles Excavation has only been used by Omega on two other occasions. Ten years ago, they were used in Egypt. Omega bought some company and completely leveled it and excavated it for four years, digging. Jess can't find one reason why Omega purchased the company or what they were looking for.

"Then five years ago, Omega spent another vulgar amount of money for a nearly bankrupt family business in Greece. They did the same thing there. Everything was legal, they obeyed all environmental laws, but they leveled the business and excavated the land for two years. Again, Jess could find no reason why they bought the business or why they were digging up the property. Jess said it was as if it never existed.

"Trust me, folks, we have a marvelous research department. If Jess can't find it, it either never happened or someone with a superior information system is keeping it hidden. This may be the case with The Omega Group. I told you they had millions," he said, frowning, but continued. "However, other companies also use this British Isles Excavation. Mostly excavating and salvage," he said, looking over the notes.

"Salvage?" I asked curiously.

"Yep, used in the Mediterranean. Some ship sank and they salvaged what there was. Then they were in the South Seas, doing what appears to be the same thing: getting the contract to salvage whatever from a sunken vessel." The phone rang again, Mac answered. It was Jess for Charlie.

He came back in a few minutes shaking his head. "This is getting weirder. Kate, you have a nose for this, I'll give you that," he said, looking at his notes.

"You *are* amazing," Maggie agreed. "What is it?"

"Jess had one of the staff call this British Isles, pretending to be from The Omega Group. This employee, who is probably being fired as we speak, told our staff, this is verbatim: The owners of the Oceanview Woolen Mill are dragging their feet, but steps are being taken to make sure the mill is sold within the week." He looked at me.

I whistled and looked at Mac and Teri. Mac was frowning and holding Teri's hand. "This might be bigger than I had thought. We need to find out who killed Brian and fast. Once that's in the open, I don't think this Omega Group will want any publicity. What do you think, Charlie?" I asked, trying to ignore the uneasy feeling in the pit of my stomach.

"Well, you could be right. I don't know much about this company, but they have always stayed within the law. Jess was strong on that point. That doesn't mean they haven't bent the hell out of it. However, no one has ever sued them or had any injunctions against them. Jess checked with our legal department and this company has never violated one international or environmental law. Whatever they do, it's legal," he said. "You've got to figure this out fast, Kate."

Now I was extremely nervous.

Mac looked uncomfortable. "What did you find out about Peter?"

Charlie took a deep breath. "Kate was right again. Mr. Sullivan," he started and looked at his notes, "was not born in Kenmare, but Dublin. He grew up in the city, nowhere near the country. No family to speak of and has lived with an elderly gentlemen for the past three years. He's twenty-eight, single, does have a girlfriend, and her name is Deirdre Morrissey, that much was true."

I was looking into the fire. "He went to college, didn't he? I'll bet he knows why The Omega Group wants this land." I looked up at Charlie, who was smiling.

"How would you like a job at our research department? I could get rid of half the staff if you joined," he said and winked.

Mac and Teri smiled. "God, Kate behind a desk." They both shook their heads.

"Talk about having your wings clipped," Maggie added with a hint of sarcasm.

"No, thank you, Charlie," I said and ignored Maggie's look.

"Oh, well, it was worth a try. Anyway, you're right again. He went to Trinity College, graduated with honors four years ago. Earned his master's and..." he stopped and gave me a prodding grin.

I thought for a moment. "He's a teacher."

"Bingo. A professor, actually. Give the lady a cigar," Charlie said with a polite bow.

I stood and paced in front of the fire. A professor of what, I thought. He knew about the mausoleum and the architecture. He's been hanging around the rocks, the cavern. My mind raced. I stopped and looked at Charlie.

Charlie grinned and said, "I can tell you know what kind of professor he is."

"History," I offered confidently.

Charlie nodded. "He's been teaching Irish history/archaeology there for four years. So far, he's as clean as a whistle. Not even a traffic ticket." He closed his notebook and slapped it against the palm of his hand and sat down.

"Why is he here? What does that mill have that would make a huge company want it?" I looked at Mac. "We need to talk to Peter. We'd better be careful, Mac. He knows something and we have to find out quick," I said and rubbed my aching neck. The thunder boomed and lightning flashed. I looked at the clock, one thirty.

Mac stood and stretched. "Well, this is enough for one night, let's get some sleep. I have a feeling tomorrow is going to be a busy day."

I couldn't sleep. I paced in my room and finally went downstairs and raided the icebox. I made a sandwich and poured a glass of milk and sat at the kitchen table. It was pouring rain as the lightning flashed and the thunder rumbled through the sky.

I was stretching my aching neck when I noticed the brochures that Mac had picked up. I looked at them, reading about Grace O'Malley and her exploits. I turned the page and read the history of the monks during the time before St. Patrick, how they had to hide their beliefs and their scriptures. There was a good deal of history in the west of Ireland. Then I thought about Peter, the archaeologist. *Wait till I see him.* What did he know? I felt close to something. I could smell it. I finished my snack and went back to bed. It was freezing and damp in this house.

I went into my room, yawing wildly, took off my robe, and walked over to the radiator. It was a little warm but not nearly as warm as it should have been. I rubbed my arms.

Just about in bed, I heard a soft knock at the door. I opened it and Maggie stood there rubbing her eyes.

"Hello, little girl, have to go to the bathroom?"

"Here. It's for your neck." Maggie glared as she tossed a tube of something at me. I plucked it out of the air and gave her a superior glance.

"For my stiff neck or am I—a pain in the neck?"

Her eyes flew open on that one.

"Speechless and dumbfounded. I didn't think that was possible. I rather enjoy this look. Hold on, don't move. Let me savor it for a moment. I know it won't last long," I said and closed my eyes. "Okay, got it. Thank you," I said triumphantly and waved the tube in the air. "Good night, Doctor."

As I closed the door, I heard a quiet "Good night" from the other side.

Chapter 17

The lotion actually helped. I woke for the first time since I got to this damp country without a pain in my neck. I remembered Maggie's blue eyes and her dumbfounded look and laughed openly.

Mac, Teri, and Charlie were in the kitchen. Teri was making breakfast. "Hey there," she said, smiling. "How'd you sleep?"

"Good morning, all. Actually, I slept very well. Maggie gave me some kind of lotion for my neck, and it worked," I said.

Maggie came into the kitchen looking like she hadn't slept at all. Charlie looked at her and said, "Hey, sis, you look terrible."

She groaned and got a cup of coffee and sat down.

"Didn't you sleep well?" I asked with a grin, which she ignored.

"No, I don't know why, but I tossed and turned all night." She yawned and drank her coffee.

"You should have used the stuff you gave Kate," Mac said.

"Really, whatever that is, I slept like a baby," I said.

She glared at me over her cup. "I'm so glad," she mumbled sarcastically. Maggie was not a morning person.

After breakfast, we tried to piece all of this mess together. We were sitting around the table drinking coffee when a voice came from the doorway.

"Hello?"

We all sat perfectly still and looked at one another. The kitchen door slowly creaked open and Tim Devereaux's head appeared. At first, none of us remembered that he spent the night.

"Good morning." He looked out the window. "Fog and damp. I'm sick of it," he said and sat down.

"Me too," I agreed wholeheartedly. "Does the sun ever shine?"

"It will today. I'm sure," he said. "I appreciate your

hospitality, Mac."

"No problem. I'm only sorry James didn't want to come," Mac said sincerely.

Tim sighed and drank his coffee. "I am, too."

"Tim, last night, you said you didn't think Brian stumbled and fell. What do you think happened?" I asked curiously.

He thought for a moment. "I think someone pushed him over the cliff. If you're thinkin it was James or me, we were together that night in Galway. With plenty of witnesses. It couldn't have been James," he said. "But I don't trust that Sullivan boy."

"Why not?" Mac asked defensively.

"I mean nothing, Mac. He showed up and Brian took him right in. Horse trainer," he snorted. "I came here a few months ago, he doesn't know a Connemara for a Shetland," he smirked.

Well, he was right there.

"But Brian trusted him for some reason. When I asked about him, Brian would get a smile on his face and say, 'Timmy, don't worry about that boy, he's doin' a grand thing. He means well.'"

"I think Peter means well, too," Mac said.

"Doing a grand thing," I repeated as I looked out the window. "What in the world is he doing?" I turned back into the kitchen. "Tim, did Brian say anything to you before he died about what Peter was doing?"

"Not much. Brian wasn't much of a talker. It was hard to tell what in the world he was thinking. Ever known anyone like that?" he asked.

Maggie cleared her throat. "Yes, and isn't it frustrating?" She avoided my glare completely.

"Indeed, Maggie. I've smacked Brian on the back of the head on many occasions to get him to talk," he said as if remembering fond memories of beating up his brother-in-law.

"Did it help?" Maggie asked with mock curiosity.

"Once or twice." Then he got serious. "Brian was up to something. The only thing he confided in me was the will. I remember he told James and me when he was going to change it. If my memory is correct, he died days before it was changed. So when we found out that Mac here was to inherit all of this, James was furious and I was shocked. I thought he died before he changed it. This is not the case. That's why I thought he was murdered," he said, looking at all of us.

"Who else knew Brian was changing his will?" Charlie asked.

"Bridget had to know," I said and everyone agreed. I looked at Tim. "Are you sure about this time frame?"

He nodded. "Quite sure. When I found out he died, it's the first thing that came to mind. I'll be honest with ya. I thought of James and thanked God he was with me. Then I prayed for his forgiveness for thinkin' somethin' so terrible about Colleen's brother."

Well, brother James isn't out of the picture yet. I looked at Tim who looked around the kitchen. "I remember Colleen's mother, God rest her, was always in this kitchen, cookin' and hummin'. She always had a song in her heart."

I looked over at Maggie who was remembering her own mother, I'm sure. She had a melancholy look on her face and tears sprang into her eyes. She looked at me and I gave her a reassuring wink.

She smiled and blinked, sending the tears rolling down her cheeks. How does she do that? How can one look so beautiful and cry at the same time? She picked up a napkin and dabbed her eyes. Charlie put his arm around her and kissed her head.

"Tim, how would you like to spend the weekend?" Teri asked, smiling. "We have plenty of room."

"And you can help us solve this," I said.

Tim gave us a suspicious look. "Now what would I be helpin' ya solve?"

"Brian's murder," I said.

The boys wanted to check out the mill. We ladies went to Anne's shop at the corner of the street. She had a shingle outside that read, "Annie's Corner." The bell tinkled on the old wooden door as we walked in.

The shop was adorable. Lotions, healing herbs, and books on the topic artfully graced the shop. Three other people were at the counter, and Anne was ringing up their purchases.

I don't usually go for shopping, but I get a kick out of watching Maggie and Teri, so I walked behind them as they browsed. They stopped and I stopped, they continued and I continued. I was looking around and wasn't watching where I was going. The girls stopped, and I bumped into Maggie who bumped into Teri. They both looked at me.

"I'm sorry," I whispered, and as I raised my hand, I knocked over some books. I quickly fumbled and caught them before they went crashing to the floor. "Geez, do the aisles have to be so close?"

Maggie was watching me. "Good grief. You're a walking disaster area."

"You should see her in a crystal shop," my loyal sister whispered.

Anne walked over. "Good day, ladies," she greeted us and looked around. "This is it."

"It's adorable," Teri said.

"What a great idea. I have a doctor friend of mine who thinks very highly of aromatherapy, healing lotions, and herbs. She was in Africa and China for a few years. This is wonderful," Maggie said.

I leaned in between them. "The lotion works, too."

Anne beamed. "Wonderful, I'm glad."

Maggie laughed and looked at me. Then Anne blushed and said, "Oh. You're…"

"The pain in her neck."

She cleared her throat. "Thank you. I work hard and read everything I can get my hands on. It drives Rory mad," she said, laughing.

Teri looked at a few books on magic, superstitions, and the like. "You have a great collection here, Anne."

"I'm not into that sort of thing. My mother and grandmother were witches of sorts." She then told us about spells for the harvest and a potion they concocted for the farmers. Teri and Maggie listened intently.

"Stranger things have happened, right, Maggie?" Teri asked.

"Indeed they have," she agreed.

Anne looked interested and Maggie told her about her mother and the problem we had six months before. How Miranda's spirit lingered until she knew Maggie was fine and how she helped me find out who murdered her twenty years before. Maggie told her of the hyacinth, how the fragrance filled the room when Miranda was present. I listened and watched Maggie's face as she talked. That was a horrible time for her but she came through it, and I admired her for that.

When Maggie was done, Anne said in amazement, "You're not pullin' my leg, are ya?"

"It's the truth, scary but the truth," I said. "Like the other night, when I thought I saw someone outside the cottage." I watched Anne who looked at me with a thoughtful gaze.

"A few months ago," she said, "I remember Rory telling me that Brian had some weird happenings outside the house. Rory said he looked spooked, but he didn't know who it was. I guess it happened on several occasions."

"I hope it happens one more time. I'm not letting him go this time," I said decisively and looked at Teri. "I mean it."

We browsed for a while as Maggie and Teri bought a few items. The day turned warm and sunny as we walked to the pub to meet the guys.

"This would be a good day to see the cliffs," I said and looked up at the sun. No clouds, this is a first.

The guys were at a table having a beer. Over lunch, I couldn't get my mind off those cliffs. I glanced at my watch, one thirty. "Everyone done? Good, let's go," I said and started to get up.

"Whoa, Sherlock, what's the hurry?"

"It's a gorgeous day. I want to see the cliffs," I said frankly.

Mac got up. "Good idea. Let's go."

We stood there and no one else got up. "C'mon, let's go," I said impatiently. "I've got to go back and change."

Teri and Maggie looked at each other. "We decided it's not safe for you two to go down there," Teri said and Maggie looked at me.

We? I got a little indignant, well more than a little. "Look. I know it's risky, but we've got to see what's down there. We'll be fine."

"Someone will get hurt," Maggie said, and I knew she meant me.

I was going to say something when Mac put his hand on my shoulder and squeezed too hard. "Okay, you're right," he said and glanced at me before he continued, "Whatever is down there will stay down there. Peter has been going down there for months.

153

Maybe he'll find out what it is. Maybe he'll let us in on it. If he doesn't, Kate will have to figure something else out. I'd hate to see Peter get deeper into trouble. Kate thinks he's in over his head. I agree," he said frankly.

I understood what he was doing and sat down. "Let's think of something else," I sighed and Mac sat next to me.

"Don't you see that someone might get hurt?" Teri tried to explain.

Mac nodded. "Yes, honey, I see what you're saying and you're right."

Boy, Mac is good at this.

Maggie looked at me. "Kate, you know if something is going to happen, it's going to be to you," she said.

I am not good at this. I understood what Mac was doing, but I got irritated and my pride was about to take over. I didn't need anyone's permission, being in my safe detached loop for so long. I shifted angrily in my chair.

Mac could see I was about to say something rash and said quickly, "I know how you both feel," he said and glared at me.

I was drumming my fingers on the table.

Teri looked at both of us. "Please, please, please, be careful," she conceded.

Mac stood up quickly and said, "I will. I promise."

I jumped up and sent the silverware clanging to the floor.

Maggie put her hand to her forehead. "God, this is a mistake, I can feel it."

"Don't be a pessimist. It doesn't suit you, Doctor." I laughed, kneeling next to her. I picked up the wayward silverware and looked up; our eyes locked for a moment. "I...we'd better get going."

Maggie grinned slightly and took the knife from my hand. "Before you kill someone," she offered seriously.

"We'll meet you over there in twenty minutes. We gotta change. C'mon, Charlie," Mac said, sounding like a little kid.

Charlie grudgingly got up. "I thought they'd forget about me," he said and followed us.

As we dashed out the door, pulling Charlie with us, we heard Teri, or was it our mother? "Don't drive too fast!"

Chapter 18

Mac drove too fast. "I hope we find something, Kate." He was as excited as I was as he drove around the curve. "I do, too. There's gotta be something down there."

"Water. We're gonna get wet," Charlie said from the back.

We pulled up to the house and jumped out. We ran upstairs to our rooms and changed. I put on my work clothes, as I call them— old jeans and heavy boots. A shirt and my old baggy sweater. I was ready.

I ran out of my room as Mac came out of his, pulling on a sweatshirt. Charlie was already downstairs. I made a detour and grabbed a flashlight from the kitchen drawer. We laughed like a couple of kids as we ran to the car.

As we pulled up to the cliffs, we saw Maggie and Teri were leaning against the car waiting for us. The wind wasn't too bad. That was a good sign.

"What's the game plan?" Charlie asked hesitantly as he took off his sunglasses.

I had forgotten mine. I squinted and held my hand in front of my face to see him. "I thought I would go down first, then Mac. Charlie, would you mind taking up the rear?"

Charlie shook his head. "Your ballgame, Kate. Lead on."

"Okay, let's go," I said and turned to Maggie.

"Kate, please be careful. You know how you—"

"You're gonna jinx me. I'll be fine. Can I borrow your sunglasses? I forgot mine." She took them off and handed them to me. "Thanks, I'll bring 'em back."

"I couldn't care less about them. Just bring... Oh, get out of here," she said anxiously and looked away.

"You worry too much," I said and put on her sunglasses.

She hesitated, then hugged me around the neck. "Don't do

anything reckless, Miss Ryan," she whispered against my cheek.

I pulled back and laughed. "I cannot guarantee something like that," I said and playfully patted her cheek.

Tim was giving instructions to Mac and Charlie. "I'll tell you from experience, mind the swells and the wind. When the waves go out, do most of your movin'. Stay low and watch the swells."

We all walked to the edge and looked down. It wasn't that steep. Starting out, it was a gentle slope, but it did get steep later. I looked up at the sun—still no clouds and it was almost hot.

I pulled the sweater off and tossed it to Maggie. "If I don't come back, you keep it."

"Dammit, Kate!" Maggie said.

Teri agreed, "Don't talk like that."

"Sorry, I was kidding. Teri, *you* can keep it."

I started down the path, which was only fifty feet or so. Mac followed at a safe distance, then Charlie. It took us roughly thirty minutes to travel the short distance. Once on the shore, we noticed there wasn't much room to maneuver.

"Well," I said, raising my voice. "The cavern is over there." I pointed south and led, staying as close to the cliffs as I could. The waves were not nearly as high as they were two days before.

We slowly made our way around the rocks. As we got closer to the cave entrance, the waves started crashing against the rocks. One good wave showered us and we were soaked.

I yelled back. "Stay low. Once the next wave hits, we move."

They both nodded. We started climbing the low slippery rocks; this was where I slipped the last time. The waves ebbed and we moved as quickly as we could. When the waves came again, we almost lay on the rocks. The cold seawater washed over us, and we started again.

The opening of the cavern was about forty feet away. I was exhilarated and impatient to get there. I heard Mac yell to me to take it slow. I nodded and continued along the slippery rocks. Then it happened.

We heard Charlie cry out as he slipped. I saw the panic on his face as the wave carried him out. My heart raced and I made my way back to Mac. We both lay flat on the rocks and reached for Charlie. He floundered for a moment, getting a mouthful of seawater, then reached for us.

Mac and I caught him by the sweater and frantically pulled him onto the rocks.

We went to a high point and sat there for a moment with the waves crashing around us. "Thanks," Charlie yelled.

"You owe me a beer," I yelled back.

Poor Mac looked petrified. He's not a swimmer at all, which quite possibly made him the bravest of us all.

Once we caught our breath, we started to the cavern entrance. I looked at Mac, his poor forehead bleeding. We slowly made our way until we were in front of the entrance. I looked out to the sea, and from there, I'm sure, you couldn't even tell there was a cave. "I bet nobody has a clue this is here. Look at how hard it was to get here. Who would ever want to come down here?"

Charlie nodded. "This is remarkable. It's not very big."

I pulled the small flashlight from my back pocket and turned it on, grateful it survived the drenching. "There may be bats," I said.

"Lead on, Sherlock," Mac said and cautiously looked around.

We peered into the cave entrance, which was completely dark. The waves that crashed on shore flowed in and out of the cavern. We stood almost knee deep in water as we waded into it.

"How far should we go?" Mac asked as his voice echoed in the darkness.

"I have no idea. Let's just see," I said and motioned forward.

We trudged onward. I looked up for bats. Nothing so far. I instinctively scratched my head. I hate bats.

"Knock it off. You're making me itchy," Mac said absently.

We had only gone perhaps sixty yards when the cave narrowed so that we could go no farther.

"I guess we're stymied," Charlie said.

I noticed the flashlight beginning to dim. I banged it against my hand. "Dammit, the batteries are going."

Charlie reached into his pocket and took out a cigarette lighter. "Maybe it'll work," he said. The flame flickered to life.

"Do you feel the breeze?" I asked and looked around in the darkness. There was definitely a breeze coming from somewhere. "Charlie, hold your lighter there." I motioned to my right.

As he did, the flame flickered wildly. "Guys, look at the flame on the lighter." I took my dimming flashlight and banged it on the heel of my hand once more and it flickered to life. I pointed it in the direction of the breeze.

We were astonished to see another passageway. "Why not?" I said and we walked slowly. The water had receded and was now only ankle deep. As we walked, we felt the breeze getting stronger.

"Do you feel that?" Mac asked.

"Keep going," I urged as we kept walking.

Then against the far wall of the cave, I saw a shovel and blinked in disbelief.

"Guys," I said. They both looked at me and followed my gaze.

"What in the hell?" Mac said and started for the shovel.

"Don't touch it," I said quickly. "I don't want anyone to know we've been here." *Like it wouldn't be all over the village anyway.*

Charlie's lighter pooped out and my flashlight was not far behind.

"I think we need to come back with better equipment," I said decisively.

Mac concurred. "We need more light."

We made our way out of the cave and back through the rocks. I led, and as a huge wave engulfed us, I felt myself thrown against the rocks. I felt a stabbing pain in my side as I clung to the rock, completely soaked.

Mac and Charlie were instantly at my side. "Are you all right?" Charlie yelled and I nodded.

Mac grabbed me under the arm. I put my arm around his neck and winced painfully when Charlie pulled me up.

We got back to the bottom of the cliff and looked up. Maggie, Teri, and Tim were anxiously looking down at us and we waved confidently. Teri had her hand on her chest and I could tell she was relieved.

All of us were breathing heavily. Mac's head was still bleeding and Charlie handed him his handkerchief. Tiredly, we started back up the path, getting our footholds and climbing slowly. Mac was leading now and I was in the middle.

By the time we got to the top, we were completely breathless. Teri hugged Mac.

I stood there breathing heavily holding my side. Maggie stood by me. "Take a deep breath," she ordered.

I looked at Mac. He was leaning against the car and Teri was holding the handkerchief on his head.

Maggie knelt next to me. "Are you all right?"

"I'm fine. Just pooped. Sorry, I lost your sunglasses."

"You can buy me another pair," she said. As she helped me up, I winced.

"You're not all right," she said quickly.

I stretched my side. "Yes, I am. I'm just horribly out of shape."

"The way you got Charlie out of the water, you look all right to me," Maggie said. "C'mon, let's get you adventurers home."

As I was changing my clothes, there was a knock at the connecting door. "Come in, Dr. Winfield."

Maggie was smiling as she walked in with her doctor's bag. "Making your midday rounds?" I asked. "Didn't we do this last fall?"

"Yes. It's becoming an annoying habit with you. You're my last patient of the day. I should start charging you." She gave me a stern look. "Now what did you hurt?" She put her hand up as I opened my mouth. "No sarcasm, no lying. Tell me."

"My back. I felt it when I hit the rocks," I said and she walked behind me and lifted my shirt.

"Dammit," she said angrily and opened her bag.

"Nice bedside manner, Doctor," I grumbled.

"Oh, keep still. You scraped your back and it's turning a nice shade of black and blue, for something completely different," she finished with sarcasm. "Now—bend over," she said flatly.

"Very funny," I snapped as she lifted my shirt. I leaned on the dresser and gritted my teeth. *She likes inflicting pain, Dr. Demento.*

I heard her opening a bottle, and at once, an antiseptic smell filled the air. She leaned closer. "This is goin' to sting like the devil, Miss Ryan." She tried her best at an Irish brogue.

"And you enjoy this far too much." I grimaced as she held the cloth on my back. "Thanks," I grumbled when she had finished.

"You're welcome. I hate to tell you I told you so," she started, and I gave her a challenging glare. Maggie glared right back. "I told you so," she said defiantly.

My outstretched hands reached for her neck as I visualized the wringing process with eyes bulging and tongue hanging out.

Mac knocked on the door and poked his head in. He noticed my strangling posture. "Uh, I'm sorry to interrupt this tender scene, but Bridget's downstairs. She needs to talk to you. It's about the Dublin car."

"Perfect timing," I grumbled as I walked out the door. I thought I heard Maggie say something. I turned back as she was slamming the bottle into her bag. "I'm sorry, were you saying something?" I asked innocently.

"Yes, I said I'll send you a bill," she snapped.

I met Bridget at the foot of the stairs. "Good day, Kate. How are ya?" she asked, smiling.

"I'm fine, thanks. What's the good word?"

"Constable Reardon wasn't as much help as we would have liked. The car belongs to a Russell Devine from Dublin," Bridget said, standing close to me. "That's about all the constable could find."

"That's it? Nothing more? Charlie is having his office check him out," I said and looked at Bridget, who looked a little nervous. Mac and Teri noticed it also. I watched her carefully. "Well, Bridget, thanks. This is very helpful. Is there something wrong?"

"No, nothin' at all. I'd better be headin' back to Donegal. I hope this helped," she stood and I walked her to her car.

Once outside, I put my hand on her shoulder to stop her. "If you know something or think you do, please tell me. Maybe we can figure out if it's important or not."

She took a deep breath. "Whether it's important or not is irrelevant. I cannot and will not divulge any information on a client," she said very professionally.

I was shocked. "Russell Devine is a client of yours?" When she said nothing, I continued, "You can at least tell me. I can find that out on my own."

She shot an angry look my way. "Your tactics might work back in Chicago, but don't try to threaten me." She turned and opened her car door and stopped. "He is not my client. That's all I can tell ya."

"Thank you, I'm sorry if I offended you," I said and she turned and put on her sunglasses.

"Ya didn't, it's my temper. I'll be in touch."

I went back into the library. "He's not her client, but she knows something." I sighed and plopped myself back into the chair. "Dammit, everybody knows something around here but me! We need to go back to cave with better lighting." I looked at Mac who agreed, as did Charlie.

"Not today. The tide's comin' in, so you'll have to wait until tomorrow."

We all agreed, even Maggie and Teri, that the next day would be better. I looked at Charlie. "Is your girl finding out about Mr. Devine?"

"Yes, she is. She said she'd be calling back later this evening."

"Someone has to know about Mr. Devine," I said absently.

I sat there thinking, Russell Devine is from Dublin and so is Peter; that in itself is no great concern. However, given the circumstances, it might be. I looked at Mac. "What did Peter have to tell you last night?"

"Oh, I nearly forgot. He's gone to Dublin to see Deirdre, said he'd be back later tonight. He did look worried, though he wouldn't say why."

"He's up to his ass in this. If he's an archaeologist, he's got to be digging in that cave for something. What does it have to do with the mill? What is Russell Devine's reason for being here?" I got up and paced. "And why is The Omega Group offering so much money?"

"I thought you and I were going to take a ride to Donegal today," Mac said.

"I nearly forgot. It's only four o'clock. We can be there and back by dinner," I offered, but Teri stood.

"Mac, remember, Rory Nolan is stopping by to see you," she said.

"No problem, I'll go myself." I shrugged and picked up the car keys. Maggie followed me into the foyer.

"Want some company?" she asked as she grabbed her sweater and walked out the door.

"No."

She was already in the car.

Chapter 19

The Donegal Inn was very crowded. We walked up to the desk and the young girl smiled.

"Back again? I'm afraid we're completely booked."

"No, no. Is Mr. Collins still here?" I tried to get a glimpse of the registry book. Maggie noticed and tried to do the same. The young girl skimmed the page and looked up. "Yes, he'll be here for another day. He's in the lounge right now," she offered and pointed in the right direction. Maggie, God love her, seized the opportunity.

"My, what a lovely ring. May I see it?" she asked and the girl offered her hand, smiling.

"My boyfriend gave it to me," she said.

"May I look at it in the light?" Maggie asked and took her away from the desk and straight to the window. I quickly turned the book around and scanned the pages. I found Russell Devine's name and dates, as well as Mr. Collins. Then I hastily turned the book back as Maggie and the girl returned to the desk.

"That is a beautiful stone. Thank you," Maggie was saying as the girl stood behind the desk.

As we walked to the bar, I took her by the arm. "Very clever, Doctor," I whispered.

"I had a Sherlock moment."

We sat at a small table in the lounge. The room was crowded, but I saw Mr. Collins at the end of the bar. I asked our waitress to tell him who I was and ask if I could speak with him. We watched as she talked to him. He looked our way and smiled slightly.

"Here goes nothing," I said, and Maggie patted my knee as he walked toward our table.

"Miss Ryan? We meet again," he said and looked at Maggie. I made the introductions.

"You wanted to speak to me?" he asked politely and sat down.

"Yes, I did. Mac was telling me about your offer. I was curious as to the amount. It seems very generous," I said as the waitress set down our drinks.

"We've been interested in Mr. McAuliffe's property for quite some time now," he said.

"Why would a mega company like yours want a small woolen mill?" Maggie blurted out and I cringed.

Jarred Collins raised his eyebrows and smiled. "A mega company? Seems you've been doing a little research, Dr. Winfield. I'm not privy to the company's plan. I am here merely to present the offer. Now if you'll excuse me. It was very interesting meeting you." He stood and bowed slightly and made his way through the busy lounge.

I sat there for a moment not saying anything. Glancing at Maggie, she avoided my look completely. After another moment of silence, I picked up my drink.

"Okay, okay. I shouldn't have blurted that out," she admitted, completely dejected.

"It's time for a couple of questions, Doctor," I said firmly, hiding my grin. "Who's the private investigator here?"

"You are." She sighed unhappily.

"And who is the doctor?"

"I am," she answered. I saw the forlorn look.

"And who has helped me more than she will ever know?" I asked. *What's getting into me? It must be this country air.*

Maggie quickly looked up and grinned. "I sincerely hope it's me."

"It is," I said and took her hand.

"I thought I could help," she said, looking at our hands.

"I know, and I appreciate it, truly I do," I said.

"Kate," she said slowly.

"Wait, let me say something. About the other night. I was wrong when I said it didn't mean anything. I'm so out of touch here. I have to be honest. I don't know what the hell I'm doing. And I'm not sure it's fair to you."

"Don't you think I'm a better judge of what's fair for me?" she asked and sat back.

"Maybe. I know I care for you. God knows, you've been the best friend I've ever had. I don't want to lose that—"

"Neither do I."

I sat there and tiredly rubbed my forehead. Maggie was watching me with a grin. "Are you all right?"

"No," I said childishly. "I have a headache."

"Aw," she said, and to my surprise, she leaned forward and kissed my brow. "Better?"

"No. I-It's a little sore right here," I said and pointed to my cheek.

She raised an eyebrow and gently kissed my cheek. Some dope in the crowded bar let out a deep groan. I think it was me.

My heart raced as I tried to find some moisture in my mouth. "W-We'd better get back before something else starts aching."

Maggie let out a healthy laugh and I joined her. I tossed some money down on the table as we quickly exited the crowded bar.

Maggie and I went for a walk before dinner. We strolled down the path toward the cottage and Maggie stopped to look at it.

"It is a pretty cottage. All it needs is a little paint and touchup on the thatching," she said, smiling.

I knew she would like the cottage. "I agree. I stayed there the other night, before you got here. With the fire going, it's warm and cozy."

"You and your fires again."

We sat on the stone wall looking out at the Atlantic. The sun was descending, and the clouds seemed to engulf the sky once again, but it was still warm, almost summer-like weather.

"I certainly hope this weather holds up for a couple more days. I feel close to getting to the bottom of this. I do." I rubbed my neck.

"You're going down there again tomorrow, aren't you?" she said.

I heard the worried tone in her voice. "Yes, we need better lighting. I think we should go earlier in the morning when the tide is completely out, as Tim suggested."

I glanced at Maggie as she looked out at the ocean. "I know you have to. However, you can't ask me not to worry about you."

"We'll be fine. Really," I said, trying to convince myself, as well. We continued walking farther from the cottage and the house.

"So it seems like your anxiety attacks are less frequent. You do feel better about talking, don't you?" she asked.

"I do. You know me pretty well. Talking about myself is not one of my strong points. However, you do have a way of getting me to open up. Aggravating as it is at times." I heard her chuckle as we strolled down the path. "I do appreciate you listening. It was a horrible time in my life. Probably the worst. I can't believe how foolish I was. How..." I ran my fingers through my hair and started thinking about it. Maggie watched me, waiting for the wave of anxiety to start, I'm sure. It did, but not nearly as bad as it usually does.

"It's getting better," she said.

I nodded, although I was perspiring and I wiped my forehead.

"You've kept it bottled up for so long. That's not good for you. I'm your friend and I'll listen, but you need to get certain things said out loud. It makes it easier to deal with," she said.

I watched her as she spoke. "Why do you bother?"

She stopped and gave me a curious look. "This is going to be like pulling teeth for you, isn't it?" she asked with an affectionate grin. "Kate, you and I need to—"

All of a sudden, the thunder rolled in the distance. We both looked up.

"Get back fast," I finished quickly, looking at the sky.

"No, wait a minute," she said and held my arm. The wind started to blow.

"C'mon, tell me later," I said and grabbed her hand.

We ran back to the cottage, barely missing the cloudburst. We stood on the doorstep waiting for the rain to stop. "Let's go in. I don't think it'll stop too soon," I said.

"What a downpour," I said, looking out the window.

Maggie was admiring the cottage. "This is adorable," she said, looking around.

"Yes, it is, very cozy," I said. The thunder boomed and Maggie jumped. Remembering her fear of thunder, I put my arm around her shoulders and gave her a reassuring hug.

"C'mon, sit, I wish we had time, I could build a small fire."

"Can I ask you a question?" she asked.

"Maybe..."

"Is there a bad scar?"

I wasn't expecting that. Honestly, I don't know what I was expecting. I said nothing for a moment or two. "Yes, there is," I said and instinctively felt the back of my neck. "I've never—"

"May I see it?" she asked, interrupting me.

"Maggie," I groaned self-consciously. "Why would you want to see an ugly scar?" I got defensive. This was way too much attention for my liking.

"Call it a doctor's morbid curiosity—call it anything you like," she said, being gently persistent.

"You're not going to let this go, are you?" I sighed, turned my back to her, and unbuttoned a few buttons of my shirt. "God, you're a pest," I said as she pulled my shirt down, exposing my back. I thought for sure she was going to gasp or make some disgusted noise. I remembered a woman I dated a couple of years before, in an intimate embrace, she saw the scar and was revolted. It was a definite mood killer.

Maggie, however, was too kind for that. If she felt the same revulsion, I couldn't tell. I felt her fingers on the scar, probing professionally. *There she goes touching me again.* Goodness, she had a soft touch. My back tensed and I shivered for a moment.

"Sorry, did that hurt?"

"No, you've... No, that definitely didn't hurt."

"She certainly did a number on you," she whispered. "Whoever the surgeon was did a magnificent job."

I knew the jagged scar ran from my hairline on the back of my neck down and across my shoulder blade. I felt her trace the scar with her fingertips. She pushed my shirt back up around my shoulders. It seemed as though her hands lingered on my shoulders for an instant. Then I felt her soft fingers lightly run through my hair for one wonderful moment and they were gone.

As I buttoned my shirt, I laughed thinking about the revolted woman, and when Maggie asked, I told her. "So thank you for not passing out or running, screaming into the night in terror," I said, buttoning my shirt.

"Did you think I would do that?"

"It wouldn't have been out of the question. It's a hideous scar," I said defensively as we stood and faced each other.

Suddenly, a window shattered. I instinctively grabbed Maggie and stood in front of her. "What the Christ?" I yelled and looked around.

Someone had hurled a bottle through the back window and it exploded into a small ball of flames by the front door. Maggie screamed and I picked up the rug in front of the fireplace and threw the blanket on the fire, smothering it. I stomped until the fire was out. The smell of kerosene permeated the cottage.

I turned around and looked at Maggie. "Are you all right?" I asked urgently. She only nodded.

"Don't move," I said and opened the front door and ran out. There was no one, nothing. I looked in all directions. "Sonofabitch," I cursed and went back inside.

"Christ, Kate, that scared the life out of me. Are you all right?" she asked.

"I'm fine. Let's get back to the house, though," I said anxiously.

Charlie bounded down the stairs when we made our noisy entrance. "What's the ruckus?" he started to joke, then saw our faces. "What happened now?"

Mac and Teri joined us and I explained.

Mac was furious. "I've had about all I can take."

"Mac, please don't lose your head, honey," Teri said.

I looked around. "Where's Peter?" I asked suspiciously.

"He's still in Dublin. At least that's where he said he'd be," Mac said.

"Where's Tim?" I asked, running my fingers through my damp hair. I looked at Maggie; she was staring at the fire.

"He went out about an hour ago, said there were a few old friends he wanted to meet. He should be back anytime," Teri said.

During dinner, we discussed what had been happening. I became extremely tired and yawned wildly. Tim followed suit. "It's a contagious thing. Now are you goin' back down there tomorrow?" he asked, drinking his wine.

"Yes, but we need to be better equipped this time," I said. "Hey, Mac, you have those keys, let's check out the cellar after dinner and see what's down there. Maybe we'll get lucky."

We continued with dinner and Charlie asked, "So this Molotov cocktail was another scare tactic?"

I thought about it for a moment. "I don't know. Why start a

fire?" I said and absently picked at my food.

"You certainly can't stay in the cabin anymore. The smell of that kerosene is enough to keep anyone out. We can clean it up later," Maggie offered.

"I'm glad neither of you were hurt," Teri said.

My mind was racing. *There was a reason for that fire...*

"Let's get back to the cliffs. If we need more equipment, maybe it's in the cellar. We haven't been down there yet," Mac said and pushed his plate away. "I'll get the keys." He left the dining room and came back holding the cellar key and the other smaller one. "I wonder what this little one is for."

I looked at it. "Let me have that one. I'll check every lock in this house," I said with a determined nod.

As Mac opened the cellar door, he pulled a string and turned on a light bulb that dangled from the cobweb ceiling.

"Ah, modern electricity," Charlie said sarcastically.

We all cautiously descended the stairs and once at the bottom, there was yet another string and another light bulb. "Oh, allow me this time," Charlie quipped and pulled the string.

The light illuminated the cellar and I took inventory of the damp area. There was a long table with assorted tools on it. Mac found two lanterns and a couple of large flashlights. He turned them on.

"Hmm. I didn't expect them to work," Mac said absently.

Charlie was busy on the other side of the cellar. "We don't know how old those batteries are," he said. He picked up a gallon can and shook it, opened it, and smelled it. "Kerosene," he said.

I noticed something next to the containers. "Hell-o."

There were four or five long thick ax handles with rags tied to the end of them. I picked one up. "It's like right out of the movies. I wonder if these would be better to use. They might stay lit longer," I suggested.

I looked around the cellar and noticed pickaxes, shovels, and a pair of heavy work boots all together with the cans of kerosene and torches. "Looks like someone was getting ready to do some digging."

"Let's leave this and you can take the torches in the morning," Teri said.

Tim was at the top of the stairs, we told him what we found.

"The last time I saw Brian, I asked him to borrow, oh, I can't remember now what it was, but he didn't let me down there. He went himself and closed the door behind him," he said and scratched his head.

"Everybody, up to bed. Doctor's orders," Maggie said seriously. "If you're going to go climbing again, I don't want you exhausted and falling into the ocean. I don't care how good a swimmer you might be." She pushed me toward the stairs.

I took a hot bath, and as I laid my head back, my mind went to work. Why would someone start a fire in the cottage? Then my mind went to Bridget and Peter. Peter is definitely involved in whatever this is. Bridget knows something, as well. She knows the man in the dark coat who now had a name—Russell Devine.

Maggie was right, which irritated me to no end. I was exhausted as I went back to my room meeting Maggie in the hall.

"Did you leave me any hot water?" she asked.

"Yes, Dr. Winfield, it's all yours," I said, just as the thunder started again.

We looked at each other for a moment. The memory of Maggie lying next to me flashed once again through my mind. "If during the night, there's a storm and you—" I stopped and had no idea what to say.

Maggie raised her eyebrow and gave me a sarcastic grin. "Perhaps someday, Miss Ryan, you won't need a tropical storm, hail, and damaging winds," she whispered and kissed my forehead. "I'll wait for that day. Good night."

Perhaps someday...

Chapter 20

The morning offered the usual weather—damp and foggy. I strolled down the path toward the cottage. When it came into view, I got a little nervous thinking about the events of the day before. I opened the door and noticed the smell of kerosene had dissipated. I took the burnt rug and tossed it outside, then took a broom to the small pieces of glass.

The room didn't look right. Scanning the area, I realized a chair had been moved and the desk drawer opened. I cautiously walked through the rest of the cottage. Each room was in some stage of disarray: mattresses slightly moved, drawers opened, kitchen cabinet doors ajar.

It didn't take a finely honed ex-P.I. to know someone had been in here. Someone carefully searched the cottage, but didn't take the time to make sure all was back in order. Then I shivered at the thought—perhaps I interrupted someone.

"I thought you might be here," Maggie said from the doorway. "Good morning."

"Someone was in here," I said quickly.

"What do you mean?" she asked as she looked around. "What were they looking for?" I showed her all the little differences.

"I have no idea, but look around. The desk, cabinets, and dresser drawers look as if someone was looking neatly through them, not merely ransacked. Whoever it was knew what to look for."

She followed me down the hall to the bedrooms where I showed her the mattresses.

"Someone looked under the mattress. What do you keep under a mattress?" I asked, scratching my head.

"Money, for one," Maggie said, fixing the bed.

I helped her with the mattress. "Yes. Maybe letters, documents," I said as we remade the bed.

"That's the reason for the fire," I said. "It got us out of here. A small fire would do the trick. Scare us into staying in the house, so they had a chance to look around. Dammit, but for what?"

Maggie looked around, as well. "I'm stumped and I'm starving. You have the honor of making me breakfast," she said decisively.

"You deserve it, after taking care of me for the past couple of days. I appreciate it," I said. "So what'll it be? Ham and eggs? Bacon?"

"All of the above."

Mac and Teri were sitting at the kitchen table. They both looked up when we walked in. "Where have you two been?" Teri asked, smiling.

Maggie sat down. "At the cottage. Kate thinks someone was in there looking for something. I think she may be right."

I poured both of us a cup of coffee and sat next to Maggie. "Someone was definitely in there nosing around." I explained how the cottage looked and Teri shrugged.

"You're the expert. I bow to your expertise." She lifted her coffee cup.

"Thank you, milady," I said and raised mine.

Mac was drawing something on a piece of paper. Maggie looked on. "Color by numbers?"

Mac snorted. "Very funny, you've been hanging around Kate too long."

"What are you drawing?" I asked, looking across the table.

"I'm trying to get the distances correct. Where's Charlie?" Mac asked.

"On the phone," Charlie called from the hallway as he entered the kitchen. "I called Jess, are you ready for this?"

"No, but go ahead," I said eagerly.

"Okay. Russell Devine is from Dublin. He's twenty-seven, single. He went to Trinity College during the same time Peter did. He didn't graduate. And he has a police record. Six arrests, no convictions. All for assault. This boy has a temper. He beat a man in Cork so badly that the man was in traction for two weeks. Jess, God love her, called a friend at the Dublin police. Someone with money and a good lawyer got him out each time. That's the police version anyway." He took a drink of coffee and continued. "He has no permanent address but is seen frequently in Dublin. Jess can't find whom he works for or even if he works.

"Also, Peter's last known address was in Dublin with an elderly gentleman, who passed away six months ago of natural causes. His name? Daniel Carroll, and guess what he did for a living."

"Another history professor," I said.

"Right. He taught ancient Irish history at Trinity. And," he added smiling, "he did work for the National Museum in Dublin in his spare time," he finished and closed his notebook.

"Jess has done a fine job, Charlie. Please thank her for me." I looked out the window, the clouds were rolling by and the wind had picked up, but no rain yet. It was seven thirty. We all sat there in silence. I didn't know what to do next. I needed to organize my thoughts.

Charlie looked down at Mac. "What are you doodling there?"

We watched as Mac concentrated on his work. "Charlie, look at this. It's a scale drawing," he said and handed him the paper.

Charlie studied it. "This looks good. I don't know if the mill is that close, though," he looked up and handed it to me.

Mac had drawn a map of the cliffs and the mill. He had marked the distances above ground and below to see how far we had gone in the cave. It appeared that we were at least two hundred feet from the mill.

"I'm not sure how much farther we could have gone. Maybe fifty or sixty feet," I said. "Although it was getting narrow."

Charlie agreed. "A shorter, skinnier person would have no problem, but that ain't us," he laughed and I agreed.

Maggie coughed and we looked at her. "I'm shorter and skinnier."

"No," I said quickly.

"No?" she repeated slowly.

Mac and Charlie took their coffee cups off the table and sat back.

"Maggie, you're not going down there," I said.

She took a deep breath. "The last time I looked, I was an adult. I don't need your permission."

"You're not going down there. It's too dangerous," I said

173

calmly.

When will I learn to watch for the telltale signs like the twitching left eye?

Her face was turning a scary shade of red. "It's too dangerous," she repeated calmly. "But not too dangerous for you," she added and gave me a challenging look.

"I'm used to this. I won't allow—"

"You won't allow?" she asked slowly. *Wrong word.* She had her hand on her coffee cup and I wasn't at all sure she wasn't going to bounce it off my forehead. "Don't pull this macho—I'm in charge—with me, Kate. If I can help with this, I'll go. You don't have the right to tell me not to."

I leaned forward on the table. "In charge? When am I in charge? You bossy—"

Maggie stood and nearly sent the chair across the room. "I'm going!" she announced angrily and stormed out.

I got up and looked at my comrades. "Not the wisest thing I could have done."

As I dashed out of the kitchen, Maggie was at the top of the stairs. "Wait a minute," I said.

She turned and said rather rudely, "Oh, go blow it out your ass." She went into her bedroom, slammed the door, and locked it.

"Blow it out my ass?" I repeated. I dashed into my room and got to the connecting door before she locked it.

"Don't come charging in here like a bull," she said, her eyes blazing. "I will not be treated like a child," she said with her hands on her hips.

I was about to tell her she looked like said child but thought better of it. "Look, I'm not treating you like a child. I was down there and it's dangerous. I don't want you hurt, that's all," I said with my voice raised as I continued. "However, you're right. You can do anything you want, and I don't have a right to tell you not to." I took a deep breath. "I'm sorry."

She softened and ran her fingers through her thick hair. "I'm sorry. My temper always gets the better of me."

"Yes, there is that."

"I have a chance to contribute. If I can help, don't you think I should take the chance? You would."

I walked to the window and tried to come up with one good

reason why she shouldn't help. She was right, and I had to admit it. I was being protective and wasn't being fair; she had a right. "When we go down there, you follow me and stay close," I said as I turned around to face her. "I mean it."

"I will," she said too quickly. "Whatever you say."

I looked down into those damned blue eyes. "It's a gift—that you can stand right there and lie with a straight face. It is a gift," I said and avoided the innocent beguiling smile.

By the time we got everything together, it was nearly eight thirty. Tim was helping Mac and Charlie, making sure we were prepared for our expedition.

Teri and Maggie were talking as I bounded down the stairs. I stopped in my tracks when I heard Teri.

"What are you going to wear?" she asked.

"Gee, I don't know," Maggie said thoughtfully.

I groaned and pinched the bridge of my nose. "We're not going to the prom, Maggie. What you have on is fine—it goes with your eyes. Do you have boots?"

She nodded. "Yes, but not as good as yours." I believe she was trying not to aggravate me, which I thought was sweet since I wanted to wring her neck.

"Fine," I said. "Put them on and we'll meet you both by the car."

Tim and Charlie were checking the flashlights as I walked up to them. "I don't know about this, Charlie," I said.

"I know, but you can't tell Maggie anything. Seriously, though, she might be able to get farther than we can. Don't worry, among the three of us, nothing will happen to her," he said.

It was still foggy and damp and my neck ached horribly as we finished packing the car. I stretched my neck back and forth.

"Pretty bad this morning?" Mac asked.

"Yeah, this stinking weather," I said miserably.

The fog was very dense and the eerie silence was deafening when we pulled up to the cliffs.

Mac finished placing the flashlights into the small backpack and slung it over his shoulder as we started down the rugged path.

I led, Maggie followed. Charlie and Mac brought up the rear.

We had a relatively easy time of it; without the wind, the waves were calmed. It didn't hurt that we were in an alcove and the rocks blocked some of the wind off the ocean. I was relieved and glanced back at Maggie. She gave me an encouraging nod. She was having the time of her life, the goof. There were no slips or faltering as we finally got to the opening of the cavern.

"Okay, all set," I said as I looked at Maggie. "Stay close to me."

The waves washed in and out of the mouth of the cave. It was not as deep as the day before, but still the seawater was cold.

As we waded through the entrance of the cave, Mac handed each of us a flashlight. Maggie said from behind me, "Boy, it is dark."

"I know, so far no bats," I said.

As we walked into the cave, the water now was only ankle deep. We walked for another hundred feet or so. Even through the beams of our flashlights, it was dark as pitch in front of us. The only sound was the water sloshing around our ankles.

"We should be there soon, shouldn't we?" Mac's voice echoed behind us.

"I think so. It can't be very far ahead." I looked up. "At least no bats."

Maggie instinctively scratched her head.

"I know the feeling," I said.

We kept on—that's when we saw him.

"What in the hell?" I exclaimed and ran ahead of everybody. It was Peter. He was lying on his side, almost completely in the water. He looked terribly still.

I knelt beside him, he was freezing. "Maggie!" I called, but she was already by his side.

Mac and Charlie lifted him out of the water. His head was resting on Mac's lap. "Is he alive?" Mac asked.

Maggie checked the pulse in his neck and wrist. She opened his eyes and did the doctor thing. "He's breathing, but he's ice cold. We need to get him out of here quickly." She checked his limbs for signs of injury. "Nothing appears to be broken. Let's go and be careful."

Mac and Charlie lifted him up and Mac slung him over his shoulder in a fireman's carry. We went out as quickly as we could.

I led and Mac was right behind me, followed by Maggie and Charlie. Soon we were at the entrance and out onto the shore. We looked up and Teri and Tim waved, then saw Peter. Tim yelled, "Are you all right?"

The wind of course had picked up and whirled around us as I gave Tim the thumbs-up sign. Now the waves started.

"Dammit, great timing," I said.

Mac had laid Peter down, he was groaning but still out of it. The waves crashed around us. Maggie yelled over them, "We need to get him out of here!"

"We have to get moving," Charlie yelled out. Mac once again carried Peter over his shoulder.

We all stayed close to one another and started across the slippery rocks. Mac was undaunted. How he carried Peter, I will never know. We slowly reached the bottom of the path. The waves still came on shore, but in our little cove, they subsided.

We all sat there for a moment, completely drenched, surrounded by fog. As Mac laid Peter down, Maggie knelt and checked him. She looked up at Mac and said, "How in the hell are we going to get him up there?"

"Don't worry, I'll do it," Mac vowed.

He and Charlie lifted Peter once again onto Mac's shoulders. It seemed to take forever, but we made it to the top quickly enough.

Teri was immediately at Mac's side. "Where did he come from?" she asked.

Mac fell to his knees, completely breathless, and laid Peter down. "He was in the cave, almost dead, I'm sure," Mac said, gasping for air.

Maggie knelt beside Peter's still body. "Okay, we need to get him warm quickly. In the car, let's go," she ordered.

An anxious feeling rippled through me as we got Peter into the car. I gave the cliffs a backward glance as we pulled away. What was in that cave?

Chapter 21

Back at the house, we put Peter in one of the remaining rooms. He looked awful.

"Kate, please get my bag," Maggie said firmly.

I ran down the hall, my boots squishing all the way. When I got back, Mac and Charlie had stripped Peter's wet clothes off him and wrapped him in several blankets.

"We've got to maintain his body temperature," Maggie said in a worried voice. We rubbed his body and dried his hair; he looked ashen.

He opened his eyes and smiled. "My angel," he whispered.

"Lay still, Peter." Maggie checked his pulse and his eyes once again. Thank God for her. She was calm and reassuring as she sat on the edge of the bed and examined his neck. "He's got a nasty gash," she said to no one in particular. She opened her bag and got to work. A few minutes later, she had cleaned and dressed his wound.

"That's about all we can do. It's imperative that he stay warm." Maggie ran her fingers through her wet hair. She looked around at all of us. "We all need to get dry and warm, no one needs to get sick," she ordered and ushered us out of the room.

I was in dry clothes but was still chilled to the bone. I stood by the fireplace playing with the odd little key. I had tried every lock I could find in this bloody drafty house and nothing. It fit no door, desk, or cabinet. What the hell is it for?

"What's wrong, Kate?" Maggie asked. I jumped and put my hand to my heart. "Sorry, you looked deep in thought," she said, watching me play with the key. "Found the lock yet?"

"Nope, but I will," I said stubbornly. "It has to fit something in this house and I'm gonna find it. Besides, this business with Peter has got me stumped." I went to the window.

The fog was now as thick as pea soup, as the saying goes. I

turned back to Maggie, who was giving me a worried look. "I have a bad feeling. Something's about to give here. I can feel it. If what Charlie said is true, the British Excavating company feels certain Mac will sell. How can they know this?" I asked, rubbing my neck.

I paced back and forth. "Bridget and Peter," I said absently, trying to think.

"What about them?" Maggie asked.

"When we first met Bridget, there were a few times I thought they exchanged glances, as if they knew a secret. I passed it off, though, at the time. Then I remembered being in her office, looking at her diploma. Dammit, what did it say?"

"What did what say?" she asked.

"Her diploma on the wall," I said thoughtfully. I had an idea and ran to the phone.

Maggie had a puzzled look on her face as I picked up the phone. It was then Mac, Teri, and Charlie came in and looked at Maggie, who shrugged and said, "I have no idea."

I looked at her and winked. I got the operator. "Can you connect me with Trinity College in Dublin, please? Registrar's Office."

I looked at them. "I want to make sure..." I started and a voice came over the phone.

"Registration, may I help you?"

I cleared my throat and said in my best Irish brogue, "Yes, I'm from Bridget Donnelly's office. She graduated from the law school there not too long ago. She'd like to continue her education in the history department, but she can't remember the professor's name. Is there anyway ya could find that out for me?" I asked sweetly and waited.

"If ya can hold a moment, I can pull up Miss Donnelly's records. You're from her office, you said?"

"Yes. She's an attorney in Donegal now. I'm her personal secretary," I added. She put me on hold. "She's checking her records," I whispered to the questioning faces.

Maggie looked at me with raised eyebrows. "You're very good at this, it's scary."

Mac nodded. "She should've been a cop."

I shook my head. "I hate guns."

Teri gave me an exasperated look. "You carried one for nine years."

"But I never used it," I said defensively and noticed Maggie's horrified look. "Maybe once, but the damn squirrel was bothering Chance."

The woman's voice came back on the line. "Well now, you say Miss Bridget Donnelly, you mean Miss Bridget Donnelly-Devine correct?" she said and I went cold.

"Yes, I'm sorry. She goes by Bridget Donnelly now, not Devine," I said, and my four companions on this merry chase gave me a collective incredulous look.

"I understand," the woman said. "She did graduate, with honors, it looks like. She took a course in Irish ancient history. Professor Carroll taught the class. Unfortunately, he passed on a few months ago. Professor Sullivan now teaches the classes. Did you want to register Miss Donnelly?" she asked nicely.

"No, I'll let her know and I'm sure she'll be contacting you. You've been a great help. Thank you," I said.

We all stood there in the hallway stupefied. "I'll be damned," I said. "She was married to Russell Devine. I think that was the name I saw on her license that hung on her wall."

Charlie took the phone out of my hand. "We'll soon know for sure," he said and dialed. "Jess. Charlie. One more person. Bridget Donnelly-Devine. Graduated Trinity College. She's an attorney in Donegal. Goes by Bridget Donnelly now. Need to know if she was married to this Russell Devine creature or has any connection to him at all. Soon? Thanks. I…" Charlie gave us a pleading glance.

We gave him some privacy and headed to the kitchen; Maggie checked on Peter.

"What's next?" I asked, shaking my head. I put the kettle on the stove.

"What in the world made you think of this?" Mac asked.

"I don't know. I was talking to Maggie, and all of the sudden, it popped into my head. I remembered looking at her diploma, seeing her and Peter stealing glances at each other. I passed it off." I shrugged.

Charlie came into the kitchen. "Jess said it shouldn't take too long. If Kate found out that much in ten minutes, she can find out the rest in an hour or so." He looked at me. "It's a challenge thing with Jess."

"Dating you, I can see the challenge," I said with a sweet smile as I finished making the tea.

"Well," Maggie said as she joined us, "Peter is breathing normally and his body temperature is much warmer. We got him out of there in time. He needs to rest now." She wearily rubbed her forehead.

I took the pot of hot tea and a small mug. "Follow me, Doctor."

Once in the living room, I motioned to the chair by the fire. "Maggie, you look pooped. Sit for a while."

"I'm fine."

I gave her an unwavering look. "Sit down, please."

She sat in the chair by the fire while I poured a cup of tea. "Let someone take care of you for a change," I said and handed her the steamy cup. I slid the ottoman under her feet.

"Thanks, Kate," she sighed.

"Hey, where'd Tim run off to?" I asked and looked around the room. With all that had happened, I completely forgot about him.

"I think he went to see Sean and Mary. Said he'd be back later."

"We need to get our information organized here," I said. "Now the newest wrinkle is Bridget. She's involved in this, as well, which I truly suspected anyway. She took a class from Professor Carroll that somehow links her to Peter, maybe. I thought he knew her because of Brian, but it appears he knew her long before. Why would she lie about that?" I asked absently. "We'll know soon enough. Peter is going to have to spill his guts now.

"What the Christ is going on and who in the hell killed Brian?" I looked out at the fog, as if it were going to answer me.

For the next few hours, we took turns looking in on Peter. He slept peacefully and Maggie was sure he'd be fine.

As Maggie and I sat by the fire, I heard the phone ring. Teri rushed back into the library. "Kate, it's Bridget, she needs to talk to you. She sounds terrified."

"Now what?" I ran to the phone.

Bridget *was* terrified. "Kate, I'd never ask ya for a favor, but if ya could, would ya come get me? I'm at my office. Things are gettin' a mite out of hand and honestly I'm scared to death."

I heard the panic in her voice. "Stay where you are. I'll be there in twenty minutes," I said and hung up and went back into the library. "Something's wrong, she's afraid to leave her office. I told her I'd pick her up." I looked over at Mac.

"I'll go with you."

Charlie offered to go, as well. "Would you mind staying here with Maggie and Teri? I'd feel better."

Mac drove too fast once again. We said very little until we got into Donegal. I looked around; the town was quiet, not many tourists in this damp foggy weather.

We pulled up to Bridget's office. Mac honked and she came running out and got into the backseat, out of breath.

"Thanks. I..." she started crying. Mac pulled away and drove out of town back toward Duncorrib.

I turned in my seat to face Bridget. "What the hell is going on?"

"Peter's missing. I was supposed to see him this morning at eight. He never showed. Then I saw Russell Devine, and I got scared. I've had four phone calls with no one on the other end. Then this bloody fog rolled in, and I got spooked. I'm sorry to do this to you," she said and took a deep breath.

"Bridget, Peter is at the house," I said.

Her eyes widened. "Thank God, I thought..." she let out a sob and covered her face with her hands.

"He was dead?" Mac finished for her. He was getting fed up, I could tell. Mac is a very easygoing man with a high boiling point. However, once his kettle starts...

Bridget shot a look up at him. "Why would you say something like that?"

"Because we found him in the cave knocked unconscious and almost drowned," he said, not hiding his anger.

I put my hand on his leg in a warning gesture. He took a deep breath and continued driving through the fog. We drove slowly through town and onto the private road leading to the house.

"Christ, this is thick fog," Mac said.

Then out of the corner of my eye, I saw him—a man stumbled out of the dense fog and onto the road. "Mac, look out!" I yelled.

Mac skillfully swerved and missed him. The man now lying

on the road was Tim. There was blood all over his face from the gash on his forehead.

Mac and I dashed out to help him into the car.

"Sonsabitches," Tim whispered thickly and put his head back. Bridget took a hanky and placed it on his forehead.

Mac pulled away quickly. "What next?" he asked loudly and banged his hand on the steering wheel.

I'm sure he didn't expect an answer. "Easy, Mac," I said, but I agreed with him completely.

We helped Tim into the house and Maggie came running over. "What in the world…" she said.

Once in the kitchen, we eased Tim into a chair.

"I got my licks in before they got me," he flexed his hand, his knuckles bloodied. Maggie looked at me, and once again, I was running for her doctor bag.

"What happened?" I asked when I came back. I handed Maggie the bag.

"I was walking back in this blasted fog. I thought I was being followed, but with the fog, I thought it was my imagination. Then all at once, they were on me, two young bastards. Pardon me, ladies."

"A redhead and a bald kid," I said.

"That's the ones." He winced as Maggie cleaned his forehead.

"Stitches?" I asked.

"No, I can fix this," she said confidently and continued.

"Good, nobody leaves this house. Nobody." I looked at Bridget. "Peter is upstairs."

"I'll go to him," she said and started to leave.

"He's sleeping, you can see him later," Maggie said firmly without looking up. Bridget glared at her. Maggie glanced up at her and continued mending Tim's forehead. "Sit down before you collapse. You're as white as a ghost," she ordered soundly.

Bridget looked angry. "Look. I don't have to—"

Maggie interrupted her and said harshly, "Yes, you do. I think between you and Peter, enough has been accomplished for one morning. Now sit down and keep quiet until I'm finished."

I gave Bridget a pleading look. "You'd better sit."

She grudgingly sat down. Maggie, without a word, finished Tim's forehead and started on his bruised knuckles.

Mac reached over and grabbed Tim's arm. "I'm so sorry."

"Don't be. I say we go find them young bastards and show them a thing or two," he said angrily.

"You're not going anywhere, Tim," Maggie said and looked at Mac and me. "No one is."

Mac and I looked at each other like scolded children. Bridget sat there glaring at Maggie.

I watched as Maggie finished with Tim. She was far too calm for my liking. She closed her doctor bag, walked over to the sink, and washed her hands. She grabbed a towel and dried them, looking at Bridget the entire time. "Kate, why don't you and Mac take Tim in the library?" This was not a request.

As we helped Tim up and walked to the door, Bridget stood and Maggie said, "I'd like to speak with you for a moment, Bridget."

I gave a curious look at Maggie while Mac guided Tim out of the kitchen. Maggie was frowning, still drying her hands and avoiding me completely. *What was this now?*

"Maggie..." I started to say and she gave me a look I had never seen before. It stopped me dead in my tracks. I stood there for a second just blinking.

"I'll be out in a moment," she said clearly and succinctly. There was such resolution in her voice that it sent a slight shiver up my spine. For future reference, I made a mental note of that tone. I had no idea what she wanted with Bridget.

"It's been nice," I mumbled to Bridget and walked out.

In a few minutes, Teri came out of Peter's room as I had my ear to the kitchen door.

"Kate," Teri called down to me.

I jumped and whirled around. "What? I'm not doing anything," I replied in guilty fashion, just as the nuns taught us.

Teri gave me an odd look. "What were you doing? Never mind. I don't want to know. Peter's awake, get Maggie."

As I walked into the kitchen, I heard Maggie say, "I hope we understand each other, Bridget."

I stepped into the kitchen and looked at Maggie. "Peter's awake," I said. "And Teri needs you."

Bridget quickly walked out.

I opened my mouth to say something, but by the challenging

look on Maggie's face, I closed it quickly. "Good idea," she said evenly.

She grabbed her doctor's bag and walked out of the kitchen with a purposeful gait. "Maggie…" I started and let out a grunt as the swinging kitchen door greeted me. I rubbed my forehead. "That's gonna leave a mark."

Chapter 22

I walked into Peter's room, still rubbing my forehead, to find Maggie sitting on the edge of Peter's bed. "Welcome back again." She checked his pulse and his eyes and his neck.

"You're a pretty lucky man, Peter. If we hadn't been in that cave, you'd certainly be dead," Mac said as Peter sat up and looked at Bridget.

"Peter, that's where they found you."

"I don't remember," he rubbed his forehead.

"What's the last thing you remember?" I asked.

He glanced at Bridget. "I don't remember exactly."

"Okay," I said. "We'll talk to you later."

He gave me a suspicious look as did everyone else.

"Kate's right. Enough, you need rest," Maggie ordered.

"Would it be all right if I stayed?" Bridget asked sarcastically.

"Yes, for a few minutes," Maggie said with authority.

"Okay, what was that about?" Teri asked me as we walked into the library.

"Look, those two know what's going on," I said. "My guess is they're both in over their heads. Let them talk and mull it over. I think Bridget is scared to death. Teri, you heard her voice. She'll talk before Peter. Trust me, she'll talk."

Tim was sitting with Charlie, playing cards. "Penny a point, young man," Tim said with a wink.

"You're on," Charlie said in a confident tone.

The day was still foggy and damp. Mac and Teri sat on the couch talking. I sat in the chair by the fire. Maggie came up and sat on the ottoman facing me.

Teri came up to us. "Looks like we're going to have houseguests tonight."

I put my hand in my pockets and felt the small key. I took it out and looked at it. "Where, oh where, do you belong?" I asked absently. I thought for a moment. "Every key has a label on it. Why not this little bugger?"

I looked at Maggie. "C'mon, let's do some investigating."

She smiled enthusiastically. "After you."

We double-checked every door in the house. I glanced at her while she concentrated. "Um, so what did you say to Bridget?"

"When?" she asked as she looked up at me.

"You know when, Dr. Winfield. In the kitchen."

Maggie's blue eyes searched my face. She then raised one eyebrow. "We discussed her business in Duncorrib as compared to Donegal." She smiled sweetly and walked down the hall.

As we checked the bookcase in the hall, I noticed Maggie's odd look. "What's wrong?" I asked.

Maggie took the key from me and looked at it thoughtfully. "You know…" she started and stopped as Bridget came down the stairs. I saw Maggie stiffen as she watched Bridget walk by and into the library.

I leaned into Maggie. "Hold that thought," I said and we followed Bridget.

"How's Peter?" I asked casually.

"He's asleep," she said thankfully. "He looks awful." She sighed and put her hand to her forehead.

"Bridget, he's in way over his head, isn't he?" I asked and she looked up quickly.

"N-No, he's—"

"You might as well tell us," Mac said. She looked at her hands and said nothing.

"Okay, let me take a stab at it. You tell me when I'm wrong," I offered.

"Kate, ya don't know." She sighed tiredly.

"Well, let me try," I suggested. "You, Peter, and Russell Devine all went to Trinity College, and at some point were in Professor Carroll's ancient Irish history class. I'm guessing that's where you all met. I'm also guessing that's when you fell for Russell and married him."

She shot an incredulous look at me and turned a nice ashen color, and I knew I was right. Bridget looked like someone hit her in the solar plexus. "Peter is working on something," I continued. "We know he's a professor at Trinity, taking over for Professor Carroll. We know that Russell Devine is an ill-tempered man who, for some reason, is behind all these 'accidents.' What I don't know is what Peter is digging for..." My voice trailed off as I looked toward the kitchen and back at Bridget. I had that anxious feeling in the pit of my stomach. I felt pieces of the puzzle coming together. I went into the kitchen and picked up the brochure that Mac had gotten several days before and brought it back into the living room.

I showed it to Bridget and said curiously, "The west of Ireland. Full of history, tales of piracy. Monks, hiding their forbidden works. All sorts of things. The Book of Cells found after centuries."

She sat there looking at the brochures. "Ya have no idea."

I was getting *so* impatient. "I'd like to have some idea, if someone would level with me," I said harshly.

A voice called out from the hallway, "If someone would get me some clothes, I'll level with all of ya."

We all looked up and there stood Peter, wearing nothing but his glasses and a blanket.

Charlie gave Peter some clothes and he sat drinking tea in front of the fire. He looked at Bridget, gave her a sick smile and sipped his tea.

My patience was wearing very thin. It's a virtue. *I don't have it.* I said nothing but stood by the fire warming my hands. They were perfectly warm. I needed something to do with them, instead of shaking the words out of Peter. I was about to scream when he started.

"Where should I start?" he asked thoughtfully.

I rolled my eyes and groaned, "Oh, good grief."

Maggie, standing beside me, rudely nudged my ribs. I sighed and said, "Why don't you try the beginning?"

"Well," he started. "I was twenty-one or was it twenty-two?"

Bridget said, "Twenty-two, I think."

Oh, good Christ. I sat in the huge chair by the fire. Maggie sat next to me on the hearth.

"I was twenty-two, a graduate from Trinity, working on my

professorship, or thesis, whichever you prefer. Anyway, that's when Professor Carroll came to me. It was in the spring almost six years ago. We—"

Bridget interrupted him. "I think it was in the fall, Peter. Remember, we were celebrating me becomin' an attorney."

"Oh, you're right, it was," Peter said, nodding.

My leg was bouncing nervously; they were driving me nuts. Maggie very subtly, and without looking at me, put her hand on my knee and squeezed firmly.

"Are you nervous?" she asked in a hissed whisper.

"Just in that leg," I whispered back in kind and winced as I felt her nails.

"Professor Carroll came to me with a fantastic story," he said and leaned forward in his chair. "When he was younger during World War II, he came across an old book from the eighteenth century. His professor, who had it for sixty years, gave it to him.

"It told the story of a ship from the Spanish Armada that was sunk along the Atlantic coast of Ireland. Now if ya know history, the Spaniards were a plundering lot. Queen Elizabeth was at constant odds with King Phillip of Spain for decades. According to this story, what was aboard this Spanish ship was originally plundered from an English vessel. The trail of this treasure, as it were, has been hot and cold for almost two hundred years.

"We investigated the possibility. I thought it might be a hoax. However, between me, Brig, and Russell, we helped Professor Carroll, and after four years of studying every text, every map of Ireland from beginning to end, staying up till all hours of the mornin', we felt it was no hoax, it had to be real. Professor Carroll went to the National Museum with all our data. It took months before they decided to give us a grant to continue looking."

"Looking for what?" I asked.

He looked at Bridget who said, "Might as well tell them, they'll find out. They found out about me and Russell."

Peter gave me a shocked look. "It wasn't her fault. He was different back then, kind and good. Money does strange things to people, so does love."

Remembering my own mistakes, I said, "I couldn't agree more."

"Look, Peter, someone killed Brian and is terrorizing my

family. Let's get this solved once and for all," Mac said firmly.

"You're right, Mac," he said and looked at us. "Back in the seventeenth century, there was an Irishwoman who captained a small group of pirate ships."

"Grace O'Malley," Mac and I said at the same time and looked at each other.

"Yes," Peter said and continued. "According to history, she plundered this Spanish ship and scuttled it against the Irish coast, on the Atlantic—that was her base of operations, if you will.

"According to the text, whatever was aboard was taken and hidden, but not by Grace, someone else took it. It had to be someone on Grace's ship or another Irish captain. Before it could be retrieved, they died and the whereabouts went with them.

"Grace O'Malley was imprisoned by the English. For how long, we don't know. Then she was given amnesty by Queen Elizabeth, probably because she respected Grace and admired her for being a woman in control of a man's world. As you can imagine, this was unheard of. In any event, she lived to a very old age, married several times, and had many children. She died never knowing who took it or where it was hidden."

"Who took what? What is 'it' Peter?" I asked.

"According to all the text, Phillip of Spain was returning a small trunk full of jewels that he plundered from one of Queen Elizabeth's ships. As a show of good faith and not wantin' a war, he threw in etchings by one of the Spanish artists not well known at the time—his name was El Greco."

We all sat there staring at him. I voiced what I believed we all were thinking, "You mean to tell me there's a sixteenth-century masterpiece buried somewhere on this property?" *Was my voice squeaking?*

"Along with a small trunk of jewels," Charlie added with a great deal of skepticism and no squeak.

"I know it sounds fantastic, that's why we were hesitant to tell ya," Bridget said and looked to Peter.

He adjusted his glasses and continued. "Believe me, it's true. That's why that big company is lookin' to buy the mill. They believe it's here, too. Although, I'm not sure they know about the cavern. Yet," he added.

"Should this be true and you find this treasure, what value are

191

we talking here?" Charlie asked, still very skeptical.

Peter scratched his head. "It's not the monetary value I'm after."

"It's the monetary value *someone* is after, now how much? Give it your best guess," I said, still trying to wrap my mind around this.

"We have no idea about the jewels, the text is very vague," Peter said. He took a deep breath and continued, "No one knows exactly what's in the trunk. We researched the British Naval records, and some records actually show the names of the ships, the dates they sailed, and their cargo. We know the paintings, or etchings, were on board this Spanish ship and most records show that the trunk was, as well. However, as I said, we don't know what's in the trunk."

"If anything," I added.

Peter looked at me and was about to disagree but said, "I will be honest with all of ya, there could be nothing of any great monetary value. However, if there is some sort of artwork, and we are sure there is, it's priceless." He looked at all of us. "How do you put a price on a Raphael or Van Gogh? If I had to guess, millions. I'm no expert, but Professor Carroll had a friend who was, and that was his guess." He rubbed his neck. "So ya see why we need to find it before Russell's people do."

"How did Brian fit into all this?" I asked, still not convinced.

Peter smiled. "I came here a year or so ago and became fast friends with him. He knew I was no horse trainer, as did you, Kate. He confronted me and I told him. Bridget advised against it, but I knew he would understand and he did. He met with Professor Carroll on several occasions, and they talked about the possibilities of what a find like this would mean for the museum and for Ireland's place in this world. They became good friends, and we all decided to keep it to ourselves.

"I would pose as his employee so I could stay here and investigate. Six months ago, we had a breakthrough. I found the cavern. I was so close. Then Professor Carroll had a heart attack and died. The funding stopped. Who could blame them? It took us five years just to find the right area. Now I'm on my own. Well, it was me, Bridget, and Russell." He sighed and looked at Bridget.

Bridget continued, "Russell and I were married my last year at

Trinity Law. That's when we all took Professor Carroll's class. We were completely intrigued. At first, he told only Peter, but then they decided the more help they had, the quicker it might go. So Russell and I were told. It was a glorious time, we felt like we were doing somethin' for our country. Then as we got closer, Russell started talking about finding the treasure and selling it.

"That was last year. By then, our marriage had been annulled. It was a foolish young thing I did." She sighed and continued. "Needless to say, there was a tremendous fallin' out and Russell left. We never saw him again until that big company came and offered Brian the money. That's when we realized he told them and was in it for the money. He's been dodgin' us and harassing you ever since. I don't believe he killed Brian, though. I really don't," she said as if trying to convince herself, as well as us.

This whole time, I realized Tim Devereaux was listening but said nothing. It struck me as odd that he didn't think this was too fantastic. Well, I thought, the Irish and their pot o' gold, I guess they've heard a great many stories about buried treasures.

Although, now he said, "Well, young lady, someone killed Brian. Who else do ya think it could be?"

"How about James, for one?" Peter sat on the edge of his chair. "He stands to get something and so do you, Tim."

Tim took a step toward him and Peter stood up. Mac pushed Peter back down in his chair and Charlie put an arm on Tim. "Easy, fellas," Mac said.

This was too fantastic, but my gut told me too fantastic *not* to be true. "Okay, let's try this scenario. Say all this is true. Brian knows about it and allows Peter to try and find this treasure, for lack of a better word, but then he changes his will. Why? Why not leave it to the villagers instead of giving it to Mac? Why give it to someone he barely knows? Why not leave it to the museum or to Peter?" I looked at Tim. "Did Brian confide in you at all about leaving everything to Mac?"

"No, he never mentioned a word to me," Tim said.

I looked at Peter and Bridget. "Did he mention it to either one of you?"

Peter shook his head. "Definitely not. I had no idea until the day before he died. He handed me a ticket and told me to fetch Mac. That was all he would tell me. He thought I'd be 'better off not knowing.' Those were his exact words. That was the last time I saw him alive. I didn't come and fetch you till after the funeral," he said tiredly.

Bridget spoke. "Bein' his lawyer, yes, I knew. The lawyer-client privileges bound me. I told no one, not even Peter."

I believed her, then got a sick feeling in the pit of my stomach. Instantly, I started sweating. I thought of Liz and how I believed her, and the memory once again flooded my senses. As I tried to control a wave of anxiety, I knew I had to get into the fresh air.

Maggie must have seen it. She gave me a worried look. My ears were ringing as I wiped my forehead. *God, not again.* "I'll be right back," I said quickly and excused myself in a controlled panic.

I left the library and went out the front door. I stood there not knowing in which direction to go. My breathing was shallow and the ringing was still in my ears. I put my hand to my forehead—I was perspiring profusely. I ran my forearm over my face. I wanted to break into a dead run. *Great, this thing has finally made me nuts.*

I walked quickly down the path and I heard Maggie's voice calling me. Christ, I don't want her to see me falling apart. I turned and smiled as casually as I could.

"Hey, I'm f-fine. I'll be right in," I said, shivering.

She ran up to me and put her hand on my shoulder. "Here's your sweater, it's a bit chilly."

I took it from her and sat on the stone wall. She sat next to me and put her hand out. I quickly got up. "I'm fine, I needed some air," I said. My voice shook horribly. I took several deep breaths, the ringing in my ears stopped and my breathing returned to normal, although I was perspiring as if I had run a race.

"Kate, sit down," Maggie ordered. I sat a couple of feet away from her. "Another one?" she asked.

"Yep, I'm nuts," I said and sat there taking a deep breath.

"Better?"

I took another deep breath, feeling normal again and stood up, shivering.

"Put on your sweater," Maggie ordered and held it for me as I slipped into it. She ran her hands up and down my back. "Okay, get back in there," she whispered in my ear and gave my shoulders a confident shake.

Mac and Teri looked at me when I came into the library. "I needed some air."

Peter and Bridget looked worse than I felt.

"I think that's enough for the time being," Maggie said as Peter stood on shaky legs. Bridget went over and steadied him.

"Why don't you take him upstairs?" Maggie said. "Peter, you need to rest for the remainder of the day."

He nodded with a weak smile. He and Bridget walked out of the library.

"Buried treasure? Sixteenth-century masterpiece? Piracy on the high seas?" I said, shaking my head. "They've got to be kidding."

Mac nodded. "What about Kate getting tossed around in Donegal?"

"And someone trying to set the cottage on fire," Maggie reminded all of us.

"And a murder," I said absently, staring out into the late afternoon fog.

Chapter 23

The remainder of the afternoon was quiet and somber; the weather didn't help. When the dense fog lifted, the wind and rain started. I had hopes of going down to the cavern again, but that wasn't going to happen.

Mac and Teri were sitting on the couch talking. Maggie was sitting by the fire reading. Charlie was losing big money to Tim at the card table. Tim won yet another hand and picked up the pencil. "Well now, let's see, that makes it two pounds ten."

Charlie sat there with his chin resting on his hand. "I believe Ireland's currency is the euro."

Tim laughed and thought for a minute. "Pardon me, the euro. Well then, that's roughly, four euros. Double or nothin'?" he asked with a sly grin.

"Deal," Charlie said.

I watched Tim Devereaux. I knew very little about him. He was an in-law who inherited his share of the mill from his late wife, Colleen McAuliffe, Brian's sister. He was a Merchant Marine all his life, sailing around the world. Exciting stuff, I thought.

I thought of his brother-in-law, James; what a grump he must be. I wondered how far he might go to stop Brian. Strange we haven't seen him since his rude visit a couple of days before. I remember Tim had said they were together the night Brian was killed. Family might say anything to protect each other, especially a loyal Irishman. I lazily paced behind the couch, playing with that blasted key in my pocket.

There was a knock at the door. It was Sean Farrell. "Good afternoon, Kate."

"Hi, Sean, c'mon in." I stepped back and he came into the foyer and wiped his shoes.

"Can I ask a favor? Our phone's been out for a few days. Can

I make a call to my brother? He's expectin' one, and if I don't call him, there'll be hell to pay."

I laughed quietly. "Sure, down the hall."

He stopped and looked in the library and said, "Good afternoon, all." Tim and Charlie were so intent on their gin rummy game he was never noticed. Mac and Teri talked with him for a while.

After he made his call, Mac walked him to the door. "Thank you again for a grand dinner. Next time, it'll be at our house," Sean said.

"Nice old guy," Mac said as he closed the door. He put his arm around Teri. "How 'bout a nap, Lady McAuliffe?" He smiled wickedly and raised one eyebrow.

Teri matched his smile and sighed. "A nap sounds fine, my lord."

I groaned openly. "Oh, grow up, you two."

"It's time you started napping again, Kate. It wouldn't hurt," Teri said and looked at Maggie.

From the corner, Tim said, "Well, young man, I can't take your money any longer." He got up and stretched. "Think I'll go to my room."

As he walked by, a thought stuck me, and I turned to him. "Tim, have you called James at all? He must be angry that you're staying here."

Tim stopped and said, "He was at first, Kate. He'll get over it. I called him from Sean's. He's a gruff one, but he'll come around."

I watched him for a moment. "Good, I hope he can stop by sometime. It would be good for him and Mac."

He nodded. "Indeed it would." He continued up the stairs and into his room.

"This is a lazy afternoon," Charlie announced. "Guess I'll go to my room, as well. Don't forget to send the maid when dinner's ready."

Maggie was sitting alone on the couch, staring at the fire. I walked over and flopped down next to her. "This has been an interesting day," I said, staring at the fire.

"Where'd everybody go?" Maggie asked.

"Mac and Teri are taking a nap," I said and rolled my eyes.

Maggie blushed and laughed. "What's wrong with napping? You're not averse to it, are you? Or are you?" she asked and smiled sweetly.

"N-No, I'm not averse to it. I like napping as much as the next person," I said. Suddenly the room got very warm.

"Am I interrupting?" I turned to see Bridget standing in the doorway. "I'm sorry, were you busy?"

"No, no. Is everything all right? How's Peter?" I asked, grateful to change from the topic of napping. I noticed Maggie abruptly walk over to the fireplace.

"He's out like a light again. I thought I'd go back to Donegal. Peter wanted me to pick up his work. He wanted to show you all tonight. If you wouldn't mind, can I borrow your car? I shouldn't be more than an hour or so."

"You shouldn't go alone. I'll drive you," I offered.

"I don't want to be a bother," she said and glanced at Maggie.

"It's no bother," I said.

"If ya don't mind. I'll just be a moment," she said and went upstairs.

I noticed Maggie had left the library and was on the phone when I heard her getting flight information from the airport. I was surprised. She hung up and started for the stairs. I walked up behind her and grabbed her arm.

"Are you leaving?" I asked.

"Eventually, yes. I have to get back to the clinic," she said.

"But you can't leave with all this going on. Surely you can stay for another few days," I said and let go of her arm.

"I was only going to stay the weekend, remember?" she reminded.

"I know. I just thought you'd—"

"I'd what?" she challenged, sounding completely exasperated.

"I don't know. I guess I'd thought you'd stay until this was over. What about Peter? H-He needs you," I said. "You can't run off like this and leave him."

Maggie looked me right in the eye, which unnerved me to no end. "I don't know that Peter needs me. It seems he has Bridget." She turned away.

I hate talking in code. First napping—now this. I ignored my inner voice, reminding me that I started the covert code. "Maggie,

I don't need—"

Bridget interrupted Maggie as she walked down the stairs. "Ready?" she smiled.

Maggie continued to her room. Bridget grabbed my arm and whisked me out the front door.

Peter had an enormous amount of…stuff—boxes and boxes of it. Bridget and I loaded it into the trunk and backseat. "Good grief. This is a lot of junk."

"Junk, are ya crazy? This is four years of hard work, Kate. Junk, indeed," she snorted and walked by.

I followed her out to the car, my arms full of hard work.

Bridget turned and smiled. "I'm sorry. My temper again is short. Forgive me?"

"Sure, I understand. It's getting pretty tense for everybody."

"It's no excuse for my being rude." She took the box from me and loaded it in the car.

On the drive back, I could feel her looking at me. "So can I ask ya a personal question, Kate?"

No! "That depends."

Bridget didn't even hesitate. She came right out with it. "Are you and Maggie involved? I only ask because Maggie and I had a wee bit of a discussion this morning about ya. She doesn't want to see ya hurt again. She told me she has no claim on ya. I wanted to make sure she was right."

No claim, huh? "Maggie and I are very good friends. I'm not in the market for a relationship right now."

"I see." She gave me a wicked smile. "What are ya in the market for?"

"Solving Brian's murder and making sure nothing happens to my family," I said honestly.

Bridget handed me a box. "When you're in the market, let me know," she whispered and leaned in and kissed me again. It had more oomph than the other did. I was stunned and I stood there like a dope with my hands full. She laughed and continued unloading the boxes.

Charlie came out to help. He carried in a huge box, as did Bridget, and set them on the dining room table.

"Good heavens," he said, scratching the back of his head, and turned around to see Bridget come in with another box.

"Is this all of it?" he asked, looking at the boxes, not wanting to touch anything; some of the books looked quite old.

"Yes, that's it. How's Peter?" she asked, taking off her coat.

Charlie took it from her. "I'm sure he's still sleeping."

Bridget turned and walked out of the dining room and bumped into Maggie.

"Back so soon?" Maggie said affably, though I heard the sarcasm. "Go on up, he's asleep."

Bridget said nothing and went upstairs. Maggie walked into the kitchen.

"Boy, there sure is a lot of stuff here," I said and picked up one book. It was printed in 1892—I quickly put it down. "Geez, don't touch anything till Peter gets up."

Charlie agreed as we stared at the boxes. I absently looked at the pictures. "Maggie, um, says she's leaving soon."

"I know, she advised me of the same, quite angrily, I might add," he said frankly. "Now why would she be angry?"

"Because she's a stubborn—"

Charlie raised his hand. "Don't even go there. I've lived with that woman all my life. It's your turn." He pulled me up by the back of my shirt and pushed me toward the door. "Go, play nice," he said and shoved me through the swinging door.

Maggie had her head in the refrigerator and looked up as I made my entrance.

"Are you that hungry?" I asked. Come to think of it, I was starving. "What are you going to make?"

She gave me an incredulous look. "Good grief, you know I don't cook. I was hoping you would." She picked up an apple and bit into it.

"Woman, how do you survive without cooking?" I pushed her out of the way.

"Ordering out, fast food, hospital food," she said and sat down. "I suppose the only time I eat right is when you cook for me."

"Then I should cook for you all the time," I said without thinking and stopped dead in my tracks. "How can you eat like that and maintain that figure? What's your secret?" I pulled out the cheese and a bottle of wine.

"You've noticed my figure?" she asked frankly.

"Get some glasses."

I uncorked the wine and Charlie poked his head in. "Did I hear a cork pop?"

"Yep. A little something to take the edge off our appetites."

I arranged a plate of apples, pears, and cheese. Charlie took the wine, Maggie got the glasses, and we sat at the dining room table enjoying our feast. One by one, they came down and soon we were all sitting staring at the boxes at the other end. We said nothing until Peter finally broke the silence. "Well, this is it. Six years of work," he pulled out text after text, map after map. All pointed to Mac's property. It was unbelievable. He even had photos taken from a plane.

"This looks like something out of a World War II reconnaissance photo," I said, looking at the topography photo.

"That's exactly what it is. Professor Carroll got it from a friend of his at the War Department in Washington. They did a lot of that back then, took photos of everything. It took Professor Carroll two years to find that," he said proudly.

I looked at the photo and saw a circled area. "This is us?" I pointed to the circle.

"That's us," Bridget said. "The ship was reported sunk a little farther south of here, by County Clare."

Tim looked at the photo. "The Atlantic is a rough ocean. Many a ship has been tossed and scuttled along these shores," he said. "I've heard stories of all kinds."

I remembered he was a sailor. He must have heard some fantastic stories in his time and probably lived through quite a few, as well. "You've never heard of this before in your voyages, Tim?" I asked curiously. Our eyes met, and I felt the same thing as I did with Peter—something was not right here.

He seemed to look right through me; his gaze was intense for some reason. "No, Kate, nothing like this."

I shivered and Maggie glanced at me. I was spooked and I couldn't say why. I rubbed the back of my aching neck.

"You certainly have an enormous amount of data," Teri said and looked around the table. "And I'm sure all of you have an enormous appetite."

After dinner, Peter announced his plan. "Tomorrow, I'm going back to the cave. I'm too close to stop now, it has to be there," he said and looked at Mac.

"Tomorrow, we end this," Mac said. "If what you say is right and this treasure is in that cave, the quicker we find it the better."

I rested my head against the back of the chair and closed my eyes. "We still have a small problem of a murder. Somebody killed Brian. He did not stumble and fall off that cliff. I think we all agree on that. I'm afraid the logical suspect is Russell. Have you seen him lately?" I asked. "Peter, do you think Russell knocked you out?"

He paused for a moment, then took off his glasses and rubbed his eyes; he looked beat. "I don't know," he said.

"Whoever it was wanted you dead, Peter," I reminded him. "If we hadn't decided to go down there, the tide would have come in and you'd have drowned. You were already underwater." I looked at him and he shifted uncomfortably in his chair.

"Peter, does Russell know where the cavern is?" I asked.

He shook his head. "No. I don't think so. I've been careful," he started and stopped. "But honestly, I don't know anything anymore."

"When we were at the pub, the older gentleman, Patrick, knew you were playing by the cliffs. I have a feeling he may have mentioned it. Word tends to spread around this village like wildfire," I said.

"I think the police should be told about Russell," Teri said evenly. "He's got to be stopped."

"We don't know it's him," I said. "It would be our word against his. I know he has a record, but that's not evidence to hold him or even to talk to him. He's a very clever guy. I would love to know where he's staying. He checked out of the inn." I gave Bridget and Peter a questioning look.

"Honestly, I have no idea. I saw him early this morning," Bridget said.

Peter agreed. "I haven't seen him in a day or two."

I watched them both. "What happened to Russell? You said before this, he was good and kind. How can someone change that much?"

Bridget stared at the fire. "I met him my third year at Trinity. I was young and didn't know myself or anything else. Russell was outgoing, strong, and independent. A lot like yourself, Kate. I was wildly attracted to that and I thought I was in love. We married quickly. It wasn't until we had a breakthrough and knew exactly where the treasures were that Russell became greedy. He expressed his opinion about finding it and selling it. We were appalled and Professor Carroll told him to leave. We argued and we didn't see him for months." She sighed and sat back.

Peter put his hand on her shoulder as he spoke to us. "Russell is a headstrong fella and he has quite a temper. We were worried for a time, but when we didn't see him for all those months, we figured he went back to Dublin. He didn't show up until after that company visited Brian for the first time."

I looked at Bridget. "So you lied to me at Clew Bay. You knew all along about the company and that the car from Dublin was Russell's."

She hung her head for a moment and looked up at me. "Yes, I lied, and I would again, given the circumstances. I didn't know you or your family. We were not at all sure you wouldn't sell out to Omega. We've done far too much work to be stopped. This is bigger than a lie to ya, Kate. This is a historical find of unbelievable proportion. Peter and I feel passionately about this. We've spent six years of our lives on it. Professor Carroll spent nearly forty and his professor before him, as well. So, yes, I lied to ya," she said and looked right at me.

Well, she's an honest liar anyway.

Chapter 24

Honest liar or not, I was getting very impatient. "Well, somebody killed Brian. Somebody tossed his body over that cliff." I got up and paced. "The murderer had to know Brian was changing his will. Why else would someone want him dead?" I asked absently, almost to myself. I put my hands in my pockets and once again felt that bothersome key. "Bridget, you're sure no one else knew about the will?"

"No one. Brian was adamant about that. He said no one would ever know till the time came, when he died."

"When did he have it changed?" Mac asked.

"Six months ago," she answered.

"Before that, what was his will?" I asked.

"I'm not quite sure. I have a copy of it in my office. I'll check tomorrow," she offered in a hesitant voice.

"Okay, enough for one night," Maggie ordered. She walked over to Peter and felt his forehead. "Off to bed."

Peter got up and smiled. "Yes, ma'am."

"Bridget, I apologize, but we're short one room," Teri said.

Tim, whom I had forgotten was even there, said, "I was going to tell ya, Sean and Mary asked me to spend some time with them. I told 'em I'd spend the night. So Bridget can have my room if ya like."

"Well, that's settled," Teri said as Tim put on his coat.

"I'll be goin', but I'd like to go to the cave with you if you go. I'll come by about eight in the morning."

Teri got Peter and Bridget settled back in their rooms and came downstairs.

"This is too bizarre. Buried treasure, murder," Mac groaned helplessly and looked at me.

"Am I the only one, or is it odd that Tim is staying all this time? Now he's staying at the Farrells." I shrugged.

We sat for a while not saying much. Teri had her head on Mac's shoulder, he had his head against the back of the couch, sleeping. Maggie was already asleep in one of the chairs by the fire. Charlie was fading in the other. I looked over at Teri and whispered, "What the hell is going on?"

She shook her head. "I don't know. We need to figure this out fast."

I shrugged and Maggie stirred and sighed. Teri looked up at Mac. He was still asleep.

"How can they sleep through this?" she whispered, chuckling, and we laughed quietly.

Teri looked over at Maggie. "How did she react when you told her about Liz Eddington?"

I heard the name, and my stomach clenched, as it usually does. Perhaps it always will. I gazed at Maggie while she slept and smiled. *Perhaps not.* "Like I should have known—kind and sympathetic, understanding laced with logic. She's a good friend to me, and I don't have anyone like that."

"It was nice of both of them to come all this way," Teri said softly. "Charlie has helped so much."

I looked over at Charlie; he too was fast asleep. "He's a good guy. Look at them, they look like bookends." I got up and put the ottoman under Charlie's feet and did the same for Maggie. She stirred and woke.

"I'm sorry. Go back to sleep."

She sighed and smiled. "Are you okay?" she whispered and closed her eyes.

I looked down at her and watched her for a moment. I reached over and smoothed her hair back. "I'm not sure," I whispered almost to myself. I bent down and lightly kissed her forehead. I grabbed the afghan off the back of the couch and covered her.

"Someone went through the cottage, looking for something. What?" I asked Teri as I settled back on the couch. I pulled the small key out of my pocket and looked at it. "It fits something. I know it does. I have a feeling this is important."

She took it from me and whispered, "It doesn't look like a regular key." She handed it back to me.

I looked at it and remembered something. "Maggie was saying

something about the key, but we got distracted." I looked over at Maggie. "I hate to wake her again."

"It's okay, I'm awake," she answered and lazily opened her eyes.

I walked over and knelt by her chair. "Remember when you looked at this key and started to say something, what was it?"

She nodded and said dreamily, "It looks like a key to wind up something. I had a music box when I was a girl."

"Wind up something?" I asked and looked at the key. I couldn't think anymore.

"Let's go to bed. It's late," Teri said firmly, stood, and woke up Mac. Maggie and Charlie followed like zombies.

"I'll be up in a little while," I said absently, looking at the key.

Teri patted my shoulder as she yawned. "Good night, you bloodhound."

I sat there staring at the key. "Wind up something," I whispered.

The next morning, I looked out at the fog, which was getting annoying. The little key sat there on the table challenging me. Maggie said it looked like a key to a music box. I decided to take a walk. It always helps me to think. Putting the key in my pocket, I headed out.

As I walked down the path, I thought about Brian and how he died. What a horrible way to go, being tossed over a cliff. My mind went to Russell. He must have been promised a pretty penny from someone. If The Omega Group was behind this, it was well hidden. As I walked farther, the cottage came into view.

Entering the cottage, I looked around. "What was someone looking for?"

I looked around the room again and walked into the kitchen, then the bedrooms. Nothing was out of place, so whoever was here was satisfied that what they were looking for was not in the cottage. I sat at the table and looked around and thought of Tim Devereaux. He seemed at first a very nice man, coming to dinner on Friday, despite James's disapproval. He believed Brian was murdered and seemed certain it might be Russell. That wasn't so far off. I had the same thought myself.

Tim bothered me now and I didn't know why. I looked around

the room again. God, something was here, I could I feel it.

I looked around the cottage. My mind wandered. A little paint here and there would spruce it up, and a phone would be nice... *A phone.*

"The phone!" I looked to the heavens. "That's it."

Tim said he called James from Sean and Mary Farrell's house. However, Sean came to use our phone, saying his was out for several days. I stood and paced. Why would Tim lie? Why lie?

I sat back down and took the key from my pocket. I thought of Maggie and her mentioning a music box. Now with the Tim train derailed for the moment, I hunted in each room of the cottage. No music boxes—nothing that even resembled one.

"Okay, Ryan, think." I looked around the small living room. Maggie had also mentioned it looked like a key to wind something up. Okay, I thought, what do you wind up? A music box—none. A wind-up toy—that's dumb. A watch—too small.

Then it dawned on me. A watch...my heart raced as I thought I might be right. I looked across the room at the grandfather clock. I walked up to it with high expectations. As I examined it, I noticed the clock wasn't working; the pendulum was still. I knelt down and saw the small keyhole in the glass door. With a deep confident breath and a shaky hand, I put the small key in and turned it. The door instantly popped open. I pulled it opened and saw the pendulum and the chimes, but nothing else, and my heart sank.

I immediately thought of that movie. "Hell, what's the name of that movie?" I closed my eyes and tapped my forehead. *Think, Ryan, think. What's the actress's name? Gene Tierney—the grandfather clock.*

"*Laura,*" I exclaimed. "God, this has to be it!"

With a deep grunt, I pulled the clock away from the wall; it was heavy, but I managed to get behind it. There it was—another keyhole.

I slipped the key in, turned it, and a small trap door opened in the front of the clock at the bottom. "I'll be damned," I whispered.

There were papers lying in there. I looked around making sure I was alone and took the papers. There was one letter, well, scribbling actually.

I assumed it was Brian's writing. He talked about Peter,

Bridget, Russell, and Professor Carroll. As I read, I realized what Bridget and Peter had said was true. Brian totally supported them and their quest for the treasure. He knew it would take only a few more visits to the cave and the treasure would be found. He figured it was right under the mill.

He wrote how he couldn't wait to see Mac and his family. Couldn't wait to find the treasures so he and Peter could hand it over to the museum and put Ireland on center stage.

As I looked at the letter, I was excited at the thought of all of this being true. I looked at the other papers that were in the clock. I opened an envelope and was once again shocked. It was a contract, the same contract that The Omega Group had given Mac. It offered a million euros to sign over the shares of the Oceanview Woolen Mill.

A million? They offered Mac four million. I looked at the bottom of the contract. It was signed by Timothy Michael Francis Devereaux. All the copies were intact. It looked as though they were never forwarded to The Omega Group. My eyes widened as I stared at the signature. It was dated one month before Brian was murdered. I sat back and whistled. "What in the hell is going on?" *How did Brian get this?*

My mind raced as I looked at my watch, it was seven thirty. Tim would be at the house at eight. I scrambled and put the contract and the letter back in the trap door, closed it, and pushed the clock back to the exact spot.

My instincts took over—I looked at the floor, making sure there were no marks. No one could see that the clock had been moved. I made sure the key was safely in my pocket. I pushed the chair back and looked around the room, confident everything was intact.

I ran all the way back to the house. Mac, Teri, and Maggie were in the kitchen. "I was at the cottage," I started and looked at my watch—almost eight. "Look, I don't have time. Maggie, go tell Peter and Bridget to stay in their rooms and not to come down till we get them."

She gave me a curious look, but without a word, she ran from the kitchen.

I looked at Mac and Teri's startled faces. "Tim will be here any minute. We *cannot* go to the cave today with him."

With that, we heard a knock at the front door. "Please, trust me, you guys," I said when I saw the confused looks.

Maggie came into the kitchen and stood next to me. "There's someone at the door."

"It's Tim. Trust me and follow my lead. I don't have time to explain," I said.

Mac went to answer the door. It was indeed Tim. He looked a little tired but smiled affably when he saw us.

"Good mornin'," he said.

"Good morning, Tim," Maggie said. "How 'bout some coffee?"

Teri set the coffeepot on the table. Tim smiled his thanks. "It's foggy, but I expect you'll go down to the cavern," he said simply, stirring his coffee.

"I don't think so," I started and took a drink of my coffee. "Peter had a bad night. I don't think he'll be doing any climbing this morning. We might wait till tomorrow," I said and looked at Maggie.

"Kate's right. Peter has a fever. I don't want him climbing all over today. It's best he stay in bed. The cave will be there tomorrow," she said.

"That's too bad, but tomorrow is another day," Tim offered and finished his coffee. "If ya don't mind, I think I might go back to Sean and Mary's for the day. I suspect I'll be goin' home soon." He looked me in the eyes and my blood ran cold. "I hope you find out who killed Brian. I'd like to be there when ya do."

"I hope so, too," I said evenly. "I think I'm closer."

"I say we go shopping. We haven't done much, with all this happening. It'll take our minds off of this for a little while, anyway," Teri offered.

Tim looked around the table. "I think I'll be headin' to Sean's, thanks for the coffee. I'll see ya later." Mac walked him to the door.

As soon as he left the kitchen, I let out an enormous sigh and put my head down with a heavy thud.

Mac came back into the kitchen and sat down. "Okay, Sherlock, give."

I told them about the clock, Brian's letter, and finally the contract. They all sat there mesmerized. "It doesn't mean Tim

210

killed Brian, but it certainly is a motive. I need to see if Bridget has the original will. That might prove interesting."

"So Peter was right all along," Mac said. "We better go get them." He got up and walked out of the kitchen.

Soon after, Peter came in with Bridget and Charlie, and we all sat around the kitchen table. When I told them what I had read in the letter, Peter and Bridget were encouraged by the fact that Brian was so positive about the treasure. So much so, they started planning their next trip to the cave.

"Why don't we go down there today?" Peter offered.

I heard the enthusiasm in his voice. As we watched Peter and Bridget, I could feel the excitement in the air, trying to understand the magnitude of what was about to happen.

However, it was about to get much worse before it got any better.

Chapter 25

As we helped Peter prepare for the trek to the cave, Constable Reardon phoned. The news was disturbing to say the least. "Miss Ryan, I know you and Bridget were asking about that Dublin car," he started. I listened with a feeling of doom. "I have some bad news. We found a body in the car this morning with no identification. I thought perhaps you or Bridget might recognize the gentleman."

I stood there and looked at Bridget and Peter. "We'll be right down," I assured him.

Maggie came to my side as I set the phone down. "What is it?"

"We need to go to the police station. It appears they found the Dublin car, with a man's body in it. He thinks we might be able to identify him."

Bridget froze and Peter turned white. Mac and Teri offered to stay back along with Charlie. Without saying another word, I grabbed the keys, and Maggie, Bridget, and Peter followed me out the door. It was a quiet drive to Duncorrib.

It was indeed Russell Devine. "Apparently, someone struck him over the head and killed him," Constable Reardon said. He took off his cap and ran his hand across his face. Bridget and Peter were horrified—I was dying to see the body.

Maggie must have read my mind; she said, "I'm Dr. Winfield, Mr. Devine's physician. Would you mind if I had a look at the body? I'll need to make a positive identification."

Constable Reardon hesitated. "No, I don't see why not. The doctor has finished. We'll wait outside."

They turned to leave; I stayed behind. Maggie pulled at my sleeve to join her. Maggie looked around and after locating them, she snapped on a pair of surgical gloves. "You're not squeamish about this, are you?" she asked quickly.

I looked down at Russell's body covered with a sheet. "N-Not usually. Why, what are you going to do?" I asked, not entirely sure I wanted to know. I saw an odd gleam in her eye.

"I'm no forensic expert, but maybe I can find something. You never know," she said.

I stood back as she examined the body as much as she could. She picked up his hand and examined his fingers. Then she took a closer look. "Kate, look." She showed me his fingernails. They were broken and the tips of his fingers had been bleeding. "What do you make of that?" she asked and looked the door.

"Check his other hand," I said quickly. It looked the same. "It looks like he was clawing at something."

"Like rocks—" Maggie said.

"The cliffs," I said in agreement. "I wonder if Constable Reardon will let us take a look at the car."

"One way to find out," she replied and snapped off the rubber gloves and tossed them into the nearest wastebasket.

Bridget and Peter were answering questions with Constable Reardon. When he had finished, he came over to me. "I take it you didn't know him. He was a friend of Bridget and Peter's," he said professionally.

"That's correct," I said. "May I see the car?"

He nodded. "It's in back. I'll take you."

Maggie and I examined the interior of the car under the watchful eye of the constable. "Just as I suspected, not much blood on the seat or headrest," I said.

"What does that mean?" Maggie asked.

"It means he was hit somewhere else," Constable Reardon offered and looked at me.

I agreed. "And either he made it back to his car and died or someone killed him and put him in his car."

I could feel Constable Reardon watching me. "What are ya thinkin'?" he asked. "Peter told me of your exploits, Miss Ryan. If you have any idea what happened, let me in on it."

"What was he wearing?" I asked.

"Nothing out of the ordinary—trousers, sweater, boots. Although, his clothes were damp," he said. "We've got them bagged for the Donegal police. We're kinda small here, not used to murder."

We walked back in and I opened one of the bags, careful not to touch the contents. As I peered in, I instantly smelled seawater. Maggie sniffed and I knew she thought the same. I gingerly closed the bag. I itched to examine them closer but realized I would contaminate any evidence they might contain.

"Okay, this is now two murders," I said.

"Hold on there. Two?" the constable asked. "Ya still think Brian was murdered?"

"Yes, and I think Russell Devine was part of it, as is Tim Devereaux. But I have no proof." I explained what I had found in the clock.

Constable Reardon was amazed. "I'll need to talk with Tim Devereaux."

"In the meantime, I'll go back and get the contract. I'll give it to you and you take it from there," I said and looked at Maggie. "Why don't you all stay put? He's over at Sean's, so at least we know where he is."

Constable Reardon gave me a curious look. "Sean Farrell isn't at home. He and Mary left yesterday afternoon. They went to his brother's, said he called from your house and they decided to drive there. I saw them on their way out of town."

Maggie gave me a worried look. "Kate, that means Tim is…"

"A liar and God knows what else," I interrupted her. "You all stay put. I'm going back for the contract."

Maggie reached for me and grabbed my arm. "Not alone, I'm going with you."

I shook my head. "No, please stay here."

"No," she insisted. "You're not going alone."

"Maggie, don't argue with me," I said.

We all went.

They stood behind me in amazement as I opened the clock. "Pretty clever, huh?" I asked as I presented the documents.

Bridget and Peter looked stunned. Constable Reardon took the documents and shook his head. "Unbelievable."

I glanced at Maggie who smiled. "Yes, you are."

I gave a shrug. "Laura."

Maggie frowned deeply and put her hand on her hips. "Who is

Laura?"

"A movie. When I couldn't find where this key belonged, I looked at the grandfather clock and remembered the movie. See, Clifton Webb was secretly in love with Gene Tierney—Laura—who doesn't feel the same. He kills a woman in her apartment, thinking it was Laura, and hides the shotgun in the clock, then waits for a time to come back and get rid of the evidence. It's a great film noir movie. Nineteen forty-four, I think. Dana Andrews is the cop who—"

Maggie placed her hand on my arm. "Thanks, we'll wait for your review," she said dryly.

"Now what?" Bridget asked as she sat at the small table.

Peter sat opposite her. "It's early still. I'd like to get back down to the cave. It's really there."

"It looks like it," I said. "Whatever it is."

"I'm not sure it's wise for you to be going down there with Tim Devereaux on the loose," Constable Reardon said. "But I can't stop ya. Duncorrib is a small town. He'll show up."

As he walked out, Peter stood. "I'm going down there. Anyone what to join me?" he asked and I saw the gleam of excitement in his eyes.

"I'm in," I said wholeheartedly.

"And me," Bridget concurred and stole a glance at Maggie.

Only I saw the left eye twitch. She looked at me. "I have a feeling you're going to need a doctor."

Peter gave me a curious look. "Are ya sick, Kate?" he asked as he leaned into me.

I glared at him. "Can we just go?"

Charlie, Mac, and Teri agreed to stay at the house and wait for us. The four of us drove to the cliffs and unloaded our gear. Peter had suggested we take a shovel and a pickax along with the backpack that contained the flashlights. Tying them to a heavy rope we found in the cellar, we lowered everything down the cliffs to the rugged shore below. We then made the trek to the cave with no problem. The midday sun was warm enough and the waves were not crashing against the rocks so violently, as before.

Peter turned on his flashlight, and in cold ankle-deep water, we trudged through the opening of the cave and followed the same direction.

With Peter in the lead, Bridget followed with Maggie and I taking up the rear; this was their treasure hunt, after all.

At one point, Maggie stumbled and I grabbed for her arm. "Easy," I said and held onto her. "Wouldn't want anything to happen to the *doctor*." I laughed quietly at my sarcasm.

"You're such a child," Maggie whispered and pulled her arm away.

"This is the end," Peter called out ahead of us.

We stopped and looked around the eerily illuminated cavern. "This has to be it," Peter said. "There are no other entrances and nowhere else it could be."

I stood next to Peter at the smaller entrance. "None of us can fit through that small opening," I said and felt Maggie's presence right behind me.

"I can," she said and walked ahead of us. Peter followed.

"Maggie—" I started and stopped when I got the look of certain death. She looked scary in the high beam of the flashlight.

"Okay, let's try this," Peter said and handed his flashlight to Bridget.

"Peter, can she fit through there?" she asked.

"With a little grease…" I said with a laugh and cleared my throat.

The entrance was extremely narrow, not looking like an entrance at all, but the rush of air that blew through it had my curiosity on alert. "It has to lead somewhere," I said.

"Let me try and find it." Maggie took a deep breath.

Now Maggie is a small woman; I had my doubts but kept them to myself. I didn't want to play dodge the hurled flashlight. With Bridget behind us, Peter and I watched as Maggie tried to wedge her small body through the narrow opening. It was a tight fit, but God love her, she squeezed through.

Peter and I quickly stood at the narrow entrance and peered through the darkness. "I'm gonna slip a flashlight through, sweetie," I called out.

"Okay, hurry up, it's dark in here," she called back. I could tell by the echo of her voice that she had found a larger portion of the cave. I turned to Peter who already had the flashlight in hand.

It seemed like a damned lifetime, and my stomach was in

knots before we saw the high beam of the flashlight through the narrow opening. Peter and I stuck our noses in as close as we could. I could barely make out Maggie's form as she looked around the confines of the other cave.

"Whattaya see, Maggie?" I called out.

"Nothing. It looks the same as out there. The water is not as deep here, though," she called back. "Just around my ankles. Wait…"

Peter and I jockeyed for position. "Maggie!" I called out. Damn this woman. "Maggie!"

"Hold on, Kate," Bridget said from behind me. "She'll be fine." She sounded far too confident of this; I was not in the least bit sure.

"Maggie, what do ya see?" Peter called out.

"I-I think there's another …" Her voice trailed off.

The beam of the flashlight dimmed and my heart pounded in my ears. "Maggie!" I yelled.

"Kate, will you stop yelling?" Maggie called out. "Good grief, I'm fine."

"Then answer me!" I yelled through the small opening. "Dammit."

"I *am* answering you!" she yelled back.

"Where are you? I can't get to you if something happens!" I continued to yell.

"Nothing is going to happen!" Maggie shouted in return.

I growled angrily and ran my fingers through my hair. It was then I caught a glimpse of Peter and Bridget just watching me as they listened to our tirade. Peter shook his head. He gently pushed me out of the way.

"Maggie? Is there another entrance?" Peter asked in a loud, but calm voice.

"Yes, I think so. Let me do a little exploring," Maggie called back.

"No!" I exclaimed and stuck my face in the narrow opening. "Hey, I think we can squeeze in here."

"Kate, will you quit shouting?" Maggie shouted.

I turned to Peter, who was painfully pinching the bridge of his nose. He was getting exasperated, I could tell. It was all Maggie's fault—she's so stubborn.

I peered back through the opening and watched as Maggie walked back toward it. "Peter, do you think you can use that ax on this entrance? It's really thin on this side," Maggie called out.

I looked back at Peter who shrugged. "Might work."

"Yeah, and it might collapse on Maggie," I offered firmly.

"No, it won't. Although," he said and examined the rock, "it looks as though these walls may have shifted through the years." With that, he reached out and pushed on the large rocks. By the look on his face, I could tell he was as astonished as I was when a few gave way.

"That's some shift," I said sarcastically, as I too reached down to examine the loose rocks. "Peter, you're the archaeologist, what's up with these rocks?"

"They don't look like part of the cave wall," he responded thoughtfully. He held the pickax in position and called, "Maggie, stand back, luv."

I stood there with Bridget, as Peter went to work. In a matter of minutes, he had a sizable chunk of rock chipped away, enough to squeeze us through. It flashed through my mind how easily the rocks crumbled.

This time, I gently pushed Peter aside. "Ladies first," he said with a bow and stepped back.

What a struggle. Now I know what my grandmother meant when she said, "It's like stuffing ten pounds o' potatoes in a five-pound sack." All Irish deal in potatoes. I groaned and grunted as I slipped sideways through the opening.

It was then I felt Peter pushing on my hip. "Okay, okay, give me a minute!" I called out. "My hip is attached, you know. I come fully assembled, no…" I grunted "…spare…" I groaned and slipped through with help from Peter and fell face first into the shallow cold water "…parts."

"Are ya all right?" Peter called out. I heard the laughter in his voice.

"Am I all right?" I mumbled. "Yes, I'm fine." I stood and ran my hand through my wet hair and looked around.

Maggie was nowhere in sight.

.

Chapter 26

P eter slipped a flashlight through. I aimed the high beam around the dark cave.

"What's the matter?" Peter groaned as half his body was through the opening. I quelled the urge to yank on his legs.

"I can't find Maggie. Damn that woman." I started down the narrow cave. "Maggie!" I called out.

Peter and Bridget were right behind me. "She can't have gone far," Bridget offered. I was not that hopeful.

It was dark as pitch, even with the flashlights. My heart was in my stomach as we walked through the ankle-deep water; still no sign of Maggie.

Then, up ahead, we heard her. "Guys?" Maggie called out.

I breathed a sigh of relief and started to run. I couldn't see the beam from her flashlight, so when I nearly ran her over, it scared the hell out of me. All of the sudden, I had one hundred and ten pounds of shivering doctor in my arms. "What happened?" I asked quickly and tightened my arms around her.

"Nothing," she replied nonchalantly. I was still looking for my heart, and she's calm. "I dropped my flashlight when I saw it."

Peter and Bridget caught up to us. "What happened?" Peter asked breathlessly.

Maggie swept her hair off her face. I saw the big grin. "I found another passage. Come quick," she said, almost giddy, and pulled at my arm.

We ran through water as the beams from our flashlights danced around the cave walls. Maggie stopped abruptly and crouched down. It was another passageway. We all joined Maggie and peered into the dark tunnel.

I grabbed for Maggie as she started forward. "No, let me or Peter go," I offered. Peter agreed.

"She's right. You and Bridget stay here. Kate and I will go,"

Peter said.

I itched with excitement; Maggie pouted.

I followed Peter as we crawled through the tunnel. "Doesn't it seem like we're moving upward?" I asked as we sloshed in the cold water. I thought of rats and quickly dispelled it. It was too late; now I had the constant feeling of something crawling up my pant leg.

"We are," Peter said over his shoulder. "I'll wager we're headed toward the mill."

"How far do you think we've—" I was interrupted.

"Are you two all right?" Maggie's voice bellowed.

"Yes. Quit yelling, you'll collapse the cave," I called back.

Peter ran his hand over this face. "I think we've gone about eighty feet or so."

"Upward. We're headed for the surface," I said.

I got an anxious feeling. It was then we heard it; behind us, the shallow water sloshed. Something was crawling toward us. *Rats...*

I let out a small screech as the rat came into view—it was Maggie with Bridget right behind her.

"Goddamit!" I exclaimed. I heard Maggie chuckle. "What in the hell is the matter with you?"

I heard Peter take a deep relieved breath. "Brig, are ya daft? Ya scared the life out of...Kate."

"We were tired of waiting. If something's going to happen, let it happen to all of us together," Bridget said. "Now let's keep moving."

"Why didn't ya bring the flashlights?" Peter asked.

Neither Bridget nor Maggie said a word. Peter let out a sigh as we started again.

I glared at Maggie. "You forgot the flashlight," I accused.

"You screamed like a little girl," Maggie whispered back.

I opened my mouth to argue and quickly shut it. "Oh, shut up," I replied and started crawling.

Peter stopped ahead of me and raised the flashlight. It was then we were able to stand. I stood and stretched my back, letting out a deep groan. Maggie and Bridget followed. Peter cautiously flashed the light around the contour of the cave walls. "It looks as if we're at the end," Peter said in a dejected voice.

"It can't be," I insisted.

"It is, Kate," he continued and leaned against the cave wall. "It was a hoax, a dream, nothin' more."

Maggie slipped past Bridget and me and stood in front of Peter. "It was not a hoax. It's here somewhere, right here," she persisted. She turned to me. "Isn't it?"

"Don't any of you feel that breeze?" I asked with a small grin.

Peter quickly took a lighter out of his pocket. He lit it and held it up to the far wall. We cautiously followed him.

I put my hand up to the stone wall and felt the slight breeze. "I'm telling you, there is something behind there," I said.

Peter crouched down and ran his hand over the damp rock. He then lightly kicked at it. I was amazed as pieces crumbled and plopped into the shallow water. He looked up at me with wild eyes.

"The pickax," we both said simultaneously.

"I'll go." I turned and bumped into Maggie.

"I'll go with you," Bridget offered.

"*I'll* go with her," Maggie replied in that resolute voice.

"Mag—" I started.

"Let her, Kate. Then bring back another flashlight and the rope," Peter said. I heard the urgency in his voice and stopped arguing.

It took a while to crawl back through the tunnel, then we ran through the passageway. Maggie easily slipped through the narrow opening that Peter had made. I, of course, had a more difficult time. I heard Maggie as she gathered the rope and flashlights. "Don't get stuck."

I grunted and—got stuck. *Why do these things happen to me?* "I'm stuck," I groaned helplessly. I was wedged nicely. Maggie let out an exasperated groan, then laughed at my plight. "Just help me."

"Hmmm, interesting position, Miss Ryan."

There I was, at her mercy. "Maggie..." I warned as I struggled.

"I like you like this—all struggling and needing my help," she said. She laughed and gently pulled at my arm. I wriggled and squirmed and finally slipped through, both of us stumbling backward. I grabbed her around the waist to steady both of us.

"Th-The flashlights and..." Maggie whispered as she looked

up.

I swallowed and nodded. "Right." I let her go.

I gathered the length of rope and the pickax as Maggie grabbed the other flashlight.

When we finally got to them, poor Bridget and Peter were standing in the dark. Peter quickly took the ax as we stood back. He raised the ax and started. The rock crumbled easily, and I immediately thought of the rocks by the narrow entranceway.

"This is not part of the cave wall. It's breaking away far too easily," Peter said as he swung away. "It's as if…"

"Somebody built this rock wall," I finished for him.

Maggie moved close to me and I put my arm around her. This was so bizarre, I couldn't say anything. We just watched, but my mind was racing—something didn't fit.

"This is new," Peter said and stood back.

I walked up to him. "What's new?" I asked. "The wall?"

Bridget and Maggie stood beside us. I leaned over and pulled the rocks away.

"Somebody's been here," Peter whispered, and I heard the worried tone in his voice.

I had the same feeling. "And not just an Irish sea captain two hundred years ago. When was this wall constructed, professor?" I asked.

Peter picked up a heavy rock and examined it. "Certainly not two hundred years ago, that's for sure." Peter nodded as he continued with his task. With a couple of strokes, the wall gave way. I pulled at him and we backed out of harm's way, as the rock wall crumbled. We stood there, once again in amazement. Peter grabbed the flashlight from Bridget and crawled over the pile of rocks. We quickly followed.

Once over, I bumped into Peter who was standing there, just staring. I heard Maggie gasp. I followed Peter's stare and saw it.

"You have *got* to be kidding me," I said and blinked in amazement.

It was just sitting there in the open on a ledge. It looked like a steamer trunk. About three feet long and two feet high. We all slowly walked up to the trunk and looked at it. I was actually stunned.

"Please, don't touch it," Peter said.

As if...

He knelt down and peered at the trunk. Bridget joined him as Maggie and I stood a safe distance away. *It would be my luck to lean on that thing and...*

"This is amazing," Maggie whispered and leaned into me.

I agreed. However, the question of how this trunk got in here was still nagging me.

"Well," Peter said as he stood. "Whatever is in the trunk is sealed tight."

"How do you know?" I asked, and for the first time, I cautiously stepped closer.

He shined the flashlight beam to the edges of the trunk. "Paraffin. It was used as a sealing agent back then and still is. Whatever's in there must be in mint condition."

"So that's what happened, right?" I asked and Peter nodded.

"It's just as they said. Phillip of Spain was on his way to deliver this to Queen Elizabeth. However, Grace O'Malley or some other captain had other ideas. Somebody captured a vessel from Phillip's armada and took this trunk, buried it here, and never came back." He took a deep breath. "I'll need to make a call," he said quickly. He then laughed openly. "It *is* true! I can't believe it."

Bridget threw her arms around his neck as they laughed like little kids. Maggie and I couldn't help ourselves from grinning as we watched.

"How are you going to get it out of here?" Maggie asked.

Peter took a deep contemplative breath and scratched his head. "I have no idea. It'll never fit through that narrow..." he stopped, and I knew what he was thinking.

He looked at me and I nodded. "How in the hell did they get this through that narrow opening? And why drag it through the tunnel and wall it up here?" I asked and looked around. "Dammit, it's driving me nuts!" I exclaimed.

I thought for a moment, as I glanced around the small confines of the cavern. Peter examined the trunk once again. "It looks as though it was indeed dragged up here. Perhaps this was the end and he could go no farther. It was a good hiding place."

"Yes, it is a good hiding place, but why didn't he come back for it? Why leave it here?" I asked.

"Maybe to let some time pass," Bridget offered.

I had to agree that was a good point. "Maybe he died before he could get back here…" Maggie offered.

"I'd really like to know," I replied. I watched Peter and saw his eyebrows disappear in his hairline. I shivered uncontrollably as he slowly walked farther and peered behind the trunk.

"Perhaps *he* knows the answer."

"He?" I asked, trying so hard to hide the terror in my voice. All at once, I was standing beside him, following his amazed look. "Is that what I think it is?"

Lying on the ground was a corpse, well, a pile of bones, really, covered with the tattered remains of his clothing—a saber and pistol still clutched in the bony fingers. It was like something out of some pirate movie, with the skull smiling up at us with a hideous grin.

With that, Maggie was at my side. She let out a small gasp and held my arm.

"He must have run out of paraffin," I offered and felt the nails in my forearm once again.

I heard Peter chuckle quietly as I wrenched my arm away from Maggie's death grip.

"That explains why he never came back," Peter said. "He never left."

"But why not?" I asked and looked around.

"Why would he just lie down and die?" Bridget asked as she crouched down next to the skeleton.

"Careful, Brig," Peter warned softly and knelt beside her. "Poor bastard."

Maggie knelt beside the skeletal remains. "Perhaps he didn't just lie down and die."

I joined her and aimed the flashlight beam at the skeleton. "What are you thinking, Dr. Winfield?" I asked.

Maggie reached out and Peter quickly stopped her. "Please don't disturb anything."

Maggie agreed. "I was just going to point out the reason why he never left. Take a look at his skull."

We all leaned forward and blinded the poor sea captain with our flashlights.

"Okay," Bridget said. "What are we lookin' for?"

We examined the bones, and I hid my impish grin and said, "Well, the thigh bone's connected to the...hip bone and hip bone's—"

"If I'm not mistaken," Maggie interjected, "I believe that's a bullet hole in the left frontal bone."

"Gee, I love anatomy talk," I said and glanced at the smirking doctor. "So we can assume that someone else was here and killed the poor slob, or he was very careless with his pistol."

"I opt for someone else," Peter said.

Suddenly, my mind raced. "Okay, how's this for a scenario," I started. "This sea captain came down here with an accomplice because quite frankly, he couldn't carry this trunk by himself and they found this hiding place. The other guy got greedy, shot this poor bastard, and walled up this place, and the narrow entranceway back there, effectively creating a good hiding place. He waited until the dust cleared but obviously never got a chance to come back for his ill-gotten booty."

There was silence for a moment or two until Peter spoke. "I would tend to agree with most of your scenario. However, as we said, those two rock walls we just broke down came down far too easily. I'm no geologist, but I will wager those walls were recently formed."

I gave him a curious look. "How recent is recent?"

Peter scratched his chin in thought. "Is yesterday too recent?"

"Are you saying what I think you're saying?"

He looked a bit confused. "I-I'm not sure. What am I saying?"

"You're saying that these walls were constructed recently, which means someone has to have found the treasure before we did," I said and glanced at my fellow adventurers.

"Tim Devereaux," Maggie said and looked at me.

"Why not Russell?" Peter interjected. He looked at Bridget. "You're quiet, Brig. What do you think?"

"I have no idea," she said.

"Why not both?" I offered. "Okay, let's run this up the flagpole and see who salutes: Maybe Russell found the treasure and walled everything up. He called Bridget who said he sounded excited, and this would be a good reason why. He then gets killed for his efforts. Now who killed him?"

"All points lead to Tim Devereaux." Peter shrugged.

"What about The Omega Group?" Maggie said.

I was stumped.

Peter stood slowly. "I have to call the museum, but I hate to leave this down here unprotected. However, I don't see how that can be avoided."

"Why don't you go back and get Constable Reardon, make your call, and I'll stay here—" I said and knew the interruption was coming.

"Not alone, you won't," Maggie countered seriously.

I tiredly rubbed my forehead. "Do you think that pistol still works?" I asked.

"I think I should stay," Bridget offered.

I could actually feel Maggie glaring in the darkness.

"I think Brig is right, Maggie. I'd feel better if one of us stayed with the trunk," Peter offered.

Maggie grudgingly agreed and left with Peter.

"Please don't touch anything," Peter begged me as he walked away. I noticed he didn't include Bridget in his plea, which annoyed me, but I said nothing.

With Maggie and Peter promising to come back as soon as possible, Bridget and I sat on the pile of rocks with one flashlight, one shovel, one pickax, and one skeleton. I glanced at Bridget who gave the darkened cave a nervous glance. I gently bumped shoulders with her. "Come here often?" I asked.

Bridget laughed. "You do know how to treat a woman to a good time, Miss Ryan," she said.

"Only the best. There's a cemetery I'd like to show you tomorrow."

As we were laughing, I heard a voice, "Glad you're enjoyin' yourselves."

I immediately stopped laughing and gave "dem bones" a skeptical glance before I aimed the beam of the flashlight toward the tunnel entrance.

There stood Tim Devereaux, grinning slightly and holding a gun. "This is unexpected. And where is Sullivan and everyone else?" he asked.

"Bridget and I got adventurous on our own," I said, keeping my eye on the gun.

Tim stepped into the beam of the flashlight. "That's

unfortunate."

"You can't be thinking of killing us," I said, although I thought otherwise.

"And why is that, luv?" he asked.

"I found the documents and Constable Reardon has them, so Omega is out of the picture and you'll never get your money."

"Kate, darlin', Omega has been out of the picture for a little while now. Seems they're pulling out—"

"Why is that?" I stood. Bridget stood, as well, and took a step away from me.

Tim took a step back and raised the gun but said nothing.

"Could the reason be murder?" I asked. "I believe The Omega Group wanted the property to excavate this historical find, but murder is too high a price. But not for you, right, Tim?"

"You're treadin' on dangerous ground," Tim warned.

I was going to heed the warning. However, I was on a roll now. Pieces were falling into place. "The documents I found had you signing over your portion of the mill for a million bucks," I said, then it dawned on me. "Which is why you killed Brian, am I right? Somehow he gained possession of those documents, and when he didn't tell you they were hidden in the grandfather clock, you threw him over that stone wall."

I noticed Bridget inching away from me and wondered what she was doing. I had a nervous feeling she was going to try to be heroic.

"Hidden in the clock?" Tim asked and laughed. "Brian was a clever man, but troublesome, this is true. So was Devine. He played the double-cross to perfection. I believe Devine gave Brian the documents, trying to see how far he could go with him. At the same time, Devine, the lying bastard, was telling me about Omega and how I could make a lot of money if we found the treasure first," he said and laughed. "And he did. I can't believe Devine found it. He was actually giddy when he told me, the fool. He was even going to tell Sullivan. And ya know I just couldn't let that happen." He stopped and took a deep tired breath.

I just stood there and hoped he'd keep talking until Peter came back with the constable. "So you killed Russell, as well," I said.

"Yes, I did," he said. "Once he helped me block off the two entrances, I waited until we got out of the cave and hit him with the shovel."

"I hoped the tide would take Russell as I hoped it would have taken Brian." He stopped and I noticed he looked a bit perplexed. It was then it became clear to me.

"What's wrong? Can't understand how they found Brian's body so quickly? You thought the sea would take him. After all, you replaced the rocks on that wall, didn't you?" *I knew I was right about that.* "Made it look as if nothing was out of place. It was a nice clean murder until Constable Reardon found Brian's pipe by that wall. You must have overlooked it. Pretty careless."

Bridget chuckled quietly and shook her head. "I told ya, they'd find the body. I told ya not to kill him that way. You have such a nasty temper. You almost bungled the whole thing."

I shot an incredulous look from Tim to Bridget, then back to Tim, who shrugged in a helpless gesture. "It was dark, Brig. I didn't see him drop the bloody pipe."

I must have looked like a prize jackass, gaping at both of them.

Chapter 27

I was still gaping like a jackass. Bridget chuckled quietly. "Poor Kate. Ya didn't figure on this, did ya?"

"No, I did not," I answered her. I was stunned. "Why?"

Bridget smiled slightly. "Money, what other reason? Do ya have any idea how much this is worth? Peter was right, the idealistic fool. It's worth millions, tens of millions. When Brian changed his will, and I saw that he was giving the whole thing to Mac, I knew we needed to move quickly. Russell was sent to stop Peter. However, that didn't work."

My mind was racing. "Russell tried to kill Peter," I said. "He tried to scare us into leaving by tossing me around after I had dinner with you in Donegal."

"Yes. Russell was to kill Peter and I would take care of Brian's will. Tim would take care of James's unwillingness to play nice. Unfortunately, we are at this point," Bridget said.

I looked at Bridget. "So when Mac and I picked you up the other day, there was no phone call from Russell, was there?" I asked, knowing the answer.

"No. Tim was with Russell at the time and I needed—"

"And you needed to make sure you were with us for what... an alibi?" I asked, trying to fit this piece together.

"Partly. I also needed to make sure you picked up Tim, so both of us would have an alibi," she said with a smug grin. "Ya see? But I have to tell ya, you're very good. Ya had me worried when ya found out about my being married to Russell. How did ya, by the way?"

"I remember seeing your name on your diploma that hung on the wall. It said Bridget Donnelly-Devine. The university corroborated that fact," I said. "You conniving bitch."

Bridget let out a rude laugh. "I told ya: All men kill the thing they love—Oscar Wilde."

Then I set my attention to Tim. "So you killed James, as well?" I asked, but knew the answer to that, too.

Tim nodded. "At first, he was all for it, then he talked to Brian and wanted him to keep the mill in the family. Bridget and I knew that Brian would never do that. James got cold feet and refused to sign," he said and grinned. "In the end, he did. It was nice and clean, they'll never find him. You're a pain in my arse, Kate, and as I said, I thought for sure the tide would have taken Devine, and they'd never find him." He took a deep breath before continuing. "Who knew he had the strength to struggle up the cliff," he said and looked at Bridget. "He was a strong lad."

I looked back and forth at them. "You two are some piece of work," I said and didn't hide the disgust in my voice.

Tim glared at me and took a step closer. The beam of my flashlight shining in his face gave him a menacing look.

"Well, enough prattle. We've been trying to think of a way to get this trunk out of here. You can help us." He handed Bridget the gun. She smiled happily, as she waved it in my direction.

"Take an end, Kate. Let's go." She motioned with the gun and stepped back.

"Hurry up. The tide is coming in," Tim said with a groan as he grabbed the metal handle and lifted.

I lifted my end, as well; this thing was heavy. "What does the tide have to do with this?" I asked.

"Not that it matters, but we have a boat waiting. When the tide comes in, we'll be signaling it. We'll be far off the Irish coast before they find you. Poor Kate is going to have a bit of a problem with the tide," Tim said with a grunt.

"Keep still, Tim. Let's just get this out of here. Be careful with it," Bridget ordered as we struggled past her.

"So you're the brawn, huh, Tim?" I asked and glanced back at him. "And Bridget's the brains."

"Something like that," Bridget called out. "I've had this planned for years. Once Professor Carroll died and was out of the way, I knew the time was at hand. Enough talk. Keep movin'."

It took a while to get the trunk through the low cave tunnel. We moved in complete silence. I was desperately thinking of a way out of this mess. By the time we reached the narrow passageway, I was exhausted. By the look of him, so was Tim.

Bridget handed him the pickax. Tim groaned and took the ax and started at the narrow entrance. I looked at Bridget, who avoided me.

"So you're in this for the money, huh?" I asked. "All that bullshit about it being a historical find for Ireland. You were just waiting for the right time to take it. You played Peter and us very well." I glanced at Tim who was chopping away at the crumbling rock. Bridget ignored me but kept the gun aimed right at me.

"You played Russell well, too—even married him. I wonder who else was in on Russell's double-cross," I said thoughtfully. I noticed Tim stop in mid-swing…

"Keep going, Timmy, she's baiting ya. Keep focused," Bridget said firmly and glanced at her watch. "It's almost time now. He'll be here soon."

Tim grunted and swung the ax one more time. He had enough room to get the trunk out, and my time was running short.

"All right then," Bridget said. "Let's get this to the shore. C'mon, Kate."

I grabbed my end of the trunk. "She sure is bossy, Tim. Hope you…"

Tim dropped his end of the trunk and grabbed me by the shirt. "Shut up or I'll kill ya right now!" He was deceptively strong as he tightened his grip and squeezed. "Do ya hear me?" he said in a low voice and roughly let me go.

I stumbled back and felt the pain rip through my neck. Bridget sighed deeply. "There ya go again, Timmy. You've a nasty temper. Let's keep moving."

We sloshed through the ankle-deep water and finally reached the entrance of the cave. The smell of cool sea air blasted me as we set the trunk down on a nearby boulder. I coughed deeply as I sagged against the rock.

Suddenly, Bridget was right in my face with the gun pointed to my forehead. "You've been bothersome, Kate, too bothersome, but nothing will stop me now."

I felt Tim behind me. I then heard his voice in my ear. "Poor Kate, when the tide comes in, you'll be going out with it. No one will find ya."

I turned my face toward him. "Your breath stinks, Tim." I

suppose I deserved the rude shove, which landed me painfully against the rocks. "That hurt," I groaned and tried to get up.

"You've got a sarcastic bite to ya," Bridget said and looked out to sea. I followed her look and blinked the blood out of my eyes. In the distance, I saw a small fishing boat. "It's time. Hurry up, Tim."

Tim shoved me again against the rocks and quickly grabbed the big flashlight and signaled the small boat. I watched as a light flashed back from the vessel.

"All right then. He'll be here soon. Let's get this over with," Bridget said, and I heard the nervous tone in her voice.

"You don't honestly think this will work, do you?" I asked. I blinked and the pain knifed through my head. I felt nauseated and dizzy.

"Shut up," Bridget said and glanced out at the boat. "Go, Tim."

"What's the matter, Bridget? Don't you have the stomach for murder? Or only when someone else does it?" Tim grabbed me and pulled me by the arm. "You'd better be careful, Tim. So far, you're behind the eight ball. You've killed three times and Ms. Donnelly here has clean hands, plus she's a lawyer," I said quickly, hoping that would jar Tim. It did. I felt his grip loosen, so I went on. "See, you're the one who'll go to prison, not Bridget. She's holding all the cards. I wonder who's out in that boat."

Tim shot a curious look at Bridget, and I continued, "You think she's going to let you have any part of this? Not after she's spent nearly four years trying to find it," I said. "She married Russell Devine for chrissakes…"

With that, Bridget raised the butt of the gun and slammed it against my cheek. The pain rippled through me and my knees buckled. I was in a daze as I folded like a deck of cards onto the rocky shore.

All at once, the wind started and waves crashed against the rocks. I looked up to see Peter and Constable Reardon making their way down the rugged path. Through my foggy brain, I thought I heard Tim arguing with Bridget. She had the gun aimed at his midsection.

"Don't fuck with me, Timmy," Bridget yelled over the wind and waves. I glanced at the trunk, which lay precariously on the rocks. One good wave and it would be taken out to sea.

"Stay where you are!" Constable Reardon called out.

Tim whirled around and Bridget raised the gun behind him. It was then I saw Maggie running toward us.

With all my might, I leapt at Bridget and grabbed for the gun. As we tangled, both of us stumbled and fell headlong into the icy water. We struggled under the cold waves as I maintained my grip on the gun in her hand. Then the waves took us under. I heard Bridget's muffled cry as the gun went off and I lost my grip completely. I felt my lungs starting to tighten as I frantically reached out for her. I knew she was shot—she had to be.

I quickly swam for the surface. As I broke through the crashing wave, I heard Maggie and Peter calling me. I was nearly paralyzed from the icy water as I tried to swim to shore. All at once, I was being pulled in, and I heard Maggie's voice beside me as I was hauled up onto the rocky shore.

I was amazed at how much seawater I coughed up. Maggie was holding me close to her. "Kate, are you all right?"

I nodded as I continued to cough. She wrapped her arms around me and I watched as Constable Reardon handcuffed Tim Devereaux and dragged him up the path.

Peter rushed up as Maggie helped me to my feet. "What in the hell happened? What happened to Bridget?" Peter asked.

"She was in on it, Peter," I said and shivered violently.

He looked completely undone. "That can't be!" he exclaimed and looked out at the sea. Maggie quickly stood between us.

"We need to get you off these rocks," Maggie said to me.

"We need to get that trunk off these rocks," I argued as my teeth chattered away.

"Kate Ryan, will you for once shut up and do as you're told?" Maggie yelled.

I gaped at her. *She's yelling at me?* Peter put his arm around me. "Maggie's right, Kate. We need to get ya out of here. When we couldn't find Tim, Reardon came back with me. We'll get Mac and Charlie down here to help with the trunk. You can tell us all about it."

Constable Reardon stood over me as I lay in bed, with the blankets pulled up to my neck. I couldn't stop shivering.

"I'd tell you to lie still, but I think that's impossible," Maggie said as she tended to my cheek. "You've got a good bruise going," she said and nodded professionally as I watched her.

"Everything in working order?" I asked tiredly.

"Everything but a functioning brain," she said dryly. "Are you all right?"

"Yeah, I'm fine." I fought the feeling of contentment hearing the soft concern in her voice.

"Kate, can ya tell me what happened?" Constable Reardon asked.

With that, Peter dashed into the room. "Are ya all right then?"

"Yes, I'm fine. Where's the trunk?" I asked and tried to sit up.

Maggie held me down and glared at me. "I'll tie you to this bed if I have to," she threatened.

"Hey, nice bedside manner," I grumbled and looked at both men.

"Bridget was in on it from the get go, along with Tim and Russell," I said.

"Why?" Peter asked in a quiet voice and sat on the bed.

"Money," I replied.

"Well," Constable Reardon said. "Tim Devereaux has at least three counts of murder to his discredit."

"And an attempted murder, mainly mine," I added and glanced at Peter's sad face. "I'm sorry, Peter. She fooled everyone and I mean everyone. She said she had this planned for years." I stopped and closed my eyes. My head was pounding. "I don't suppose you found her?"

Constable Reardon let out a deep tired breath. "There's no way of knowing unless she washes up on shore." He gave Peter a sick look. "Sorry."

"I understand," he said.

It was then I thought of it. "Hey, Bridget had signaled a boat."

All three of them looked at me. "What boat?" the constable asked.

"That's how they were going to get the trunk off the shore. When the tide came in, whoever was out there was going to pick them up. Tim signaled him. I watched him."

"We saw nothing," Peter stated.

"There was no boat out there," Constable Reardon said.

I looked at Maggie who nodded. "I didn't see one, but then I was a bit preoccupied watching you wrestle that woman right into the ocean. What happened?"

I took a deep breath. "I heard the gun go off and heard her muffled scream, then I lost her."

"God rest her poor soul," Peter said and stood very stiffly. "Well, the museum people will be here shortly. I'd best go get ready for them." He smiled and patted my leg. "Rest for a bit, Kate. Then come down. I wouldn't want ya to miss any of this."

He and Constable Reardon left. Maggie sat on the edge of the bed and put her hand on my cheek.

"I'm telling you, there was a boat," I insisted.

"I believe you. You need to rest for a while. You scared me to death."

"I did?" I asked. Maggie closed her eyes and I heard her mumbling.

I grinned and held her hand. "You want to smack me right now, don't you?"

"You have no idea how much," she agreed and laughed as she held my hand.

Chapter 28

When I was tired of lying in bed, which was all of one hour, I went downstairs and avoided Dr. Winfield's glare. Peter looked ill and I wasn't sure if it was because he found out Bridget was a lying conspirator to murder and whatnot or that the historical find was safe and sound. Either way, he looked as if he was about to vomit.

There was a busload of archaeologists, historians, and museum curators from Ireland, Scotland, and England on their way to Mac and Teri's. Now *they* looked ill.

Peter sat there staring at the trunk that sat in the middle of the living room.

"Shouldn't this be in a museum or someplace safe?" I suggested quietly. Mac and Teri shrugged in confusion.

"Yes, it should and it will, but for now, I want to make sure where this trunk will end up. As it stands, it's Mac's property," Peter said and looked at Mac.

He shook his head. "Not mine, Peter. You deserve to decide where it belongs. It's the least we can do for Brian."

I glanced around the living. "Where are Maggie and Charlie?" I hadn't seen either of them.

Teri gave me a cautious glance. "Maggie received a phone call from Hannah. Doc's been called away, he needs her at the clinic as soon as possible."

My heart dropped. "Really?" I then let out a wry chuckle. "Well, the woman couldn't stay here indefinitely."

"She couldn't?" Teri asked. I noticed the maternal smirk.

With that, Maggie and Charlie walked into the living room. "I cannot believe how this turned out," Charlie said. "And I really can't believe Bridget Donnelly. She certainly had me fooled."

Peter looked up then; the sadness evident on his face. "She fooled everyone for a long time. I still can't believe it—just for

239

money."

"How do you suppose it all came about?" Mac asked and looked at me.

"Hell, I don't know. It's one convoluted mess," I said and figured I'd give it my best shot. "It looks like Bridget, Tim, and Russell were in it from the get go. Bridget said Russell was sent to take care of Peter. I'm assuming he was to do more than just injure you back in Chicago, Peter."

Peter frowned deeply. I could tell he still couldn't believe any of this.

"Bridget was then supposed to take care of Brian's will," I said. "When she found out he'd changed it and left everything to Mac, she knew it called for drastic measures. The problem was Russell Devine. I'm thinking after Tim showed Russell the contract he had signed with Omega, Tim and Bridget offered him a piece of the action. I don't think they realized how greedy Russell really was.

"I think Russell stole that contract and took it to Brian, looking for more money by telling him of the double-cross. Russell saw a great opportunity in working both ends. He didn't count on Brian's devotion to the people of the village or his part in securing the legendary treasure for Ireland. Brian hid the contract in the clock and changed his will immediately, which tipped off Bridget that something was wrong.

"I'm sure Brian planned to expose the double-cross when Mac came to Ireland. Poor Brian probably never considered Tim to be a murderer. He certainly never suspected Bridget. It would never have occurred to Brian that money, no matter how much, would drive a man to murder—but murder he did. He threw Brian over the cliffs, killed Devine because he knew too much, and murdered James to complete the deal with Omega and get James's signed contract.

"Unfortunately, for them, I'm sure Omega wanted no part of the deal when people started dropping like flies. They pulled out, and I'll wager you won't be hearing from them again. And that, as they say, is that," I said.

"I cannot believe Bridget was in on this. I never, ever expected it," Peter said sadly and let out a huge sigh. He smiled then and gave me a kiss. "Thank you, Kate." He glanced at his watch. "The media and the museum folks will be here shortly. I'm sick to my stomach."

Mac patted him on the shoulder. "I don't blame you one bit. This has been one crazy ride."

On schedule, the media did indeed arrive. The house was buzzing as men and women, all snapping on rubber surgical gloves, surrounded the old trunk, which still sat in the middle of the living room. I was itching to see if there was anything of value in it. After what seemed like hours of discussion, the powers that be decided to open it.

I was amazed. "You're gonna open this thing in a living room?" I asked.

Peter laughed as did the others. "Yes, I don't want to take the chance of anything else happening to this," he said and took a deep breath.

Cameras started flashing. I held my breath and glanced at Mac and Teri who were wild-eyed. Maggie was smiling and holding Charlie's arm as we all stood back and let Peter continue.

Peter nervously knelt down and snapped his rubber gloves in place. He had some instrument that looked decidedly like a crowbar and gently pried the trunk open.

"The paraffin did its job of sealing this nicely," he said.

Everyone held his or her breath as we watched. "Unbelievable," he said in amazement.

I stood on my tiptoes to get a look. I only caught a glimpse, but what a glimpse it was. I heard Teri exclaim softly and knew she must have seen the same thing. There were jewels, gold and silver coins, necklaces. It was amazing, like something out of an old pirate movie. I expected to see Errol Flynn waltz in at any moment. The bounty looked very tarnished but still and all, it was amazing.

Peter and the rest of his colleagues logged and categorized all that was in the trunk. Then at the bottom of it, they found a smaller box, also sealed in paraffin. Peter gingerly took it out as we all looked on. Mac leaned forward, his arm around Teri. I stood there and watched.

There they were—several small etchings, all perfectly preserved. Peter now donned a pair of soft, white gloves and handled the etchings as little as possible, laying them out, describing them to the others, who were taking notes and recording the event as cameras continued to click wildly.

The look on Peter's face was priceless. He grinned like a kid at Christmas as he gingerly held the etchings. "All signed by El Greco in fifteen sixty, before he became a master. These were thought to be lost. Phillip of Spain had commissioned his work but later rejected it. What an idiot," he said and everyone laughed.

He turned a nice shade of crimson and gently coughed. "Strike that. What a miscalculation of judgment," he amended. He was a master himself and had the entire group hanging on his every word.

As I shook my head in amazement, I turned to say something to Maggie, only to find her nowhere in sight. I slipped away and walked upstairs.

Maggie was in her room as I opened our connecting door. Her bags were packed and sitting by the door.

"You're leaving in a hurry." I stood against the door. All at once, my head ached. I didn't even want to think about my heart.

She met me in the doorway. "You should have rested more. You're still pale."

"Why do you have to leave now?" I asked.

"C'mon, lie down," she said, and I grudgingly lay back against the pillows. She sat on the edge of the bed. "I have to get back to the clinic."

It was then Charlie walked into the room. "Well, Kate, I'll say my goodbyes now. I hate them." He smiled and bent down and kissed me. Tears welled up in my eyes as he sat on the edge of the bed.

"I can't believe you did it again. You are quite an amazing woman. When you get back, you'll have to stop by and tell Aunt Hannah all about it. She'll pout because she missed it, so be prepared to tell the story a dozen times. See you later, sweetie. Remember, if you ever want to change careers, you let me know. You and Jess would make an unbelievable pair."

I fought back the tears. "I'll remember. Please tell Jess thanks for all her help and yours, Charlie. I never could have done it without you." He patted my hand and gathered Maggie's luggage and left.

My chest ached as I watched Maggie pick up her coat.

"Maggie—"

She was quickly at my bedside. "Lay still." She reached down and touched my face again. "Take care of those bruises."

"I don't know why you have to leave," I said, swallowing my emotions. *I don't know how to make you stay.*

"I'm needed back at the clinic," she reminded me.

For a moment, we sat there in silence. I reached over and took her small hand in my own. I took a deep breath and said, "I need time, Maggie. I don't know what the hell I'm—"

She lightly rested her fingertips against my lips. "I understand, more than you know."

"Really?" I asked and couldn't hide the incredulous tone.

She rolled her eyes and said, "Just call me when you get home." She then lightly kissed my cheek and whispered, "Please, come home."

I wanted to say something, God knows what, but she quickly walked out and closed the door behind her.

KATE SWEENEY

244

Epilogue

By the next afternoon, Peter had finished with the media. The trunk and all its bounty were safely on their way to the National Museum in Dublin. We heard from Constable Reardon. Bridget Donnelly's body was never found. The tide that Tim hoped would take Brian and Russell to hide his murders apparently took Bridget.

In the back of my mind, that fishing boat off shore still nagged at me...

Peter looked exhausted but perked up when Mac broke out the champagne.

The early evening had turned very chilly. I stood by the fireplace and pulled the collar of my green cardigan up around my neck as I sipped the champagne.

The vision of Maggie and me sitting on this hearth flashed through my mind. I then remembered holding her that wonderful night after I told her about Liz. I could still feel her body trembling.

Please come home. Maggie's plea rang in my ears. I looked up to see Mac standing there with the bottle of champagne. I chuckled and offered my empty glass.

"Remember our conversation on the plane ride over here?" he asked as he poured. "I told you if Maggie was not for you, then she was not. These past few days since she's been here, I've seen a change in you—a good change, Kate. You'll know when, or if, the time is right for you and Maggie. Until then, stay good friends."

"So you're a philosopher now?" I asked softly and swallowed my tears along with the champagne.

He laughed and poured himself a glass. "Nope, just a brother-in-law who loves his klutzy sister-in-law. You know," he stated philosophically, "you're a smart logical woman. It's time you started dealing with your heart."

There was silence for a moment. "Oh, shut up, ya landlord," I grumbled as he laughed and walked away.

"Well," Mac said and raised his glass to all of us. "I never would have believed it, but there it is. I'm proud of you, Peter, as I'm sure Brian would be. You were true to yourself and your belief. No one could ask for more."

The rest of us followed suit and raised our glasses.

Peter cleared this throat. "Thank you. However, it would never have happened if Brian left this mill to anyone else. In his heart, he knew it was the right thing to leave it to you, Mac. Thank you for being honest and loyal. You saved the day. Well, you and Kate," he said sincerely.

We were silent until Peter broke the pensive mood. He gave us a wide smile. "What does the future hold for the McAuliffes and Kate Ryan?"

Teri put her arm around Mac's waist. "Mac and I are going to stay in Ireland for a while. How about you, Kate?"

I stared at the dancing flames and smiled. "I have no clue what the future holds, but for now—I'm going home."

-The End-

About the author

Born in Chicago, Kate Sweeney is the author of *Kate Ryan Mysteries*. *A Nice Clean Murder* is the second installment. The first in the series, *She Waits*, was released through Intaglio Publications in May 2006. In addition, her short story *Out of the Crowd* in *Wild Nights*, a forthcoming Bella After Dark anthology, will be released by Bella Books in the near future.

Kate also has a collection of short stories, other novels and novellas. Her sense of humor is evident throughout her writing, which runs the gamut from funny to sad, erotic to romantic, and anything else in between. Please visit her Web site at www.katesweeneyonline.com or feel free to drop email Kate at Kate@KateSweeneyOnline.com.

Kate currently resides in Villa Park, Illinois.

OTHER TITLES FROM INTAGLIO

Accidental Love
by B. L. Miller; ISBN: 1-933113-11-1

Assignment Sunrise
by I Christie; ISBN: 978-1-933113-40-1

Code Blue
by KatLyn; ISBN: 1-933113-09-X

Counterfeit World
by Judith K. Parker; ISBN: 1-933113-32-4

Crystal's Heart
by B. L. Miller & Verda Foster; ISBN: 1-933113-24-3

Define Destiny
by J. M. Dragon; ISBN: 1-933113-56-1

Gloria's Inn
by Robin Alexander; ISBN: 1-933113-01-4

Graceful Waters
by B. L. Miller & Verda Foster; ISBN: 1-933113-08-1

Halls Of Temptation
by Katie P. Moore; ISBN: 978-1-933113-42-5

Incommunicado
by N. M. Hill & J. P. Mercer; ISBN: 1-933113-10-3

Journey's Of Discoveries
by Ellis Paris Ramsay; ISBN: 978-1-933113-43-2

Josie & Rebecca: The Western Chronicles
by Vada Foster & BL Miller; ISBN: 1-933113-38-3

Misplaced People
by C. G. Devize; ISBN: 1-933113-30-8

Murky Waters
by Robin Alexander; ISBN: 1-933113-33-2

None So Blind
by LJ Maas; ISBN: 978-1-933113-44-9

Picking Up The Pace
by Kimberly LaFontaine; ISBN: 1-933113-41-3

Private Dancer
by T. J. Vertigo; ISBN: 978-1-933113-58-6

She Waits
By Kate Sweeney; ISBN: 978-1-933113-40-1

Southern Hearts
by Katie P Moore; ISBN: 1-933113-28-6

Storm Surge
by KatLyn; ISBN: 1-933113-06-5

These Dreams
by Verda Foster; ISBN: 1-933113-12-X

The Chosen
by Verda H Foster; ISBN: 978-1-933113-25-8

The Cost Of Commitment
by Lynn Ames; ISBN: 1-933113-02-2

The Flip Side of Desire
By Lynn Ames; ISBN: 978-1-933113-60-9

The Gift
by Verda Foster; ISBN: 1-933113-03-0

The Illusionist
by Fran Heckrotte; ISBN: 978-1-933113-31-9

The Last Train Home
by Blayne Cooper; ISBN: 1-933113-26-X

The Price of Fame
by Lynn Ames; ISBN: 1-933113-04-9

The Taking of Eden
by Robin Alexander; ISBN: 978-1-933113-53-1

The Value of Valor
by Lynn Ames; ISBN: 1-933113-04-9

The War between The Hearts
by Nann Dunne; ISBN: 1-933113-27-8

With Every Breath
by Alex Alexander; ISBN: 1-933113-39-1

You can purchase other Intaglio Publications
books online at StarCrossed Productions, Inc.
www.scp-inc.biz or at your local bookstore.

Published by
Intaglio Publications
Walker, LA

Visit us on the web:
www.intagliopub.com